Samuel Rogers

Autobiography of Elder Samuel Rogers

Third Edition

Samuel Rogers

Autobiography of Elder Samuel Rogers
Third Edition

ISBN/EAN: 9783337118747

Printed in Europe, USA, Canada, Australia, Japan

Cover: Foto ©Raphael Reischuk / pixelio.de

More available books at **www.hansebooks.com**

AUTOBIOGRAPHY

OF

ELDER SAMUEL ROGERS.

EDITED BY HIS SON,

ELDER JOHN I. ROGERS.

THIRD EDITION.

CINCINNATI:

STANDARD PUBLISHING COMPANY, 180 ELM STREET.

1881.

INTRODUCTION.

BRETHREN of superior wisdom, and on whose judgment I rely, having urged me to give the world the benefit of my father's autobiography, I have endeavored to answer their wishes, though in an imperfect manner; and in the form of this unpretending volume to give mankind a part of the experiences of one whose toils and travels in the cause of his Master began almost with the beginning of the present century, and have continued well-nigh to the present day. Abundant material has been at hand, in the form of letters, and articles from our periodicals, to make a volume twice as large as this; but we have chosen to give his own account of his work, and as nearly as possible in his own language, leaving men to form their own judgment concerning his eventful life. We regret that the plan of this volume has made it necessary to cut off so many chapters and parts of chapters of his autobiography, which might have been interesting and profitable to the reader. Doubtless there will be found many errors in the book, but we think they are not of a nature to impair its usefulness. As it is, we commit it to the world, praying that it may be as good seed sown in good ground, bringing fruit abundantly to the praise of God.

The concluding years of my beloved father were his happiest. Being quite deaf, and almost blind, he gave himself to meditations upon things divine. His hope grew brighter every day. He conversed as one whose home is beyond the clouds. He dwelt by faith in regions so sublime, that he was enabled to see all things, even the darkest clouds, from the heaven-side. When anyone inquired of him if he were not lonesome, being in his room so much alone, he answered promptly, "No, for God is always with me." He retained his mind and memory in full vigor to the last moment of life. When informed that he had but a few moments to live, he was exceeding joyful; and turning his almost sightless eyes upwards, he said, "Is it possible that the old pilgrim is so near his journey's end? O, to think that in a few minutes I shall meet my Father, who has led me all the journey through; and Jesus, my blessed Saviour; and that I shall so soon be with the soldiers of the cross who have gone before; and then to meet your mother, and your little children [addressing me] — this is joy too great to express!" — and closing his own eyes, he slept the blessed sleep. May such an end be mine, and yours, dear reader, is my prayer.

JOHN I. ROGERS.

CINCINNATI, August 12, 1880.

CONTENTS.

V.

vi CONTENTS.

CONTENTS.

CONTENTS.

AUTOBIOGRAPHY

—OF—

ELDER SAMUEL ROGERS.

CHAPTER I.

Birth in Virginia.—Emigration to Kentucky.—Settlement near Danville in the year 1793.—Removal to Clark County.—Manners and Customs of those times.

I was born in Charlotte county, Virginia, November 6, 1789, and was the eldest son of Ezekiel Rogers, whose father emigrated from Smithfield, England, a few years before the middle of the eighteenth century, and settled in Bedford county, Virginia. The family had no means of tracing any direct relationship to the distinguished martyr, John Rogers, who was burned at Smithfield in the year 1555. But my aunt Susan, a maiden lady of vivid imagination, was able to make out the connection quite to her satisfaction, suspended, however, upon very flimsy calculations — certainly too flimsy for the settlement of ancient honors upon our family. My ambitious aunt, as if sensible of the weakness of her cause, was in the habit of closing her argument with a flourish of the following facts, viz.: That her father came from Smithfield, England, where the distinguished martyr suffered; that his family were all Protestants; that all were partial to the name John; and last, though not least, that, as far back as their genealogy could be traced, not one of the name had ever been known to show the white feather. This last mentioned fact was compensating and comforting, indeed, inasmuch as it is far better to have the spirit of a martyr in the breast than to have the blood of a martyr in the veins. When my father, Ezekiel Rogers, was but an infant, my grand-

1

father embarked for England to obtain a small patrimony that had been left him by his relatives, and he was never heard of afterwards. After exhausting every available resource to obtain information, no tidings could be had either of the ill-fated vessel upon which he sailed, or of its crew. This sad circumstance weighed so heavily upon the widowed mother that both her body and mind gave way, and she soon died, leaving four little orphans, Ezekiel being the youngest.

The waves of the sea having carried away the father, and the waves of sorrow having borne the mother to an untimely grave, the little ones were thrown upon the charity of the world. By a happy providence they were kindly cared for, and found as much comfort as ordinarily falls to the lot of fatherless and motherless children.

At the age of fifteen my father joined a company of light-horse, belonging to the regiment of Colonel Washington. He was at the battle of Cowpens, where Tarleton was defeated and pursued so closely that he lost his cue. He continued in the service to the close of the Revolution, was present at the siege of York, and witnessed the surrender of Cornwallis. Soon after this he married Rebecca Williamson, of Charlotte county, Virginia, a woman of strong mind and deep devotion to the Christian religion. She was a member of the Church of England, but, under the teachings of the Wesleyan Reformers, she early took her stand with the Methodists, and had me christened by Bishop Asbury, who was the first American Bishop after the separation of the Methodists from the Church of England in the year 1784.

In the year 1793, my father, with his little family, joined a band of emigrants bound for Central Kentucky. Passing through Cumberland Gap and the Crab Orchard, he sojourned for a few months in the neighborhood of certain Virginia acquaintances, who had preceded him a few years and settled on the waters of Salt River, a few miles southwest of Danville, then in Mercer county.

The country was, for the most part, a tangled wilderness. The thick cane and undergrowth so obstructed the way, that the faithful packhorse was the pioneer's main dependence for conveying his family and household effects.

A few rude culinary instruments, with bread and meat for the journey, constituted the contents of one end of a large sack, called a wallet, made somewhat after the fashion of saddlebags; while a small bed and bedding, with now and then a little fellow too small to retain his equilibrium on horseback, were ordinarily stowed away in the other, the head of the little one protruding just far enough for breathing purposes. The mother sat enthroned between this moving kitchen and nursery, guiding the horse and administering to the wants of the babes, while the proud father, with unerring rifle on his shoulder, and his faithful dog by his side, led the way, dreaming of contentment and plenty in the Canaan of the West.

It was somewhat after this fashion that I found a safe and comfortable passage across the wilderness to the new home in Kentucky. Finding an opportunity of making a more favorable settlement, my father moved with his family to Clark county, and located on Stoner Creek, eight miles from Winchester, in what was called the Gay and Patton neighborhood. His family found comfortable quarters at Strode's Station, two miles from Winchester, while he and his faithful servant-boy built their cabin in the deep forest.

Seventy-five years have made great changes upon the face of the country and in the habits of the people about Winchester, and in my father's old neighborhood. Seventy-five years ago, dense forests and thick cane covered the face of the earth, except here and there, where some emigrant had reared his cabin and cleared out the cane and undergrowth in small patches, that he might raise a scant supply of the necessaries of life. The man who could boast of an orchard of young seedlings was almost an object of envy. Poultry-yards and pig-pens were not altogether unknown in the country, but wild turkeys supplied abundantly the place of tame fowls, while venison or bear meat was a good substitute for pork. Tea and coffee were rare luxuries, to be indulged in only on Sunday, and then in small quantities, and of poor quality. Sassafras and sage teas were most common, and reluctant children were induced to drink them from the consideration that the free use of these beverages would purify the blood and prevent the use of senna or the lancet. The maple supplied us abundantly with molasses and sugar. Even the thought of sugar-making now stirs the old blood in my veins, as some of my most pleasant memories are associated with the old-fashioned sugar-camp. I have watched the boiling sugar-water for hours, waiting with impatience for the consummation of my joys—the time of "stirring off." Always I have regretted the destruction of our beautiful maple forests of Kentucky—not only because the forests themselves were beautiful, and full of sweet memories, but especially because of the short supply of pure maple molasses, which, to my taste, has no parallel in the world. If I were to have the appointment of my winter breakfasts, I would always have, among other things, a stack of hot buckwheat cakes and the old family jug of home-made tree molasses, and, to crown the feast, a good strong cup of tea.

What would the Clark county children now think of the breakfasts and suppers of those early times? A breakfast of boiled milk and bread, or of milk and bread cold, according to taste—a supper of mush and milk, in a pewter dish, eaten with a pewter spoon, while sitting either upon the uncarpeted floor or upon the three-legged stool.

I can tell them that their grandfathers and grandmothers were happy and contented with such living, had fewer aches and pains, had more rosy cheeks and slept more soundly, had better dreams and clearer consciences, I doubt not, than their more aristocratic and wealthy descendants. Those hardy pioneers had few of the luxuries of life, but they had what was far better—good constitutions and good common sense. They had no time to sigh for what was out of reach, but brought their wants within the limits of their supplies. They had no plank, but laid their floors with rough puncheons. Instead of the large windows of the present day, which put the housewife to so much extra trouble and expense in draping and shading them to exclude the flood of light, they had a square opening in one side or end of the cabin, which they covered with paper, or muslin, which they then oiled, so as to make it translucent. The people had very little money then, and they needed but little. He was satisfied who had enough to pay for his salt and leather, and, at the end of the year, to pay his taxes. They were often without either salt or leather, and without the money to buy with. In such cases I have known clean hickory ashes to be used for salt, and buckskin moccasins instead of leather shoes. As a rule, the children went shoeless until they were large enough to engage in profitable out-door labor. For some time after we settled in Clark county we had no school near; and, while we remained in the county, I do not remember of having heard of a religious meeting or meeting-house. Our first school was taught in the neighborhood of Gateskills, by a young Mr. Stewart, in the year 1799, as well as I remember.

Hornback, on Strode's Creek, built the first mill in the neighborhood. Before that was done, we used hand-mills and graters. The grater was used in the fall of the year, before the corn became hard enough to grind. A Mr. Vert built the first mill I know of on Stoner; this was near North Middletown, and is now called Lidner's Mill. Here I had my first battle. Bowie knives and pistols were seldom used in those days, although fist-fighting was of frequent occurrence. My father never quarreled with any one, but was ever ready to resent an insult with blows, and he generally brought his adversary to speedy terms. He warned me against his example, both as to fighting and using profane language, declaring that one in the family was enough to do all the fighting and swearing. Poor as was this argument, I knew better than to disregard it. It was frequently my misfortune to be imposed upon, and, at times, quite roughly handled, by a boy named Jack Kirk, who lived near Vert's mill; and, although I believed myself capable of punishing the insolent tyrant, the remembrance of my father's admonition restrained me. Still I felt it degrading to be compelled to bear insult upon insult without resentment. A small circumstance changed my father's mind, and had the effect of quite changing his counsel. As he and I were passing Kirk's house together one day, this boy Jack, watching his opportunity, hurled a stone at my head, which, missing its mark, struck my father in the back. The youngster beat a hasty retreat, and was soon out of sight. My father turned to me, and said: "Sam, the next time Jack insults or abuses you, if you do not whip him, I will whip you as soon as I hear of it." This pleased me. The first time I went to the mill after this, the much coveted opportunity to redress my wrongs presented itself. I soon brought the insolent fellow to terms, made him beg my pardon for past offenses and promise to amend his life in the future. Shortly after this, we parted to meet no more until, as soldiers in the war of 1812, we met on the Northern lakes, when Jack Kirk thanked me for what I had done, saying that I had made a man of him.

CHAPTER II.

His father makes a prospecting tour Westward.—Passes O'Post, now Vincennes.—Crosses the Mississippi at Paincourt, now St. Louis.—Purchases land on the Missouri, twenty miles above St. Louis—Removes with his family to his new home in 1801.—He is pleased with his new home.—Fertile lands.—Wild game and fruits.—The first water-mill.—Night overtakes him in the forest.—He is pursued by wolves.—Makes a narrow escape.—Fishing and swimming his delight.

In the year 1799 a pamphlet fell into my father's hands which gave a glowing description of New Spain, or Upper Louisiana, now called Missouri. It set forth the great fertility of the soil, the rare beauty of the country, the abundance of game, and the vast extent of range for stock, besides the gift of six hundred and forty acres of land to every *bona fide* settler. All this was too much for my father, who, by this time, had contracted a great fondness for border life. Accordingly, in company with a Mr. Bradley, of Clark county, he mounted his favorite horse, and, with rifle on his shoulder, faced the boundless wilderness. They crossed the Ohio at the Falls, and took the Indian trail to O'Post, now called Vincennes, on the Wabash river— the oldest settlement in the West, I believe. Thence they passed through to Paincourt, now St. Louis. This place was an insignificant village at that time, inhabited chiefly by Spaniards and French. There was not a brick house in the place until several years afterward. The two most respectable dwellings were occupied, the one by Chouteau and the other by Gratiot, men who were for years the leading merchants of the place. They dealt extensively in furs, by which they amassed large fortunes. Furs and skins were the chief circulating medium of that time. There were two Spanish forts near the river, the one a little below and the other a little above the town. My recollection is that these forts had round towers, twenty or thirty feet high. My father was offered one hundred and fifty acres of land near the village for a fine horse, which he prized very highly. That land is now covered with blocks of the finest business houses in the city of St. Louis. There was then but little promise of the future prosperity of the place. Indeed, it has always been my opinion that it was the accident of its having been the first trading post of that region, rather than any peculiar advantage in situation on the Mississippi, that gave it the start of all other places in the West. But I will venture the prediction that, without some great misfortune to the place, the man who lives to see St. Louis in the middle of the next century will see the largest city this side of New York, if not the largest in the United States. This will be in no small degree owing to the fact that St. Louis, from the time of the Chouteaux until now, has been peculiarly blessed with enterprising and public-spirited men, without which no city has ever attained to great distinction.

From Paincourt my father passed on to what was called the Bonhomme settlement, on the Missouri river, twenty-two miles from St. Louis. There he bought a tract of six hundred acres of land at one dollar per acre. On the tract were two log cabins, and there were about four acres of the land under cultivation. This place he rented out for one year, and laid his *claim* in what is now Franklin county, about fifty miles west of St. Louis, in the vicinity of South Point.

Returning to Kentucky the same season, he purchased a small drove of cattle, which, with the assistance of his faithful man, Cy, he took, in a second journey through the wilderness, to New Spain. There he sold his cattle at a profit of eight hundred dollars; and with a part of the money he paid for the land he had purchased. The remainder he expended in moving to his new home.

In the month of September, 1801, we loaded eight pack-horses with such things as were most useful, and started for our home in New Spain. I, being the oldest child, had to walk and carry a rifle, and help to drive the cat-

tle over the entire route. My father advised my mother
to leave her Bible with her friends in Kentucky, as the
country whither we were going was under the control of
the Catholic Church, which prohibited the use of it
among the common people; and that the discovery of
her Bible might involve the family in trouble. She
would not listen to such counsel, however, but determined at every hazard to carry her Bible with her, saying she could not think of rearing her children without
it, and would not be willing to live in any country where
she could not have the benefit of the Word of God. To
avoid the vigilant eye of the priest, she sewed it in a
feather bed, and carried it safely through, and found it,
indeed, a "lamp to her feet and light to her path" in
her wilderness home. The priest never gave her any
trouble. We carried with us a large tent, under which
the family found ample protection from the storm.
Before the door of our tent we built large fires, which
afforded us both comfort and light by night, as well as
facilities for cooking, etc. We camped several days on
the little Wabash, very near the place where the village
of Maysville now stands. This was in what is now Clay
county, Illinois. Here my father killed and jerked
venison enough for our journey. The common practice
of jerking venison and beef in those days was carried on
by cutting the meat into thin slices, and exposing it to a
moderate heat, until it became perfectly dry. It then
might be put away and kept for a long time without the
use of salt. While camping on the little Wabash, my
father killed a young buffalo, the first one I had ever
seen running wild. The tenderloin of this young animal
was very delicious. I went to the little river that ran
close to our camp, to assist my father in washing the wild
meat which he had brought in, and I was astonished at
the quantities of fish that inhabited those waters. When
we threw the offal into the river the hungry fish fairly
made the water boil in struggling after it.

We were about four weeks, altogether, on our journey,
and to me they were four happy weeks. My experiences

1*

were the richest of my boyhood life. In the neighborhood of the Missouri river I had my first experience in eating persimmons. A stranger gave me a few ripe ones, and they were so delicious that I sought and found the tree upon which they had grown. In my eagerness, I failed to discriminate between the ripe and the half-ripe fruit; so I ate rapidly for some minutes until I found my mouth so contracted that I could eat no more. I came down from that tree, if not a better, certainly a wiser boy. I had learned to discriminate to a better advantage afterwards.

We were all delighted with our new home. I, especially, was pleased to find game and wild fruit so abundant, and so easily obtained. Our table was rarely without venison, turkey and fish of the choicest kind. The most delicious honey was obtained, not only in the forest, but also in the prairie grass. The glades afforded strawberries in their season, and along the streams I found the fox grape, and the summer grape, and a large white grape, more delicious than anything of the wild-grape kind I have ever known. Indeed, the white grape of the Missouri river-banks would rival in sweetness our best cultivated varieties. Also, we had gooseberries in abundance, and no thorn upon the fruit or bush.

The lands were very fertile, and produced as fine crops of grain as any in the State. Frederick Bates, afterwards Governor of Missouri, bought this place of my father, and lived and died upon it. I have always regretted that sale, and longed to repossess that home, around which so many youthful associations cluster.

For two or three years we had no grist-mills, except such as were run by hand. These were made of two rudely dressed stones, about twenty inches in diameter, placed one upon the other. The lower one being fastened permanently in a wooden frame, the other was moved by a small upright shaft, working in a round socket above, and let into one side of the stone by a similar socket. Taking hold of this shaft, the stone could be turned with great rapidity, but the grinding by such a process was tedious and very laborious. Sometimes we geared our hand-mills with bands, so that we could turn them by an ordinary crank; but this increased the expense of the machinery, and, on that account, was rarely used.

In the year 1804, Mr. Lawrence Long built a water-mill on Bonum Creek. This was considered to be a long stride toward civilization. My first trip to this mill was an eventful one for a boy only fourteen years old. Getting to the mill rather late in the day, and having to wait my turn, I was detained until after nightfall, and, therefore, had a dark and lonely journey before me. However, with a brave heart, I mounted my pony, and struck out for home. Having passed about half the distance—sometimes singing snatches of rude songs, and sometimes whistling to keep up my courage—there suddenly fell upon my ear sounds of distant music, which had not a very tranquilizing effect upon my nerves. At first I tried to persuade myself that what I had heard was only the echo of my own voice; but, after listening for some minutes, I caught the sound again, and knew that a pack of hungry wolves were on my trail. Every moment shortened the distance between us, until soon their wild howls began to make the night hideous. The sound of their approach animated my horse, so that I needed neither whip nor spur to bring him to his best speed, which he kept up for the rest of the way. The wolves followed us to within a very short distance of the house, and seemed quite reluctant to give up the chase; but, after lingering awhile about the premises, they departed, and I heard no more of them that night. I do not suppose that I was in any great danger from them, unless I had fallen from my horse, and, even then, it is doubtful if they would have attacked me. Nevertheless, the experience was such as to leave a vivid impression upon my mind, never to be erased in time. I can yet hear the fiendish yells of that hungry pack, as if they were just at my heels.

My father, being a very industrious and enterprising man, kept us all at work, except on Saturday afternoons and Sundays, when we were free to engage in any sport we might choose. The "*Muddy River,*" which is the meaning of "Missouri," had the greatest attractions for me. In this river I learned to swim, and I became so accustomed to the water that I often performed the feat of swimming entirely across it and back again. In these waters I learned the art of angling, which all of my friends know is yet much practiced by me. The Missouri has always been famous for large cat-fish and buffalo-fish; of these, in a few hours on Sunday morning, I have caught a large load for a packhorse to carry. Although I often fished on Sunday, I suppose that I was not without some good impulses; but the thought of doing any good in the world had not entered my mind, I was so taken up with the wild sports of that almost heathen land. I hardly dreamed that there was any civilization or refinement in store for the country for generations to come; nor do I remember that I had any desire for a change: the glades, and forest, and river afforded charms enough for me.

CHAPTER III.

The cession of the territory to the United States in 1804.—Lewis and Clark.—They winter in the vicinity.—Emigration is stimulated.—The dawn of civilization.—The first preachers.—His father sells out and returns to Kentucky.—He settles in Bourbon, now Nicholas county.—Marriage.—A grateful tribute to his wife and mother-in-law.—Conversion under the preaching of Stone and Dooley.

Two circumstances occurred about this time which resulted in swelling the tide of emigration and bringing the dawn of civilization into our country. Napoleon having gained from Spain, by conquest, all that country called Louisiana, ceded it to the United States by a treaty, which, I believe, was ratified in the year 1804. It was stipulated that he should receive for the entire territory $15,000,000, which, at that time, was considered an exorbitant price. Jefferson's administration was subjected to severe criticism, not only on account of the large price which was paid for the land, but also because of his having exercised unwarranted authority in the premises by making said treaty. However this might have been, the measure became very popular, inasmuch as it secured to the United States a vast amount of territory of very fertile lands, as well as the free navigation of the Mississippi.

The other circumstance, of less general importance, was particularly beneficial to our part of the country. Lewis and Clark, who had been commissioned to explore the country from the mouth of the Missouri to its source, and from the headwaters of the Columbia river to its mouth, spent their first winter in our neighborhood. The accounts which they and their men sent back to their friends concerning our country were so favorable that, the following season, great numbers visited our neighborhood, and purchased homes. From this time our part of the country was destined to be settled with marvelous rapidity.

We began to see the dawning of civilization, and to hear the people talk, for the first time, about schools and churches. Up to this time, we had never seen a preacher, or a school-teacher. When we first arrived in that country, my father said, in my hearing, that, if his children lived to be each one hundred years old, wild pasture and game would there be abundant all of their lives. For my part, I did not dream that I should live to see the country densely populated, and to see great cities springing up hundreds of miles west of that place. Nevertheless, the people continued to pour into the land so rapidly, that we soon began to fear for our free pastures and abundant wild meat.

By industry and frugality, my father, in a short time, had a farm tolerably well improved, with a large peach orchard and comfortable buildings upon it; and we were quite "well-to do," for those times, in a temporal point of view. But, while success in accumulating a goodly amount of the perishable things of this life attended us, our spiritual wants were almost wholly neglected. Perhaps I ought not to say that our souls were entirely neglected, since our mother did all that she could do, under the circumstances, in the way of giving us religious instruction. But for that godly woman, with her old family Bible, we would have been in almost total darkness. She was ever vigilant and concerned about our immortal souls; so much so that my father often became greatly worried, and would lose his patience. Still she persevered in her entreaties and exhortations until she gained his consent to allow her to have the children named — *christened,* as she called it.

Preparations were making for this ceremony, when a Baptist preacher, by the name of Music, came into our midst, and preached a series of sermons on Baptism, which convinced our mother that the immersion of adults in water was the only Christian baptism. A Methodist minister, by the name of Parker, soon followed in a series of sermons; but, being unable to convince my mother that sprinkling is baptism, proposed to immerse her. She, however, declined, saying that she preferred to be immersed by one whose preaching and practice harmonized. All I knew of the Christian religion, until I had grown to the stature of a man, I learned from those two preachers, my mother, and the old family Bible, which my mother took to that country in her feather bed. I do not remember having seen any other Bible until I was nineteen years of age.

I never had the opportunity of attending school but three months in my life; at the end of those months I could read and write, and cipher to the "Single Rule of Three," when I graduated with honor. I have often regretted that my early opportunities were so poor, and that so much of my early life was spent in the backwoods. It may be, however, that the hardships and privations of the pioneer were the very means employed by our all-wise Father to fit me for usefulness in the fields I was to occupy in future years.

In the fall of 1809, on account of circumstances not necessary to mention here, my father sold his farm, moved back to Kentucky, and settled in what was then Bourbon, but is now Nicholas county, about midway between Millersburg and Carlisle. Here we were happy to find that Andrew Irvin had settled, having moved a short time before from Mercer county, Ky.

In the autumn of 1812, I married Elizabeth, youngest daughter of Andrew Irvin, and to this fact I owe all that I am, under God, and all that I hope to be. The female portion of this family was quite religiously inclined, but my young wife was especially pious. She was greatly interested for my salvation, and, by prayerful and continued efforts, was not long in leading me to the *cross* of that Saviour who had given her abounding life and peace.

My wife's family had been reared after the strictest sect of Presbyterianism. Her mother was a sister of Parson James Mitchell, of Bedford county, Virginia.

Mitchell was a divinity student, under old Parson Rice, whose daughter he afterwards married. He became eminent, both as a preacher and teacher, among the Presbyterians in his neighborhood. It was a rare occurrence for a Mitchell, or an Irvin, to contract a marriage, or associate, on intimate terms, with any who were not loyal to the Westminster creed. There are now, in the neighborhood of Danville, hundreds of their descendants — McDoughalls, Irvins, Lyles, Caldwells, Lapsleys and Rices — all of whom, so far as I have been able to learn, still adhere to Presbyterianism with the tenacity of their fathers.

A few years before my connection with Andrew Irvin's family, a fortunate circumstance liberated them from the shackles of Presbyterianism. In 1801, the family lived on Cane Ridge, in Bourbon county, near the place where Barton W. Stone, with five other distinguished Presbyterian divines, wrote the Last Will and Testament of the Springfield Presbytery. They lived even nearer to the place where Stone held the most remarkable revival meeting on record, an account of which I give in another chapter. My wife's family became early attached to Stone, and, by his persuasive eloquence, were induced to renounce the Westminster Confession, and go with the thousands who, having abandoned the church of their fathers, followed the simple teachings of the Holy Scriptures, as the only safe and infallible rule of faith and practice.

My mother-in-law, having a strong mind and retentive memory, possessed fine colloquial powers, and, being well versed in the Scriptures, was quite ready in an argument. She was altogether the most pious and godly woman I ever knew. Her godly example and conversation had a great influence on my mind and life. I became seriously inclined, and, under the preaching of Stone and R. Dooley, I became a firm believer in Christianity, was convicted of sin, and immersed in Hingston Creek, near Jackstown, a very short time after my marriage.

CHAPTER IV.

Declaration of war.—He enlists under Metcalf.—St. Mary's.—Fort
Defiance.—Meigs.—Dudley's defeat.—Sickness.—Left to die in a
blockhouse.—His friends save him.—His arrival at home.—Recruiting service.—End of the war.—Demoralization.—Fortunate
appearing of Reuben Dooley.—Revival at Old Concord.—Habits
of the young converts.—All pray.—Most of them exhort.—Views
in regard to conversion and the call to the ministry.—Strange
notions concerning Providence.

I was hopeful and zealous, and, for a long time, my
spiritual horizon was without a cloud. This state of
things, however, was not of very long duration. I was
but a babe in Christ, and poorly prepared to withstand
the temptations in store for me.

War had been declared between England and the
United States, and my country was calling loudly for
volunteers. Both my father and father-in-law had volunteered in the Revolutionary war, and had fought
through it. I had been taught to believe it disgraceful
to wait for the draft; accordingly I volunteered in Cap-
tain Metcalf's company, bid adieu to my young wife and
friends, and marched to the rendezvous at Cynthiana,
where we joined our regiment, commanded by William
E. Boswell. At Covington, we fell in with Colonel
Dudley's regiment, and we marched together to Fort
Meigs. From Pickway to Meigs, we marched through
an unbroken wilderness until we struck St. Mary's
Blockhouse, on St. Mary's river; then we got upon flat-
boats loaded with flour for Fort Defiance. Upon arriving at this fort we learned that Fort Meigs was being
besieged. At Defiance we received orders to unload our
flour, and stockade our boats. Our regiment was ordered
to land a mile above the besieged fort, while Dudley was
ordered to land on the other side of the river, spike the
cannon of the British, and return to the boats.

History tells how bravely he executed this order, and then allowed himself to be decoyed into ambush, so that he was entirely cut off. Out of his seven hundred men, only one hundred and fifty escaped. I assisted in the sad task of burying Dudley and his men, whom we found stripped to nakedness, scalped and dreadfully mutilated.

We succeeded in driving back the Indians that were on our side of the river, and were afterwards enabled to take the two British cannon that were below the fort. In this engagement I made a narrow escape from death, although I was not fully aware of it until the fight was over, when I counted seven holes in my clothing, which had been made by the enemy's balls.

Having landed above the fort, and being fairly engaged with the enemy, General Harrison discovered that the Indians were falling back, and, fearing that we might be led into ambush, sent Major John T. Johnston with orders for us to fall back, else we might share the fate of Dudley's regiment. Major Barton loaned his very fine charger to Johnston for this occasion, but a ball from the enemy killed him under his brave rider, and Major Johnston was compelled to get back as best he could. Johnston was ready to compensate Barton for his loss, but he would receive not a cent.

The success that attended our arms at Fort Meigs would have been made the occasion of much rejoicing, but for the cloud that hung over our spirits on account of Dudley's defeat. Though it may be a display of bravery, it is unsoldierlike to disobey orders. Croghan disobeyed, and succeeded; Dudley disobeyed, and was defeated. Disobedience brought death into the world, with untold misery and ruin.

Very soon after this battle, I was taken down by a very low form of fever, called, in that day, typhus. I was in an unconscious state, and entirely helpless, during a period of six weeks. Though unconscious of what was taking place around me, I seemed to be traveling in a dreamland all the time. I thought I was riding behind a heartless creature, on a rough, clumsy horse, over the roughest road I had ever known. At one time we were ascending rocky hights, with deep gorges on either side, with scarcely the width of a horse-path between them. Again, we seemed to go thundering down steep mountain sides, at a break-neck speed; and oh, how it made my head throb, and my bones rattle! I remonstrated with the wretch for carrying me over such rough ground, but to no purpose. At length my patience became threadbare, and I slid off the horse, saying, "I shall proceed this way no further;" and, for the first time, consciousness returned.

When I awoke, the boom of the cannon was roaring in my ears, and, upon learning that the Indians had again besieged the fort, I called for my musket, but soon came to myself sufficiently to realize the fact that I could not turn myself on my cot, much less use a musket. I do not believe that I had been twice changed in position during my sickness, so inattentive were our nurses. This neglect resulted in the sloughing of the flesh from the side of my limbs on which I had so long been lying. Although I have lived to become an old man, I have never been as able-bodied as I was before that sickness. When in a condition to be moved, I, with other invalids, was carried to Seneca, situated near the mouth of the Sandusky river, where General Harrison had his camp, and near Fort Stephenson, where Colonel Croghan, with one hundred and fifty men, defended himself so gallantly against one thousand, and for which General Harrison was compelled to reprimand him, though the army was so loud in his praise.

The main army soon left for Canada, and I engaged a man to take me home. I was poorly able to ride, but had no comforts where I was, and became convinced that my life depended upon my getting home. This man was so fearful of the Indians that he hurried me along at such a rate that I gave out, and was left at Scioto Blockhouse. Here, I was alone and helpless. In the evening, the occupants of the blockhouse came in, and found me almost in a dying condition. Fortunately, I knew one of the men, Tom Lancaster, from Millersburg, who kindly waited on me, until, contrary to my expectations, I began to recover, and to think again of trying to get back to my family. I now sent word, by the man who had left me at the blockhouse, to my friends in Kentucky about my condition. No sooner did my brothers-in-law, John and Joshua Irvin, hear where I was, than they got horses, and hurried on to my relief. I waited, with great impatience, for strength and opportunity to enable me to get on my way, and was almost ready to give up the idea of seeing my friends again, when the familiar voices of my two friends, saluting my ear, made my heart leap for joy. They bore me quietly along the way, by short stages, so that I really improved; though, at times, we were on the point of starvation. I arrived at home in the month of October, 1813, and remained sick for the most of the winter.

The following summer, I entered the recruiting service, having stations at Lexington, Paris, Washington and Maysville. Upon the approach of winter, I went out to Malden, and there remained until peace was declared. We received our discharge at Detroit, and, after the disbanding of the army, we crossed the lake to Cleveland, then a very small village, but now one of the most beautiful cities of the lakes. Seven of us started for home on foot, and, after much privation and suffering, we arrived safe at Steubenville, on the Ohio. Here, we got upon a keel-boat, and came down to Maysville; thence we proceeded to our home, where we found all well, and rejoicing that the war was at an end.

During the war, the people became estranged from the house of worship, and a general coldness and demoralization prevailed. Licentiousness and corruption, the natural offspring of war, had taken the place of virtue and good order. A few, here and there, who had not bowed the knee to Baal, were still holding on their way, prayerfully and trustfully looking for a better day. I, myself, was not exempt from the baleful influences of the war; exposed, daily, to the severest tests of my Christian integrity, and, having been in the recruiting service for some time, which, by the way, is the most corrupt and corrupting service of war, I had forgotten my first love, and turned back to my old sinful ways.

About this time, there appeared amongst us a most remarkable character, in the person of Reuben Dooley, from the settlements of Barren county, Kentucky. Reuben Dooley was considerably my senior, a man of great physical endurance, plain in his attire, and, in his address, humble as a little child; but zealous, prayerful, hopeful and untiring in his labors of love. His forte, as a preacher, was chiefly in exhortation. Those who have heard the elder Creath, in his palmiest days, may form some idea of his eloquence. His compass of voice was such that he could be distinctly heard by thousands in the open air, at one time. This man, providentially, came to our help most opportunely. He commenced a revival at Old Concord, three miles southeast of Carlisle, in Nicholas county. The influence of this meeting extended to Cane Ridge, in Bourbon county, and, indeed, spread far and wide, until hundreds were again rallied to the standard of the Prince of Peace, and hundreds converted to Christ. Under the searching appeals of this wonderful man of God, my heart was again melted, and, from that day to the present year of grace, 1870, I, myself, have been humbly striving to call sinners to repentance. At this revival, two of my sisters, Fanny and Lucy, and my wife, were baptized, as, also, were my brothers-in-law, William, John and Joshua Irvin, all of whom became very useful proclaimers. William Irvin soon married my sister Fanny, and moved to Ohio, where he labored, more or less successfully, until, within the last ten years, he moved to Northwestern Illinois, where, I learn, he is still laboring faithfully, in word and teaching, and doing much good.

In those pioneer times, among the converts, it was customary for almost all of them to take some part in the social meetings that were held from house to house, among the brethren. Not only did most of the young men pray, and sometimes exhort, and relate their experiences, but some of the women prayed, and sometimes exhorted with great warmth.

Brother Dooley left us, sometime in the autumn of 1816 or 1817, to fill engagements elsewhere, and, consequently, we were without any ordained minister for several months. The good work, however, went on. Many of us exhorted, and, as I have observed, nearly all prayed; so that the meetings were interesting and profitable, both to saints and sinners. When Brother Dooley returned in the spring, he found us with harness on, at work. During his absence, thirty or forty had professed religion, as the phrase went, and were ready to receive baptism at his hands. I had been exercising my gift in exhortation, teaching in a very humble way, during Dooley's absence; so that it began to be whispered among the people that I was called to the ministry. Views were entertained in those days, not only by those of us who were derisively called New Lights, but by almost all denominations, both in regard to conversion and the call to the ministry, which were very absurd, and would now be rejected by almost every one. The evidences of pardon looked for then were a light, a whisper, a dream, or exhilarating feelings after great depression of spirits, etc. The evidence of a call to the ministry was, ordinarily, an impression, either waking or dreaming, that continued to rest upon the mind with such weight that the subject could not get rid of it. We made no distinction between the ordinary and the extraordinary ministers of Christ, but claimed to be in the shoes of the Apostles; and, hence, we expected the Lord to work with us in the same way that he did with the Apostles; and we were praying and looking for some sign, or wonder, or demonstration of the power of the Holy Ghost.

We believed, as Kincaid and others had taught, that miracles would be restored to the Church, if we could only attain to the proper degree of holiness. We were, therefore, looking continually for the beginning of more wonderful signs than any yet apparent. Meanwhile, we had to content ourselves with such mental impressions as could be reasonably construed into the extraordinary workings and unutterable calls of the Spirit. We never thought of finding our *call* in the New Testament.

Brother Dooley, on his return, finding me using the little talent I had, concluded that I must have been *called;* so he took me aside, and closely questioned me as to my feelings, impressions, etc. After the examination was over, he pronounced me one of the called and sent of God, as was Aaron. I urged that I was not qualified, never having attended school but three months in my life, and, having had no early advantages, was profoundly ignorant. But he contended that the Lord's ways were not like our ways; nor His thoughts like ours; that he had "chosen the foolish things of this world to confound the wise; and weak things of this world to confound the mighty; and base things of the world, and things that are despised, hath God chosen, yea, and things which are not, to bring to naught things which are; that no flesh should glory in his presence." This was too much for me; so, confiding in Brother Dooley's superior wisdom and goodness, I was overwhelmed.

I bethought me, however, that I could command but one horse, and that a very indifferent one, very low in flesh, and not by any means able to stand a journey; for preaching, in those days, was invariably associated with *forsaking all* and taking a journey. We thought of nothing short of counting all loss for Christ. We did not look for salary, passage, or anything of this kind; we went without purse or scrip, and often without our meals, because we had nothing to buy with; and had to swim rivers, because we had no money to pay the ferryman.

Dooley met my difficulty again, saying that, if God had really called me, He would sustain my horse, and fatten him on the way. Thus convinced, I started on a tour of ten days, through the counties of Bourbon, Nicholas and Fleming. As the distance from appointment to appointment was not great, I deemed it best to go on foot, that I might allow my horse to recruit a little for harder service.

In Fleming county, I fell in with one of the most powerful men of the Stone reformation, James Hughes. He heard me exhort, and, after the meeting was over, came to me, and grasped my hand, saying, " I perceive, my brother, that the Lord has a great work for you to do; only be humble and prayerful, and the Lord will be with you." This confirmed what Dooley had said, and it gave me great encouragement. Flattery has ruined many a young preacher; hence, many good men are afraid to give a poor young preacher the word of encouragement that his soul pants for, and which is indispensable to his life and strength as a preacher. I have never, in my life, failed to give encouragement when I thought it *needed;* and this prudent encouragement I have never seen work any evil. It is very easy to temper these words with a little wholesome counsel, and greatly benefit the young preacher.

CHAPTER V.

Trial by the Shakers.—Preaching in Lewis county.—Disgraceful scene.—His opinion of those who misbehave on occasions of baptism.—A tour.—The preacher and the horse cared for.—The King's Bounty, a cut nine-pence.—The wife's parting words.—At Falmouth.—Shaking hands.—In Preble county, O.—The Dooleys and others.—Meeting in the woods.—Scores of mourners.—Mourners' benches abolished.

About this time, Dunlavy and other leaders among the Shakers made me a visit, with the view of gaining me over to the silly teachings of their Ann Lee. At the same time, they visited a Presbyterian neighbor of mine, and induced him to join them. They disturbed me no more, however, until, hearing how greatly the Lord was blessing my labors in my new field in Ohio, they sent some of their chief men to make a final trial of my faith. I treated them with courtesy, and argued with them out of the Scriptures, proving that they preached, not the gospel of Christ, but a new doctrine, and that, therefore, the anathemas of the Apostle were upon them. At length, they gave up my case as a hopeless one, saying, that the trouble with me was, that I had never been shaken. I do not know exactly what they meant by this remark, but I do know that Paul has said: "They shall turn away their ears from the truth, and be turned unto fables"—and that we are in no danger of being turned unto fables until we give up the truth of God.

I felt that my trial by the Shakers had given me additional strength and boldness to preach the gospel; so I buckled on my armor, and traveled up and down the Ohio, on both sides, preaching, from Cincinnati to Portsmouth, sometimes assisted by Hughes or Dooley, and sometimes alone. Our labors were especially blessed in Lewis county, many, being convicted of sin, demanding baptism at our hands. In this county, on the occasion of a baptism, one of the most disgraceful scenes took place that I ever witnessed. We had closed a very triumphant meeting, on the east fork of Cabin Creek, had repaired to the water to baptize the candidates, and a band of ruffians followed us, who, during the meeting, had become incensed, both on account of the reproofs which had been given them, and the loss of some of their number, who had renounced sin and turned to the Lord for mercy. Reuben Dooley had fairly begun the administration of the solemn ordinance of baptism, when this rabble band gathered on the bank opposite the congregation, and set up such wild, fiendish howls as never before saluted my ears. They cried, yelled, howled, barked, and did everything in their power that fiendishness could invent to destroy the solemnity of the occasion, and make the place hideous. We all stood our ground, however, and Dooley proceeded to administer baptism, as if nothing was occurring. At length, a ridiculous circumstance closed this disgraceful scene. A drift was lodged on the opposite side of the creek, upon which the trunk of a large tree had been caught, and was projecting out over the water, almost to the very spot where Dooley was baptizing. The ringleader of this band had perched himself out on this log, making all sorts of faces, and cutting many wild antics to attract the attention of the multitude. Evidently, he felt himself the hero of the disgraceful scene. As the baptisms proceeded, he increased in boldness, and inched himself out to the extreme end of the log, where he was almost near enough to Dooley to touch him, as he stood in the water. At length, the old log broke entirely from the drift, and man and log fell, with a heavy plunge, into deep water, and it was not because he deserved a better fate that he did not stay there. For a moment, the silence of death reigned over the scene. The man soon rose to the surface, and swam to the shore, where his company met him, and extended to him the hand of mock welcome into the kingdom. He found little enjoyment, however, in this last scene, but took a straight course up the hill until out of sight, his friends following with yells of laughter until the hill shut out all from our view. In all my life, I have seen nothing so disgraceful as this, save once.

In 1840, I was baptizing in the night the ringleader of a very wild party of young men, when his comrades gathered in a saw-mill, almost immediately over the spot where I was baptizing, and threw stones, chunks of wood, and dogs, into the water, at no very comfortable distance from us. There can be no apology for such conduct, yet, in this case, there was, perhaps, an extenuating fact. The young men believed that their leader was acting the part of a hypocrite, and I have since been convinced that they were correct, though these simpletons ought to have known that the hypocrisy of the one could not wash out the stains of the many.

There can be no excuse for willful misbehavior in the house of God, or during the administration of any divine ordinance. It is according to the experience of my long life, that the wildest natures are subdued in witnessing the administration of the ordinance of baptism, in which the burial and resurrection of our Redeemer are so beautifully and solemnly set forth. However high the pretensions of persons may be, and however much of refinement they may claim, if they are rude, and misbehave on occasions like this, it is a sure mark of coarse nature and ill-breeding, if not of really bad hearts. The reader must not conclude that, in those early times, it was at all common to witness rude behavior during religious exercises. Indeed, I think there was, ordinarily, more profound solemnity in the worshiping assembly *then* than *now*.

In June, 1818, it was arranged that I should take a tour through Preble county, with the father of Reuben Dooley, who was a very pious and devoted preacher of the gospel. I rented out my little farm, with the stock and utensils that were upon it, reserving one small horse, which was my only dependence for the journey. My horse was so poor that I expressed my fears to Brother

Dooley that he would give out on the way. Dooley
earnestly reproved me for my lack of faith. Said he:
" If the Lord has called you to this work, he will see to
it, not only that you have strength to preach, but that
your horse shall have strength to carry you to your appointments." And it really seemed so, for my horse
fattened every day of the journey. The people now
may ridicule Dooley's faith; but in those days of religious enthusiasm, it was the current belief that, if the Lord
called any one to the ministry, He would open a door of
utterance; would put words into his mouth, which he
should speak; and, by a special, if not a miraculous,
interposition of power, would give him his outfit, and
direct and sustain him on his way. On the eve of starting, I instituted a search for means of defraying any
incidental expenses of the way, but, to my mortification,
I discovered that not a dollar could be found. In one
corner of my vest-pocket I found a cut nine-pence,
which, Dooley said, was the King's Bounty, and an
earnest that I was enlisted in His service. He insisted
upon it, that this was enough, or the Lord would have
provided more.

When the hour came for bidding my family adieu, I
was completely overwhelmed with grief. My faithful
Christian wife approached me with tearful eyes, but a
heavenly and triumphant smile lighted up her face as she
said : " My dear husband, why are you so desponding,
and what occasion do you now have to weep? Did you
not leave me, and enlist to fight the battles of your
country, with little hope even of earthly reward? How
much better is it now, that you go, with a brave heart,
to fight the battles of King Jesus, with the promise of
the life that now is and of that which is to come !" With
such words of encouragement, I felt my manhood return, and, after we had all bowed in prayer and exchanged a few words of parting, we set out upon our
journey, Elder Moses Dooley being our guide.

We spent the first night near Falmouth, and, by the
second night, reached the house of a Brother Nelson,

six miles beyond Cincinnati. On our arrival, we learned, to our great joy, that the people had assembled there to hold a prayer-meeting. This looked like a special providence, and it greatly strengthened us. I was invited to speak, but not before I felt an almost irresistible impression that I ought to say something to that waiting people. After a brief discourse, or rather exhortation, we sang and prayed, and sang again and again, the congregation mingling and commingling in the old-fashioned exercise of shaking hands, which I wish we could have restored now, instead of so much stiffness and formality as we have in our worship. The *sermon* now is the great event of the day's worship, and little else is talked about or thought of as the attraction to the house of the Lord. The disciples anciently met together to break bread, and the chief entertainment, from all we can gather, was the reading and expounding of the Scriptures, singing psalms, and hymns, and spiritual songs, and making melody in their hearts — not on any *instrument*, that we know of.

The following day we had a prosperous journey, and arrived, in good time, at the home of the venerable Dooley, in Preble county, Ohio. Here I became acquainted with many of the best preachers in the Stone reformation. Among them, I met David Purviance, and Levi, his son, and John Adams — men of more than ordinary intelligence. The Purviances were originally from Cane Ridge, Bourbon county, Kentucky, and were with Stone in the great revival which occurred in 1804. Levi Purviance made a profession of religion there, and afterwards became an educated and able preacher of the gospel.

Having heard of a meeting which was to be held on Whitewater, near New Paris, Father Dooley and I at once made our arrangements to attend it. On our arrival, we found a great concourse of people assembled in the woods. A rough stand had been erected for the accommodation of the preachers, and the people were arranged on convenient seats around it. Being unwilling to enter the stand among the more aged preachers that already occupied it, I took a seat in the congregation, and was much edified and enthused by a discourse from Father Purviance. At length, having been called to speak, my diffidence left me, and I began to exhort sinners to contemplate Jesus, bleeding and dying for them on the cross. I do not remember of ever having been more completely transported in thought and feeling than on this occasion. I felt that the Spirit of the Lord God was upon me. Calling upon sinners to behold the Saviour in his suffering, I felt the warming influence of the cross in my own heart. I now have no recollection of what I said, or how I said it; I only remember my theme, and the transports of my soul in beholding the bleeding, dying One. No doubt, the effort was an humble one, but my soul was in it; the power of God attended it, for scores came to the mourners' bench, crying and praying — crying for mercy.

We had mourners' benches in those days, and they were things unauthorized by the Word of God. We long since abolished them, and we did right in so doing; but I almost fear that we did it in such a way as to abolish the mourners too.

I knew then but a part of the gospel, else scores might have been converted. This I knew—how to make sinners feel by presenting the facts of the gospel; but I did not know what to tell them to do, for, as yet, I did not understand that the gospel had commands to be obeyed in order to the enjoyment of the promises. As it was, many professed faith in Jesus and were baptized, while as many more went on mourning. I now felt confirmed as to my call to the ministry. Especially did I feel strengthened when the pious and venerable Adams approached me, and, grasping my hand, said: "Go on, my young brother; I perceive that the Lord is with you, and has filled you with His Spirit, and is giving you much fruit."

CHAPTER VI.

Going to William M. Irvin's.—Misdirection.—A strange Providence. —Robert Long.—Development of God's purpose.—A great meeting in the woods.—He sees the hand of God, and determines to move with his family.

From this neighborhood we crossed over into Indiana, and spent three weeks in the region of the Walnut Level. We found many friends scattered through this region ; had many good meetings, and some fruitful seasons. Upon returning to Father Dooley's, it was determined that Thomas Dooley, a brother of Reuben, though not so able a preacher, should accompany me back home, taking in, on our way, the neighborhood to which my brother-in-law, William M. Irvin, had recently moved. I had never been there, but knew that it was near where Greene and Clinton counties cornered. The first night after we started found us near Dayton, at the house of Nathan Worley, a venerable and able Christian preacher. On the following day we got to Xenia by noon, fed our horses, and inquired for the Irvin settlement. No one could give us any definite information, but all agreed that our nearest and best way must be through the county-seat of Clinton, which was, and now is, Wilmington. When we arrived near Wilmington, we learned that we were as far from Irvin's as we had been at Xenia, having traveled eighteen miles out of our way. Here began to open up a strange providence, which was years in developing, but which impressed me then with the fact that the Lord had a hand in leading us out of the way, and directing our steps into fruitful paths, which we were about to pass by. Though a half century has passed since then, I am, to-day, as firmly convinced that the Lord was leading us out of our way for purposes of His own glory, as I can be of any fact of which I am not absolutely assured.

When within two miles of Wilmington, we stopped at
a house to inquire our way, and were informed that we
were then as near Irvin's as we would be when in Wilmington. Having been kindly invited to alight and
stay all night, we concluded to proceed no further until
morning. Here I met the first Quaker I had ever
seen. At bed-time, we made preparations for worship before retiring, as was our custom; but we were
politely informed by our host that he did his own praying, and we might do ours. All this he said with perfect civility, showing that he was in favor of praying,
but desired to do *his* praying according to his own
faith. We were up betimes in the morning, and,
having received directions, started on our way before
breakfast. Our Quaker friend, instead of sending us by
the way of Douglass's Prairie, which was a straight
road to Irvin's, sent us, by a path, across to the Washington road, three miles northeast of Wilmington. Here
we called at the house of a very intelligent' gentleman,
James Sherman, who informed us that, though we had
been sent out of our way, he would direct us to one of
his neighbors who knew all about the place to which we
were journeying, and the people after whom we were
inquiring. Having followed the directions, we soon
found our man, Robert Long, plowing in his field. As
soon as we got near enough, I, being chief speaker, pro-
pounded the necessary questions concerning the place
and people we were seeking. But, without answering my
questions, he told us to go to the house, have our horses
fed, and he would tell us all that we wished to know.
Said I : " If the Lord has any work for us to do in this
country, we are His servants, and are on His business."
Long wept for joy, and, after brushing the great tears
from his eyes, said : " Thank God! I have been praying for preachers, and the Lord has at last sent them.
Go to the house, and I will meet you there." And so he
did. Having introduced ourselves to him in the field,
he now introduced us to his good Christian wife, Jane,
after which we knelt down and prayed. And now the

mystery of our having been misled, I concluded, was beginning to be revealed. After prayer and mutual congratulations, we were invited to breakfast. Now Brother Long informed us that he had visited my brother-in-law, and was well pleased with him; but, said he, "He is not preaching much." He further stated that he, himself, had moved from Stillwater, where there was a small congregation of Christians, but, since his settlement here, he and his family had been without any religious associations. After breakfast, he would not allow us to depart without first exacting a promise from us that we would preach for him on our return. Accordingly, we gave him an appointment, and proceeded on our journey, musing by the way and talking of the strange providence of God.

We found the way to Irvin's without further difficulty. All were glad to meet us once more. We were sorry to learn that religion was at a very low ebb in this part of the country. The cumbering cares incident to making a settlement in a new country had so engrossed the mind of Brother Irvin, that he had, in a great measure, neglected to exercise his gift, and had, consequently, accomplished but little. Dooley and I were full of fire and zeal, though quite deficient in knowledge. We knew enough, however, to tell " the story of the cross " in a simple manner, and were not slow in pressing the claims of Jesus upon all we met. Irvin soon became equally enthusiastic, and we held several happy meetings together in his neighborhood. One of these meetings we held at Cheney's school-house, in the corner of Greene county. The house, I suppose, has long since rotted down, as the meeting alluded to was held there fifty years ago, and more; and I doubt not that many ransomed souls have gone from the little band that once met at Cheney's school-house to sing the praises of God in that house not made with hands, eternal in the heavens. Irvin here renewed his vows, and covenanted with God and with his brethren, to devote himself unreservedly to the ministry. He also determined to accompany us

2*

back to Kentucky. After we had accomplished the object of our visit here, we all started to fill the appointment we had left with Brother Long. We arrived at the place of meeting before the hour, but not before the people had assembled. The news had gone forth that two strangers were going to preach in the neighborhood, and the whole region round about had gathered to hear; some out of curiosity, but others in deep earnest. The speaking, singing, praying and exhorting continued for hours; indeed, the people were so worked upon that many of them were unwilling to leave the place. Here the providence of missing our way became still more clear. I could not now be mistaken that the Lord had a great work for me to do in this very region. I, therefore, resolved in my mind, before I left this ground, that I would go home, dispose of the little property I had there, and then return to this very place to work as long as the Lord should bless my labors. I believed that, in doing so, I was following the leadings of Providence, and the sequel has satisfied me beyond a doubt of the correctness of my conclusion. We did not continue our meeting long enough to form a correct judgment of what had been accomplished; but we were convinced that the Lord had many people in this country. After we had closed our meeting many still remained upon the ground; some were weeping, others rejoicing and praising God, all seemed loath to leave the place. Before leaving, we stated publicly that we felt that the Lord had called us to this new field, and that we had resolved to hurry home, wind up our affairs in Kentucky, and return without delay to the work in this neighborhood.

Now, we started for home; crossed the Ohio at Manchester, and passed into Lewis county, and across to Cabin Creek, where my brother-in-law, William Mitchell, lived. Here we had a pleasant meeting; but, being anxious to carry out my purposes before expressed, I hurried on to my home in Bourbon county. I now recounted to my wife at length the events of the tour; how my cut nine-pence had been sufficient for the ex-

penses of the way; how my horse had fattened from the
day I had started from home—all as Brother Dooley
had predicted; how I had been confirmed as to my call,
both by the abundant fruit of my labors, and the opinions of several experienced brethren. I also related
how, by the ignorance of the people in Xenia of whom
I inquired, I had been sent a half day's journey out of
my way; and how the misdirection of the Quaker
brought me to the house of Robert Long, who had been
anxiously waiting and praying for preachers; and how
this, again, opened up before me a field all ripe for the
sickle. I told her that I had made up my mind to return to Ohio, and enter at once upon the work that the
Lord had pointed out to me by so remarkable a providence. My wife listened with profound attention to the
detailed account of my journey, and the providence attending it, and at once expressed herself as agreeing
with me in my conclusion, that the Lord had really
called me, and was directing my course. She said she
was willing to go with me to my new field of labor—
counting all things but loss for Christ.

CHAPTER VII.

Removes to Clinton county, O.—Birth of John I. Rogers in 1819.—Organization of the congregation now called Antioch.—His ordination.—Sister Worley assists.—Return home.—Forty persons immersed at the first meeting.—The Macedonian cry.—Night baptisms.—Harvey's dream.—His conversion.—Mrs. Hodson's dream and baptism.

Preparations having been speedily made, we were soon upon our journey, and by the first of September we arrived at Robert Long's, in Clinton county, Ohio. There being no vacant house in the neighborhood for rent, it became necessary for me at once to set about building a cabin. Having obtained some assistance, in a very few weeks we were established in our new house, which was a common log cabin, chinked and daubed with common clay. The roof was made of large clapboards, bound together by long weight-poles. The floor was made of puncheons; the jambs and back-wall were constructed of stiff mortar, and of nearly the same material was the chimney made. Chimneys of this kind, in those days, were called cat-and-clay chimneys. Rough as was our new house, it afforded comfortable shelter for the winter. We felt that we had no right to complain of our humble dwelling, for many of the old prophets had not one half as good as ours, and our Redeemer had none at all. On the sixth day of January, 1819, John I. Rogers made his advent into the world in this very cabin. If there is anything in humble beginnings, then my son John I. has somewhat of which to boast.

I now gathered together a little band of Christians at Hester's school-house, on Todd's Fork, a small tributary of the Little Miami, and we were constituted upon the Bible as the only rule of faith and practice. Work went on triumphantly; members were added to the church almost daily. Many demanded baptism; but, not yet hav··

ing been ordained, I did not feel at liberty to baptize. It must be borne in mind that we did not *then* make baptism an absolute condition to church membership. In order to my ordination, the brethren urged me to visit some of our old preachers in Preble county; which I did, bearing with me letters of commendation from my brethren at home.

After a journey of sixty miles, I found Brother David Purviance, and showed him my letters, which fully explained the object of my mission. He informed me that a Conference of preachers had been organized to take charge of all these matters, but they were not to meet again for nearly six months. I told Brother Purviance that I did not desire to create any disturbance, or in anything to be insubordinate, but that I seriously questioned the right of the Conference to assume any such authority; that I did not believe that they, or any one else, could impart any spiritual gift by the imposition of hands; that I thought any prudent ministers of the gospel, sitting on my case, could decide as to my call, and, by the imposition of their hands, could delegate to me the authority to baptize. Finding, at length, that the object of my mission had failed with Purviance, I urged him to send an ordained preacher with me, who could baptize the people who were impatiently waiting my return. To this proposition he made no objection, and it was arranged that Reuben Dooley should accompany me home. Dooley and I were soon on the way, but, meanwhile, we had an appointment to fill at the house of old Brother Worley. On arriving there, Dooley took Father Worley aside and told him the object of my mission to Purviance, and of my disappointment. Worley replied that, if he could hear me preach, he believed that he could determine whether the Lord had really called me. So they determined, without my knowledge, to put me up that night to preach my trial sermon. It was well that I knew nothing of the arrangement, for it would have embarrassed me. As it was, I felt quite at liberty, and acquitted myself to my own satisfaction, and, as I thought, to the satisfaction of my hearers. There was much feeling manifested in the audience, and Father Worley seemed especially pleased.

After the meeting was over, Brother Worley asked me privately if I would object to receive ordination at the hands of himself and Dooley. I answered, " Certainly not." So, then and there, they proceeded to ordain me by prayer and the laying on of hands. Old Sister Worley also laid her hands on me, and I have always believed that I received as much spiritual oil from her hands as from the hands of the others.

Early next morning we started for our home in Clinton, and by nightfall we were safely housed in our new log cabin. During the next day, news of our arrival spread like fire in stubble; so that, by the evening meeting-hour, an immense concourse of people had assembled together. After preaching, we baptized forty persons in the waters of Todd's Fork. Then I did my first baptizing; since that time I have baptized over seven thousand persons. Reuben Dooley returned immediately home; but his father, who accompanied us from Preble county, remained and assisted me no little in carrying on the great work then on hand. Meanwhile, I found it to be more convenient for us to make some changes in our location. We, therefore, gave up our new cabin, and moved to a vacant one on Robert Long's farm, where we remained but a short time, as the center of our most important work seemed to have drifted some miles to the southeast of us, in the neighborhood of Jonah Vandervort, on a branch of Cowan's Creek. In the course of the season, the neighbors and brethren built me a house in this community, where I lived and labored for twenty-seven years, save three, which I spent in Indiana, of which I shall hereafter speak.

There now seemed to be no bounds to the field of my labor. The Macedonian cry came up from every quarter. I was sent for from Highland county, where I went, and preached in the region of Snow Hill, and Old Morgantown, and down the East Fork, with marked success. I

preached both day and night; and baptized, more or
less, almost every day, and sometimes had baptisms at
night. These night baptisms were often very impressive.
The brethren prepared a number of torches for these
occasions, which abundantly lighted up the way as we
went on to the water, singing some animating song, with
a chorus like the following :

> " Jesus, my all, to heaven is gone,
> Hallelujah! Hallelujah!
> He whom I fix my hopes upon,
> Hallelujah! Hallelujah!
> His track I see, and I'll pursue,
> Hallelujah!
> The narrow way till him I view,
> Hallelujah!
> Then we'll go on; Glory, hallelujah!
> We'll go on and serve the Lord,
> Glory, hallelujah!"

It was not unfrequently the case that persons would
become convicted at the water, and demand baptism at
our hands. I have known ladies to demand baptism at
the water; and I have baptized them while they were in
their best Sunday suits.

About this time occurred a curious circumstance, which
I shall relate, and concerning which the reader may draw
his own conclusions. Samuel Harvey, who had been
reared a Quaker, had quite recently moved with his
family from the neighborhood of Hillsboro, and settled
in our vicinity. His wife, sometime previously, had
heard one of our preachers, and desired to join the
church, but her husband bitterly opposed her. One of
my meeting-places was not far from their house, and the
time for preaching there was near at hand. Mrs. Harvey
was anxious to attend the meeting, but, knowing the bit-
terness of her husband's feelings, she did not venture to
express her wishes to him. On the Saturday night
before the meeting, Harvey had a dream, and, on Sunday
morning, he astonished his wife by asking her if she did
not wish to go to the meeting that day. This was

something new under the sun to her, and she was quite
perplexed, because she could not understand its meaning. Seeing that he was in earnest, however, she answered in the affirmative. Harvey saw that she was
surprised, and at once related his dream. He said that
he saw in his dream a man arise in the stand, and quote
certain words of Scripture, which made such an impression on his mind that he had resolved to go and see
if I was the man. He further said that he had such a
distinct recollection of the features of the man, that he
could point him out in any assembly, could he see him.
As they approached the stand when they came to the
meeting, I arose and quoted my text. Harvey stopped,
and, turning to his wife, said: "Sarah, that is the man I
saw last night, and that is the very Scripture he quoted."
He sat at a distance from the stand, but his wife drew
near, and took a seat in the midst of the congregation.
At the close of my discourse I called for mourners, as
was our custom, and Harvey attempted to fly; but, being
about to fall, he turned about, approached the stand,
confessed his sinfulness, and told his dream to the whole
congregation. A deep interest pervaded the audience,
and much feeling was manifested all around. Harvey's
conversion and experience increased the solemnity of the
occasion, and deepened the impressions already made.
Many penitents came forward crying for mercy, and
many professed to obtain the hope of deliverance. Altogether, it was a meeting long to be remembered for
good.

Soon after this, a still more remarkable circumstance
occurred in this neighborhood. Upon the occasion referred to, a large assembly had gathered at the water's
edge, and, after an appropriate prayer, I was proceeding
to make some remarks upon the subject and design of
baptism, as was my custom, when an intelligent-looking
lady came from the opposite side of the stream, and,
upon approaching me, she demanded baptism at my
hands. This looked like the conduct of one crazy, but
it was not so. She related to the assembly her experi-

ence in about the following words: She said that, while living in North Carolina, and preaching among the Quakers—the Quakers allow the women to preach—she dreamed that, while standing upon the shore of a strange river, she saw a multitude upon the opposite bank, and some among them preparing for baptism. She saw a certain man approach the bank of the stream, and offer prayer, and then heard him speak upon the subject and design of baptism. This dream she had related to her husband and friends before she left North Carolina. Without ever having seen me before—she and her husband being new-comers in the neighborhood—and having heard of this appointment for baptism, she determined to attend, more out of curiosity than anything else. After I had offered prayer, and began to speak, she said to her husband: "That is the very man I saw in my dream in North Carolina;" and, being overwhelmed completely, she came directly across the stream, and demanded baptism, as before stated.*

All of these remarkable circumstances I interpreted as confirmatory of my call to the ministry. And, when Brother Campbell taught me that I must not look for the signs of an Apostle, nor rely upon vague impressions, or dreams, or visions, I was sorely tried. I must not be understood as intimating that Brother Campbell convinced me that I was not called of God to preach the gospel, or that he attempted to do so; but that he taught me to look to God's word for my call, instead of those dreams, and visions, and vague impressions upon which I so much relied for the evidence of my call. But more of this in another place.

In the beginning of our labors in Clinton county, we had arranged to have annual camp-meetings—to begin always on the Friday before the fourth Lord's day in

---

*A few days since, I visited the son of Mrs. Hodson, who is now living near Antioch, Clinton county, Ohio. He informed me that, though he was now in his eightieth year, he had a vivid recollection of hearing his mother relate her dream before they moved to Ohio; that he was present and saw her cross the stream—Cowan's Creek—and witnessed the baptism. He went on to say that he had often heard Samuel Harvey tell his experience, and how he was converted by that strange dream. Both Harvey and Hodson were members of Antioch Church.

J. I. R.

August, and to continue, ordinarily, about a week. These meetings we looked forward to as great occasions. Our preachers were in the habit of coming hundreds of miles to attend them. And the people, good, bad and indifferent, for many miles around, made their arrangements to attend; until, finally, the multitude of people completely broke down the meetings, the camp-ground having become a place of fun and mischief for every abominable character in the land. Instead of the camp-meetings, annual meetings were appointed in their stead, which proved very profitable, and which, I believe, continue to this day in that region.

CHAPTER VIII.

Building a house of worship.—He names it Antioch.—A few do the work.—Grateful tribute to the people, and especially to his wife.

As yet, we had not built us a house of worship; but, in suitable weather, had seats prepared in the woods, under the shade, and a stand erected for the preachers. In inclement weather we preached in private houses in the country, and in public buildings in the towns. Though the country was yet new, and we were all comparatively poor, we now felt that it was our duty to build us a house of worship in a central location, so that, during bad weather, we could have room sufficient to accommodate the people. The history of the building of this house, I suppose, has been repeated in a thousand other cases. A few men had to bear the burden at the beginning, middle and end of the work. He who waits in an enterprise like this until every man is ready to bear his part, waits in vain, and will die having accomplished nothing.

In the building of our house, three or four men did the most of the work; and of that, Jonah Vandervort and sons did much the largest share. It was not long until the house was ready for use, and it furnished ample room for the large audiences that were ready to assemble there. This was the first building of the kind in that part of the country. It was certainly the first house of worship built in that country for the people who wore the name *Christian*. The honor of naming the house was conferred upon me by the brethren; so I called it Antioch, after the place where the disciples were first called Christians.

It has been more than fifty years since the organization of that church, and fifty years since the erection of Antioch meeting-house; and, as far as I know, the church has prospered continuously up to the present time. I am safe in saying that thousands have been added to that church in the last half century. For many years we had ingatherings at almost every meeting, and it was not unusual at the annual meetings to have forty or fifty additions. Indeed, I think there were added there in *one day*, at a certain annual meeting, fifty persons. This, I think, was in the year 1837, when I was preaching in Indiana. Hundreds have gone up to God from that place; many more have emigrated West, and carried the light with them that has led other multitudes to God; others have gone back into the world: yet there is a large congregation of zealous disciples, holding forth the word of life, which will be a source of rejoicing to me and others in the day of Christ, seeing that we have not run in vain, neither labored in vain. It will not be long before I shall meet some of those old brethren and sisters, whom I learned to love in the days of our early struggles in Clinton county.

But for the kind attentions of Jonah Vandervort and his Christian wife, Jane, I could never have accomplished the half that I did. They took a constant oversight of my family in my absence; inquired after their welfare; supplied their wants out of their own storehouse; sent some one of their family to wait upon them in sickness: in a word, they withheld nothing that could contribute to the support and comfort of my family. Others were also kind to me; among whom were the Bashores, Lynns, and Rulons, early converts to Christ in that region. The kindness of this people can be more fully appreciated when it is remembered that, about twice a year, I made tours through Indiana, Illinois, and sometimes to Missouri, which kept me absent from one to three months at a time.

One person, however, whom I have not yet mentioned, did more than all the rest to support me in my struggles in this holy warfare. She has gone a little in advance of me to the goodly land, and has no need now of my praise. When she found me in the least desponding, she had always words of encouragement to offer. I do not now remember to have heard, in all my life, an unpleasant or discouraging word from her lips. No matter how long I might have been absent, or how much I had overstayed my time, she had no word of reproach at our meeting, but always a smile and a cordial welcome. My wife was a good manager, and very industrious. She could spin and weave the most difficult fabrics; was quite handy with scissors and needle; could cut and make whole suits of gentlemen's and ladies' apparel; and by this means she supported a large family, with the assistance our Christian neighbors gave us. She had the rare faculty of governing the boys. They loved her tenderly, and feared to disregard her wishes. She kept them busy, either at the out-door task, or at their books. Ten children she reared to maturity — six daughters and four sons. Eight of the ten children are living yet. The youngest son fell at the head of his company in a fatal charge, in Augusta, Ky., during the late fratricidal war. Our oldest daughter, wife of Elder James Vandervort, died in her fifty-sixth year, faithful to Christ. Of all my children, she was the most intelligent in the Scriptures.

I have two sons and one grandson who are preachers, and, if I had as many sons as Ahab, I should want them all to be preachers. My friends, after hearing me recount my own struggles and hardships, express no little surprise at this. I answer them that we are not here for purposes of pleasure, but to be doers of good. A real man is never so happy as when devoting himself to the interests of mankind. No man is worthy the name who wishes to live to himself, and die to himself. Suppose a man should serve the Lord in poverty and distress all his life, and die like Lazarus; is that not far better than to amass treasures, and fare sumptuously every day, and die like Dives? I say to my sons: Go on; never mind hardships, never mind adversity; these can not keep you out of heaven. Be afraid of nothing that will not keep you away from God. Let a man look to the mark, and run for the prize, no matter how difficult the way; and it will be all right with him at the end of the race.

CHAPTER IX.

Call from Missouri.—He and James Hughes start together.—They camp out.—Cook their own meals on the way.—How they made a fire.—He goes alone to Howard county.—Wild beasts.—Glorious sunrising.—A burning prairie.—Awful reflections.—The contrast.—Finds Thomas McBride, who was overcome with good news. —Return.—Stayed all night with a colored man.—Was happy. —After severe trials and dangers arrived at home in safety, having been three months out.

Not long after I settled in Ohio, a number moved from Bourbon county, Ky., and settled on Ramsey's Creek, in Pike county, Mo. Their Macedonian cry had come to the ears of Brother James Hughes and myself, and we determined to go to their assistance. We made ready for the journey and set out, prepared to take soldiers' fare on the route, as most of the country through which we had to pass was yet a wilderness. We were both fond of tea; so we carried a coffee-pot, tin cups, and a tea-canister along with us. At each settlement through which we passed, we would procure provisions enough to last us to the next one. The settlements in Indiana and Illinois were so far apart that we were compelled to camp out most of the way. I had learned to cook in the army, and now made it my business to prepare the meal, while Brother Hughes unsaddled our horses and hobbled them out for the night. I generally had a tin-cupful of strong tea for each of us, and bread and meat sufficient to satisfy the demands of nature; but this was all. I suppose the young people of this day can hardly conjecture how we obtained fire to cook with, for we had no lucifer matches then, nor for years afterwards. We carried no fire with us, and found none in the forest, where we were often compelled to camp at night. Instead of matches, we had what answered our purpose equally well. We had flint and steel, and a spongy substance found in decaying trees, especially in the ash and hickory, called spunk. When this is perfectly dry, and of good quality, it ignites from a single spark struck from the steel by the sharp flint, and may soon be blown into a flame. We were always supplied with this means of making a fire. After enjoying our repast, we would often talk of our blessed Saviour, in His self-denying life, who traversed the land of Palestine on foot, without a place to lay His head, while we, His unworthy servants, had good horses to carry us on our journey, being far better provided than was He. With such reflections we silenced all complaints.

We made the forks of White River in our route, where we met a few disciples, and had a pleasant meeting. From this place we went to what was known as the Christian Settlement in Allison's Prairie, seven miles west of Vincennes. Here we held our last meeting until we reached Ramsey's Creek, in Missouri. Nothing occurred of special interest until we completed our contemplated journey. At Ramsey's Creek we protracted our meeting for several days, and reaped a bountiful harvest of souls. We were quite satisfied with the result of our meeting, notwithstanding we did not receive as much money from first to last as we had spent. This was no new thing with us, but we rejoiced that we were counted worthy to suffer and sacrifice for Jesus' name. We were seeking souls, and not fortunes; we were endeavoring to consult the interest of the Redeemer's kingdom, and not our own interest. After the meeting at Ramsey's Creek was over, Brother Hughes concluded to return home, but I determined to go on to Howard county. Before we parted we made arrangements to make even a larger circuit the next spring, visiting all of the places we had visited on this route and many more.

Before I started for Howard county, I ascertained that, to go by way of the settlements would take three or four days to reach the point of my destination; but to go through the prairies, I could reach it in two days.

Being a good woodsman, and understanding courses
almost as well as an Indian, I chose the latter route.
There was one danger attending the traveler at this season of the year. The prairie grass was dry, and during
the autumn the winds were generally blowing briskly;
so that the fire in the tall grass often traveled almost as
fast as a horse can run, endangering the life of the traveler who should be so unfortunate as to meet a burning. By the aid of a pocket compass, which I always
carried with me in those days, I made the first day's
journey without much difficulty, and was fortunate in
finding, about sundown, a hunter's camp, in a beautiful
grove, convenient to water. Here I determined to stay
for the night. I unsaddled my good horse, Paddy, hobbled him, and turned him out to make his supper on the
fine grass that was still green in the grove. With my
flint and steel I soon kindled a fire; then I prepared
my supper, after the eating of which I was ready for
bed. My saddle-bags were my pillow; I slept on my
saddle-blanket, and covered myself with the blanket I
rode upon. I slept tolerably well until midnight, when
I was aroused by the howling of a pack of wolves in
the vicinity of the camp. I arose and renewed my fire,
knowing that this would keep them at a respectful distance, and again I retired to rest. At break of day I
was up, and, soon having my tea ready, I ate a hearty
breakfast; unspanceled Paddy, saddled him, and was off.
I entered a vast prairie just as the sun was rising. The
scene overwhelmed me. I stopped my horse to gaze
with awe and delight upon it. The god of day seemed to
come up out of the very ground, and to be struggling to
free himself from the tangled meshes of grass. From
this grand scene, I saw by faith one far more sublime:
when the King of Eternal Day—not the center of
the physical system, but the center of the spiritual
universe—arose from Joseph's tomb. I gazed, and won-
dered, and adored, while my poor soul was filled with
unutterable delight. Looking back through the clouds
of fifty years, the scene of that morning rises vividly to

view, and I seem to catch again the inspiration of that hour. The background of the past lonely night, with devouring wolves howling round my defenseless camp, was well calculated to bring out this picture in full relief. I think that solitude brings us near to God and contributes to our inspiration. Was it not so with John in Patmos? Since the experience of that morning, I can hardly blame the heathen, who are without the Bible and a knowledge of God, for worshiping the sun.

After the raptures of the scene had subsided, I turned my face westward, and Paddy and I, both having been refreshed by the night's rest, were ready for a good day's journey. A fresh breeze sprang up, and swayed the tall grass so that, at a distance, it presented the appearance of a great sea, the waves gently rolling before the breeze. In the course of the morning I saw elk, deer, wolves, and one or two bears. I was, indeed, in a solitary way—almost a day's journey from any settlement, I suppose.

About two o'clock in the afternoon, I was aroused from my meditations by a dense cloud of smoke, which appeared to be but a few miles ahead of me, in the direction of my journey. I was not much alarmed, for I understood my business, and was prepared for it. I at once dismounted, and, with my flint and steel, I lighted a wisp of grass, and fired the prairie. I then kept to the windward until a large plat of ground was burned over, into which I dashed and was safe. By this time the crackling roar of the burning prairie all around me was extremely and fearfully grand. But for the precaution I had taken, Paddy and I would have been devoured in the flames. The Western traveler now has no idea of what a prairie was fifty years ago. In many places then the grass was five or six feet high, and quite thick upon the ground. Under a brisk wind the recumbent flames seemed to fire acres at a time. There was, however, but little danger to the traveler who understood how to provide against the coming flames. His safety in such a case was to fire the grass by him, and keep well to the wind-

3

ward of it, for the wind that drives the flame so fiercely in one direction, subdues the fire on the other side, so that it can be passed without danger.

I now began to contrast the scene of the afternoon with that of the morning. In the morning the sun arose without a cloud to obscure its brightness. Now the heavy cloud of smoke that covered the heavens from horizon to horizon almost entirely obliterated the sun. The flames went rolling onward like a flood of fire, and the sun looked down upon the scene like an eye of vengeance. In the midst of the devouring elements, however, I was safe, and my spirit tranquil. How sweet to be conscious of safety in the sight of danger! The scene of the morning reminded me of the resurrection of the Sun of Righteousness, with healing in His beams. The scene of the evening reminded me of the coming of the Son of Man to judgment, when the world shall be on fire, and the elements shall melt with fervent heat. O, where then shall the ungodly and the sinner appear? The flames were now far in the rear, and, the smoke having cleared away, Paddy and I resumed our journey. Thankful, indeed, was I for the early experience that taught me how to provide against such approaching danger. Had I attempted to save myself by flight, I should have been, most likely, devoured by the flames. But I found safety, not in flying like a coward, but in facing and fighting against the danger. God has provided us against all harm, if we will put on the whole armor, and stand like men. Men who attempt to fly from adversity are frequently overwhelmed by it. It is generally the safe plan to stand and struggle against difficulties until they are overcome.

After traveling over the burnt prairie for a few hours, I came to timber, and, from the direction of the streams, I knew that I was on the waters of the Missouri. I was not long in finding a cabin, where I inquired after Thomas McBride. The inmates knew him, and gave me directions that soon led me to his cabin. He was at home, and was glad to see me. Thomas McBride was a plain, uneducated man, but he had fine sense and a sound judgment. He was the first Christian preacher who had crossed the Mississippi to preach the Bible alone, as the only basis of Christian union. He was a poor man, and led an humble life, but he was rich in faith, and had been battling alone for years against error and superstition. His home was now in the upper end of Howard county. He had recently moved to this place, but he made me welcome and comfortable in his log cabin. I related to him the success of the meeting at Ramsey's Creek, at which he seemed overjoyed. For a long time he had been in Missouri, and he had almost despaired of ever receiving any assistance from any source. When I informed him that Hughes and I had determined to make a lengthy tour through this country the coming spring, his feelings completely overcame him. We talked of old times and new until a late hour, when we had worship and retired to rest for the night. I was soon asleep, and dreaming of the dreadful fire I had escaped the previous day. This aroused me from my slumbers, and, while musing in my bed, I became a little poetical in my feelings, and composed several stanzas, which I am not able to recall, except the following lines:

> This night I lay in deep reflection,
>   A dreadful scene was now unfurled—
> The awful day of vast destruction
>   That's lowering o'er a guilty world.
> By faith I viewed the Judge descending,
>   In flaming grandeur, down the skies;
> And saints and angels were attending,
>   And began the Grand Assize.

I remember that I endeavored to describe the condition of the various classes of men in their relations to one another and to God — kings and subjects, parents and children, preachers and people — and what they must answer for to God in judgment.

On the following day, arrangements were made for a meeting to be held at Brother Cyrus Bradley's house.

We had a pleasant season, but, being anxious to see other friends and relations before I should return home, I left for Salt Creek, in the lower part of Howard county, where Brother McBride had labored for some time, and had gathered together a small band of disciples. Here I had a happy meeting, and formed many pleasant acquaintances, among whom was an old sister who, like myself, had, all of her life, been a great tea-drinker. She told me that, when she was young, the doctors pronounced tea a slow poison, and that she had lived to prove it, for she was about eighty years old and in tolerably good health yet, though she had used tea three times a day during most of the time.

From this place I went to Franklin county, where Brother McBride had lived and had made his mark. I found many here who loved the Bible cause, but they had no leader. I preached for them some days, and the people heard with gladness. We had a time of great rejoicing, for the Lord crowned our labors with abundant success. I had two sisters living in this county—Mrs. Patton and Mrs. Buckner. After visiting them, I took the most direct way home, for winter was setting in, and I had nearly five hundred miles to travel. I went by the way of Vincennes, and struck the Ohio at Madison. It had been raining on me most of the way, but it now suddenly blew up from the North and became quite cold. I crossed a small river about dark, near Madison, called Indian Kentuck. I learned of the ferryman that my way led up a small stream, and that the nearest house was about five miles distant. I suppose I could have found lodging with the ferryman, but, being anxious to get home, I determined to pass on to the five-mile house. I found the way very rough, and, I think, in going the four miles, I crossed this stream, which I was following, at least a dozen times. I now came to what proved to be the last ford I had to cross until I arrived at camp. There was a thin ice upon the water, and my horse seemed unwilling to cross. I struck him with my whip, and he plunged into the

water, which covered horse, saddle and all; but Paddy,
being an excellent swimmer, landed me safe on the
shore; but I was completely drenched up to my waist.
I had gone but a short distance when I discovered
that my clothing was frozen stiff upon me. I now
traveled at a rapid gait until I came to the house
alluded to, and saw through the window a large, blazing
fire. Never in my life had a fire appeared so inviting.
I hallooed, and a gentleman came to the fence to learn
what I wanted. I soon told him my condition, and
was not slow in making known my wants. "Light,"
said he, "and go in to the fire; my wife will assist
you in drying your clothes, while I will attend to your
horse."

I was soon by the fire, and the woman of the house
was very active and handy in waiting upon me. To my
astonishment, I discovered that she had a black face.
When the gentleman came in, I saw that he was of the
same color, but I felt that this was no time for drawing
nice distinctions. They were kind, their fire was warm,
their house was comfortable, and I was made welcome.
The whitest faces could do no better. In the course of
the conversation, the woman found out that I was a
preacher, and that I had obtained my first license from
Barton W. Stone, at Cane Ridge, in Bourbon county.
"Why," said the woman, "my father-in-law lives there
now; and we are all members of that church." Upon
inquiry, she told me her father-in-law's name was
Charles Mason. I knew him very well. We now
seemed almost like kinsfolk. A good, hot supper was
soon prepared for me, and I enjoyed it very much. We
then had worship. They then left me for the night, to
enjoy to myself a warm room, nice, clean bed, and refreshing slumbers. They were up before daylight; had
a blazing fire for me to get up by; had my horse fed,
and an excellent breakfast prepared, which I ate with a
relish. I offered to compensate them for their trouble,
but they would not receive anything. After a morning
prayer, I thanked them, and went on my way for sweet

home. I shall ever remember with gratitude the kindness of those people, and I hope they may be abundantly rewarded — here and hereafter.

The wind was still blowing from the North, and real, freezing winter had come. The way was very rough, and the weather very bitter; but I made good time, and before night had crossed the river at Rising Sun. The next day I crossed again at Cincinnati; and the day following, as the sun was setting, I arrived safe at my home in Clinton, having been gone three months—the longest preaching tour I had yet made. I found all well, and talked until a late hour, detailing the successes and perils of the way.

CHAPTER X.

Wentworth Roberts baptized for remission in the year 1821.—Stone on baptism for remission.—David Jamison baptized for remission. —George Shideler a like convert.—Dr. B. F. Hall.—Talbert Fanning.—James E. Matthews.

Not long after my return home, there came to my house a man by the name of Wentworth Roberts, a very intelligent gentleman—a school-teacher by occupation —who demanded baptism at my hands. From reading the Scriptures, he had come to the conclusion that no one could claim the remission of sins without baptism. I asked him if he believed that the Lord would then and there pardon his sins. He replied that he most certainly did. Said I, "Then, according to your faith, so be it unto you;" and I baptized him. Though this was a new doctrine, it made but little impression on my mind; not enough even to set me to investigating the subject. After I immersed him, he came up out of the water rejoicing; and made a speech at the water's edge, in which he quoted Peter (Acts ii. 38): "Repent, and be baptized every one of you in the name of Jesus Christ for the remission of sins, and you shall receive the gift of the Holy Spirit." The last I heard of him he was still faithful. This occurred, I think, in the year 1821.

After preaching a few weeks in my own neighborhood, I visited Kentucky again, especially to arrange with Brother Hughes for our contemplated trip to Missouri. While there, I attended a meeting at Millersburg, conducted by Brother Stone. The interest was very great, and the audiences very large. Many had professed religion, and many more, who were at the mourners' bench, refused to be comforted. After laboring with the mourners until a late hour of the night, without being able to comfort them, Brother Stone arose and thus addressed the audience: "Brethren, something must be wrong; we have been laboring with these mourners earnestly, and they are deeply penitent; why have they not found relief? We all know that God is willing to pardon them, and certainly they are anxious to receive it. The cause must be that we do not preach as the Apostles did. On the day of Pentecost, those who 'were pierced to the heart' were promptly told what to do for the remission of sins. And 'they gladly received the word, and were baptized; and the same day about three thousand were added unto them.'" He then quoted the commission: "He that believeth and is baptized shall be saved."

When Brother Stone sat down, we were all completely confounded; and, for my part, though I said nothing, I thought our dear old brother was beside himself. The speech was a perfect damper upon the meeting: the people knew not what to make of it. On a few other occasions, Brother Stone repeated about the same language, with the same effect. At length, he concluded that the people were by no means prepared for this doctrine, and gave it up.

Another case, which occurred before this, is worthy of notice. Brother David Jamison, of the neighborhood of Cane Ridge, had been seeking pardon for a long time, and, failing to get relief, applied to the word of God for light upon the subject. He soon became convinced that a believing penitent could not claim the promise of pardon until he had submitted to baptism. He laid his case before Stone, Dooley and others, who held a council in regard to it. Upon due deliberation, they decided that Jamison was a proper subject of baptism — that he had doubtless received pardon, but was not conscious of it. They baptized him, and he went on his way rejoicing, and was faithful to the day of his death, which occurred some years since, near Mayslick, Ky., at the house of his faithful son, Benjamin Jamison.

George Shidelcr had been praying, and reading, and agonizing for a long time, vainly seeking pardon according to the notions of our people in that day. One night, about midnight, he came to the house of Brother Dooley, and, waking him, demanded of him baptism. He said he had been seeking pardon for a long time when he had no promise; that, from the word of God, he had become satisfied that he had no right to look for pardon until baptized. Dooley baptized him " the same hour of the night " in Seven-mile Creek, above Eaton.

Elder B. F. Hall, in a sketch of his life in possession of my son, John I. Rogers, gives a scrap of history, very interesting, and which will not be out of place here: " On the 15th of May, A. D. 1825, I was, by prayer and imposition of hands, ordained by the venerated B. W. Stone and others. Brother T. M. Allen, now of Missouri, was ordained at the same time. The ordination took place at Old Union, Fayette county.

" Early in the summer of that same year, I returned and preached through Middle Tennessee and Northern Alabama. We held many camp-meetings that fall. It was a season of much religious interest. It was no uncommon thing, at a camp-meeting, to see from ten to fifty weeping sinners at the anxious seat, crying out for mercy. Being naturally sympathetic, I thought they were the most affecting, touching scenes I had ever witnessed. At many of those meetings I spent nearly the whole night singing, praying for, and trying to instruct weeping mourners how to obtain pardon. I would weep with those that wept, and rejoice with those that rejoiced.

" At one of those meetings, in the fall of 1825, an unusually large number were constantly at the anxious seat, weeping, and praying, and begging us to pray that God would have mercy upon them. Some found relief during the meeting; but the greater number remained uncomforted. At the close of the meeting, when about to leave for another meeting, a brother proposed that we sing a parting hymn, and that the Christians first, and then the mourners, who had not found peace, should come forward and give the minister the parting hand. When the broken-hearted mourners came in a

3*

long line, weeping as if their hearts would break, I could sing no longer, but burst forth in a wail of anguish of soul. My pent-up grief found vent in a gush of tears. On the way to the next meeting, I said to a brother preacher :

"'There is a wrong somewhere. Surely, we do not preach as the Apostles and first evangelists preached.'

"'Why do you think so ?' he asked.

"'Because our preaching does not produce the effect which theirs did. We nowhere read of persons who were convicted under their preaching, going away un-comforted.'

"'Wherein,' said the brother, 'does our preaching differ from theirs ?'

"I answered that I could not tell; but I was satisfied there must be a wrong somewhere. This idea haunted me through the whole series of meetings which I attended that fall.

"Early next spring—1826—I set out for Kentucky to see my friends, especially my aged mother, whom I greatly desired to see before she passed to her reward. Late one afternoon, having traveled hard all day, I reached old Brother Guess's, whose house stood on the south side of Line Creek, a small stream which, at that point, divided Tennessee from Kentucky. As I rode up, Brother Guess came out to meet me. He told me, as I was tired, to go into the house and rest, and he would take my horse. He informed me that Sister Guess had gone to see a sick neighbor, but that she would be home directly and get me something to eat. As I entered the house, I looked for a book that I could read, while sit-ting resting myself. In a small book-case in one corner of the house, I saw some books. As I drew near I saw one with 'Debate on Baptism' printed on the back. It struck me at once that it was the debate between Camp-bell and M'Calla, which took place in Mason county, Ky., October, 1823. I had heard it had been published, but had never seen it. It turned out as I expected. I knew I should have but a short time to examine it, and

began to turn over leaf after leaf to find something of
especial interest to read. Turning the leaves slowly
over, my eye caught Mr. Campbell's speech on the design of baptism. I read it carefully from beginning to
end; and I had scarcely concluded his masterly argument on that subject when I sprang to my feet, dropped
the book on the floor, clapped my hands repeatedly together, and exclaimed: 'Eureka! Eureka!! I have
found it! I have found it!!' And, thanks be to God, I
had found it! I had found the keystone of the arch. It
had been lost a long time. I had never seen it before —
strange that I had not. But I had seen the vacant
space in the arch a hundred times, and had some idea of
the size and shape of it; and when I saw baptism as
Mr. Campbell had presented it, I knew it would exactly
fit and fill the vacant space. I was converted over;
and was one of the happiest young converts you ever
saw; happier than when I was converted the first time,
and a great deal more certain that I was right. Hitherto,
I had been walking in the mud, or on the sand, and,
withal, groping in the dark. Now, all was light around
me, and I felt that I was standing on a rock; and I have
felt the same way ever since. From that day to this, I
have never doubted that baptism is for the remission of
sins. Not even a stray doubt has ever flitted across my
mind. Every brother I met on my way from Line
Creek home I told of the grand discovery. On the
south fork of Green River, I met Brother Sandy E.
Jones — he was not a preacher then — and told him of
it. He affected not to receive it — perhaps did not; but
the next time I heard of him, he was a preacher, and was
preaching baptism for the remission of sins.

"In the summer of 1826, I met Elder B. W. Stone,
and spoke of the idea to him. He told me that he had
preached it early in the present century, and that it was
like ice-water thrown on the audience; it chilled them,
and came very near driving vital religion out of the
church; and that, in consequence of its chilling effect,
he had abandoned it altogether. I insisted that it was

God's truth, nevertheless, and that I felt compelled to preach it at a meeting at Sulphur Well, to which we were then going. He begged that I should not preach it while he was present, but said he would leave after meeting Lord's-day morning; then I could do as I saw proper. I complied with his request, but preached it that night rather privately to persons who appeared to be concerned about their souls. Five, I think, was the number who were persuaded to take the Lord at his word. I immersed them the next morning for the remission of sins. Our venerable brother, Samuel Rogers, who is still living, was at that meeting, and was the only preacher who did not oppose the idea.

"The next year, in September, I think, I preached baptism for the remission of sins on Cyprus Creek, in Lauderdale county, Ala., on Lord's-day night. Talbert Fanning was present and heard the discourse, was convinced of the truth, and, when the invitation was given, came forward and made the good confession, and was immersed the next morning for the remission of sins by Brother James E. Matthews. I witnessed the immersion. Brother James E. Matthews embraced the sentiment at or soon after that time, and at my instance wrote several articles on the subject, addressed to Brother B. W. Stone, which were afterwards published in his *Christian Messenger.*"

I mention these cases to show how men would act, being untrammeled by creeds and human platforms. The light, even at that day, began to break through the clouds, in a few cases, and at intervals, giving promise of the brighter day about to dawn upon us under the teaching of that greatest of men, Alexander Campbell. As a people, though we were somewhat superstitious, and were advancing slowly towards the full day of gospel light, yet we were certainly preparing the way for this Reformation as no other people were. The sequel affords abundant proof of this, especially in Kentucky.

CHAPTER XI.

Tour with Hughes to Missouri.—Cummins Brown.—Louis Byram.—
Conversion of Elijah Goodwin, then a small boy.—Cast the net
for a fish and caught a frog.—The frog's revenge.—The home of
Kincaid.—Swimming rivers by day and camping out by night.—
Springfield, Ill.—Lost in the night.—Crossing the Snigh and other
bayous.—A severe chill.—Recovered.—Meeting at Ramsey's Creek,
Mo.—The last fall of the wrestler.—Franklin county.—Boone.—
Howard.—Taken sick.—A hymn, etc.

After arranging with Brother Hughes appointments
for a three months' tour through Indiana, Illinois and
Missouri, I returned to my home in Ohio, where I
preached in all the region round about until the time of
starting. We had sent our appointments before us, no-
tifying the brethren of our coming, and we were to meet
at Pigeon Roost, near a river of that name in Indiana.
Here we met and spent one week—the length of time
we proposed to spend at each place. From this place,
we proceeded to Lost River, where Brethren Cummins
Brown and Louis Byram came to our aid. These meetings were quite successful. From here we went to the
forks of White River, and had a glorious meeting, at
which, among others, Elijah Goodwin was baptized. My
recollection is that Cummins Brown baptized him. Then
he was but a small boy : now he is past middle age, and
has been among the most useful proclaimers in his own
State, and has done great good wherever he has gone.
He is as faultless in the matter of his discourses and
writings as any one I know of.

At this meeting, one night, while multitudes of mourners were wrestling with God in prayer, my attention was
directed particularly towards one fellow who was among
them, cutting such strange antics that I was induced to
approach him and look narrowly into his case. Stoop-
ing down until I was near enough to catch his breath, I

knew at once that I could not be mistaken in his being beastly drunk. I knew, from his manners, that he would break up our meeting if allowed to remain; so, being then a very stout and active man, I seized him by the collar with one hand, and with the other I seized his pants, and lifted him up and cast him sprawling out into the darkness of the night, saying as I did so, "We cast our net for fish, and behold, we have caught a frog." The fellow soon became sober enough to seek revenge, and for that purpose he approached the stand, intending to mutilate my hat. That he might be sure of mine, I suppose, he cut two of them to pieces; neither of them happened to be mine, however.

From this place Brother Brown returned to Kentucky; but Brother Hughes and I pressed on our way westward. We passed on to the Embarras River, stopping to preach one day in Ellison Prairie; thence a short distance beyond the river to our second appointment. Here Brethren John and Gabriel Scott 'and Brother William Kincaid were living. They were all preachers, though not very actively engaged in their calling. The people came to this meeting from a great distance, and manifested quite a desire to hear. While engaged in social conversation with the preachers of that neighborhood, a skeptic approached us, and, in the course of his conversation, administered a very severe reproof to the idle preachers of that region. Said he: "If I believed the Bible as you profess to: that it teaches men the way of escaping an awful hell and gaining an eternal abode of happiness, I could not rest a single day without using my utmost endeavors to save men. Yet," said he, "with the exception of these men (referring to Hughes and myself), I know of none of you who are not as busily engaged in the affairs of this world as I am, and you are doing little more to spread the gospel than I am. Therefore," he continued, "I conclude that idle preachers do not themselves believe the gospel." Some who heard this severe reproof profited greatly by it; for, as I afterwards learned, they began from that hour to be much more diligent, and, by exemplifying in their life what they taught with their lips, were the means of doing much good in this region of country. Truly, we may profit by the words of our enemies, though they may only design to reproach us.

From this place we had nearly three days to travel before reaching our next appointment, on the Sangamon River, beyond Springfield, where a Brother English, with some other disciples, had settled. We set out on our journey well supplied with dried beef and corn bread. It commenced raining the day we started, and continued more or less every day for about three weeks. The creeks and rivers became much swollen. There was but one ferry on the way, and that was at Vandalia, on the Okaw. We had to swim creeks and rivers during the day, and camp out at night, with no protection from the storm. Notwithstanding this, we arrived on the third day at the appointed place, wet to the skin, but in good health and spirits. Brother English, who gave us a hearty welcome, had a stand prepared in a beautiful grove, and seats conveniently arranged for the hearers. The people seemed extremely anxious to hear, coming quite a distance through the rain, and keeping their seats, or standing as if transfixed, for hours, taking spring showers as they came. Springfield had then received its name, but was an inconsiderable village, with one small store, kept by a man from Bath county, Ky., named Iles. The lands in this section were not yet in the market, though they had been recently surveyed. There were a number of small settlements in the neighborhood of Springfield at this time, awaiting the time of Government sales. I have traversed most of the western country, and have always regarded the prairie lands of this region as the best in the West.

Our next appointment was at Ramsey's Creek, Pike county, Mo., distant about two days' journey. We crossed the Illinois River late in the evening, and had but a dim path through the barrens and prairie to the ferry on the Mississippi, where Louisiana now stands.

We traveled on until late at night, with no other light than the flashing lightning, which was almost incessant. In the midst of the thunder, lightning and rain, we, at length, lost our path. After an anxious search of some time, we succeeded in finding it, and we followed it until we entered a grove. Here we concluded to tie up our horses and wait for morning. We sat upon our saddles, and rested against a large tree, while we covered our heads with our blankets to protect us from the mosquitoes, which were waiting to devour us. In this condition we slept a little, not knowing what was ahead of us. Morning found us on the hills overlooking the Mississippi. Following a dim path, we were soon in the bottom, at the house of a man named Ross. Here we fed our horses, ate our breakfast, and were ready for new toils.

Mr. Ross informed us that, to get to the ferry, which was six miles distant, we must cross an island and many bayous and creeks, which were then swimming. We crossed in a pirogue, and swam our horses by its side. The first bayou was called Snigh, and was at least one hundred and fifty yards wide. Other waters traversing the island we had to swim, so that, with difficulty and peril, we reached the ferry late in the evening, and found the waves running so high under a fresh gale that the ferryman would not venture to put us over until morning. That evening, having been so completely drenched, and so much fatigued and worn out, I had a severe chill. The ferryman kindly furnished us skins to sleep on and to cover with, and, after giving me a cup of strong spicewood tea, and other attentions, he committed us to sleep for the night. I slept soundly and perspired freely during the night, and was entirely relieved by morning. We now crossed the river and hurried on to our appointment at Ramsey's Creek. We were two hours late, but the people waited patiently until our arrival.

Here we had a glorious meeting. Eighty persons professed religion and were baptized. One of the number was a fellow-soldier of mine in the war of 1812; he was Corporal of the company of which I was Orderly Sergeant. We were both active, and, when in camp, fond of wrestling, but were so completely matched we could never determine who was the best man. As I was leading him into the water, I said to him, "Well, brother, I am going to throw you the last fall now." He has long since crossed the Jordan, but was faithful unto death.

From Ramsey's Creek we crossed over to the south side of the Missouri, and went into Franklin county, where we had our next appointment. My youngest brother Williamson, my mother, Aunt McIntyre, and a few other disciples, lived in this neighborhood. We gained a triumphant victory. In this same region I had sown my wild oats, to the annoyance and disgust of some who were present at this meeting. When in my youth, I suppose no one ever served the devil more faithfully than I did. I was not a large man, but muscular and very active, and capable of handling adversaries very roughly who were much over my size. Some of these people had witnessed my wild revels in those days, and took pleasure in speaking of a certain day when they had seen me fight three successive and successful battles. They told this, not that they delighted in this ruffian-like conduct of mine, but rather that the recollection of what I had been, and had done, enabled them to better appreciate what great things the Lord had done for me. I am of the opinion that the recollection of the fact that I was now on the ground where I had done so much for Satan, gave me additional strength and zeal to battle for the Lord. I met my old comrades in sin at the foot of the cross, exhorted them, prayed for them, and rejoiced in their deliverance. Retrospecting the past, I can say truly with David, "The Lord has done great things for me, whereof I am glad." My brother-in-law remarked to me on this occasion that, if he had been going to call a man to the work of the ministry, I would have been the last man he would have selected among his acquaintances.

"Yes," said I, "but the Lord's ways are not yours, but heaven-high above them;' hence, he has chosen 'mean things,'. which you, in your ignorance, would have passed by."

"But," said he, "I can not account for your success, reared, as you have been, in the backwoods, with little or no education, and having led so reckless a life in youth; while others, with better early opportunities every way, do not accomplish half so much."

I answered him that those men did not understand so well as I where to find a sinner. I had been in all his lurking places, and knew so well where to aim, that, shooting off-hand as I did, I could wound half a dozen while those elegant ones were looking for the game, or hunting a rest to shoot from.

From Franklin, we crossed over to Boone and Howard, holding a number of successful meetings in those counties. At one of these meetings we baptized James McBride, who married the daughter of my old friend, Philip Miller. He became one of our best preachers, moved to Springfield, and, at length, to Oregon Territory, now a State. We returned to Franklin county, held another good meeting, and then turned our faces homeward. After filling a number of appointments on the way, we arrived at home in the month of July, and both were taken down with fever soon afterwards. My attack was violent; so much so that I despaired of life. In a few days, however, I was up and able to work again.

During this sickness, as the result of febrile excitement, rather than any natural endowment, I became quite poetical, and called for pen and paper, though I was not able to sit up in bed without assistance. My wife supplied me with writing materials, and, having propped me up in bed, held a candle for me while I penned the following:

> Begone, you earthly toys of sense,
> A nobler joy attracts my mind;
> A vast, immortal recompense,
> A treasure that is all divine.

Thou King of Terror, falsely named —
     To me thou art the Prince of Peace;
With pains and fevers rend this veil,
     And give my fettered soul release.

My anchor, Hope, is still secure;
     I safely ride the swelling flood,
And shout to think I 'll gain the shore
     By faith in Jesus' precious blood.

The curtain now is drawn aside;
     I see my anchor still secure:
Through winds and waves I safely ride,
     With Jesus standing at the oar.

He safely takes my vessel o'er,
     I, fearless, pass the swelling flood,
And shout to think I 've gained the shore
     By faith in Jesus' precious blood.

Methinks I hear the angels speak,
     And say to me, "How cam'st thou here?"
"Sirs, out of tribulation deep,"
     I answer without dread or fear.

I washed my robes in blood divine,
     And stand arrayed in white above;
With all the happy millions join
     To shout and sing redeeming love.

But ah! a grander note shall sound,
     Whene'er this body meets the soul;
When Gabriel's trump shall shake the ground,
     And wreck this globe from pole to pole.

This body, then immortalized,
     Awakes, ascends the vaulted skies;
Doth in its Saviour's image rise,
     Where saints and angels harmonize.

O, then my bliss will be complete;
     With palms of victory in my hand,
I 'll lay my laurels at His feet,
     And thus conclude: Amen! Amen!

CHAPTER XII.

A tour to Virginia.—Almost without food for two days.—A witch converted.—She surprised the superstitious mountaineers by sinking.—A triumph for truth.—Home again.

In a few weeks, I turned my face eastward; traveled and preached through the eastern part of Ohio, Pennsylvania, and on to Baltimore. At that time we had a few weak churches in Southeastern Ohio, and in Bedford county, Pa. Brother William Caldwell, a good and true man, had married and settled near a place called Bloxly Run, near where were three or four small churches. In passing on to Baltimore, I learned a lesson of an African slave that has been of benefit to me ever since. The country through which I was passing abounds in beautiful springs, one of which I was approaching at the same time that a fine silver-mounted carriage halted near. A servant alighted from it, bearing a silver pitcher and cup in his hand. Upon meeting him at the spring, I asked him for a cup of water. Said he, "If you please, sir, when I have served my master." Deeply sensible of the just reproof, I waited patiently until the servant returned, and held out a cup brimming with cold, sparkling water, which I lifted to my grateful lips. I then thanked the boy, at the same time handing him a small piece of silver. This, and more, I felt was due the servant, not only for his politeness in waiting upon m⸻, but also for teaching me how to serve my Master. Here was one, bought with his master's money, who was more faithful and understood his obligations better than we who have been bought with our Master's blood. I left that spring with the words, " when I have served my master," ringing in my ears, and settling down into my heart. I adopted the motto, " My Master first; then, others."

In Baltimore we had a small congregation, but no preacher. I preached a few discourses in the city and baptized a few persons. Some twenty miles from the city, in Harford county, on Gunpowder, we had a good meeting, and I baptized a number of converts. There were a number of small churches in this region that formed quite a nucleus ready for the Reformation which soon followed. Many privations and sore trials awaited me on this tour, of which I will not now speak, except to say that I was compelled to sell my Bible and hymn book to pay ferriage and other incidental expenses on my way home. These books had been of great service to me, and, in giving them up, I comforted myself with the thought that my temporary loss might, in God's providence, prove an eternal blessing to the new owner of my books.

On my arrival at home, I found Daniel Combs waiting for me. He came to get me to go with him on a tour to Little Sandy. He had lately surveyed the field, and was enthusiastic with the conviction that it was fully ripe for the harvest. I was tired, and had no money, and my wife had none. She had been almost entirely alone for months; still she uttered no word of complaint, believing that we were called as were the Apostles, and that the same woe would attend us if we preached not the Gospel. Combs had a little money, which he generously divided with my wife; and, after I had taken a short rest, we departed, gathering, from all that we had learned, that the Lord had a special work for us on the Sandy.

On the first night, we preached at the forks of Brush Creek, and there we ate our last meal until we arrived at McAllister's, on Little Sandy, which journey consumed forty-eight hours. We had a little money to pay for feeding our horses, but not enough to pay for our meals. We obtained a few apples, and lived on them alone for two days and nights. We made beds of our saddle-blankets, and pillows of our saddles, contenting ourselves with the thought that, if we had been satisfied with such fare in the service of Cæsar, we should certainly be in the service of King Jesus. When we arrived at the place of meeting, we found the people in high spirits, awaiting our coming with the expectation of a glorious meeting; nor were they disappointed, for the truth triumphed gloriously.

Not far from our place of meeting was a settlement of very superstitious people, who believed in witches, and seriously harassed some of their neighbors who, they thought, had bewitched them. One of the most notorious of the supposed witches, who had been burnt in effigy, and whose effigy had been shot with a silver bullet, came to our meeting and was baptized. On the day of her baptism, all of her superstitious neighbors came to see her baptized, believing that she could not sink in the water, and that, therefore, she would be completely exposed before the multitude as a veritable witch. They had such a tradition among them, that a witch could not be put under water. Therefore, when they saw me baptize her with as much ease as I baptized other candidates, they seemed astounded. We knew nothing of this until about the close of the meeting, when we learned that the preaching of the gospel and the baptizing of the woman had determined those superstitious ones to abandon the persecution of witches. We baptized at the same meeting a man of more than ordinary talents, by the name of Burns, who became quite a useful preacher; but, being poor and having a family to support, he mixed law with preaching, which I have always regarded as a dangerous experiment, if not an indication of very weak faith. We preached for some time in that region, extending our labors as high up as Guyandotte, Va. Here Combs and I parted — he for Kentucky, and I, by the way of Chillicothe, home. To reach Chillicothe, I traversed a very rough country, and found but few creature comforts. We had no church there, but I found a few faithful disciples, who administered to my wants for the night. I reached home in one day from this place, having ridden fifty miles.

CHAPTER XIII.

Our mode of worship.—No choirs, nor tuning-forks.—Acre.—Shick,
—The runt calf.—Conferences in Ohio.—Our blunders.—Working
a miracle.—A disappointed enthusiast.

I now devoted myself for some time to the interests
of the churches I had planted in the region around
home. I found them doing well, and the cause suc-
ceeding in their hands better than I could have expected. It must be remembered that almost every
convert we made in those days was required to pray, not
only at home, but in the church also ; and all who had
voices to sing, sung with the spirit; whether with the
understanding or not, I will not venture to say. We
had no choirs then to do the singing for the congregation, and we certainly had no organs — not even a
tuning-fork. I can not say that our mode of worship
was after the Apostolic pattern exactly; indeed, I know
it was not. There was sometimes a want of good order
in our worship, and, on particular occasions, I have
witnessed scenes of great confusion in some of our
churches. Still, as a rule, the people came together,
one with an exhortation, one with a psalm, another with
a fervent prayer, and all believing that the Lord would
be with them, and give them a time of refreshing from
His presence ; and it was not unusual for them to go
away from such meetings shouting the praises of the
Lord. They held frequent social meetings from house
to house, and they seldom made a social visit without
singing, and sometimes praying, together.

Preachers were greatly needed then to do pioneer
work ; but, when a church was once constituted in a
neighborhood, the disciples took it for granted that,
preacher or no preacher, they must let their light so
shine before men, that others, seeing their good works,
might glorify their Father in Heaven.

After an absence of a few weeks or months from home, I found on my return persons in the different neighborhoods waiting for baptism. I was often kept busy for weeks, holding a meeting in the day-time at one point, and at night at another point, and baptizing the converts by day and night, some of whom had been converted by those who were called exhorters, but who were not authorized to baptize. Quite a number of young men now began to exhort and preach in this region, so that I could safely commit the cause to them in my absence. One of them was Jacob Acre, a German. In the beginning, he made rather an awkward appearance in public, and at times, from a want of familiarity with the English language, he made ridiculous blunders in attempting to select the proper word from synonomous terms. I was present on one occasion when he attempted to repeat his text from memory—"Behold, I stand at the door and knock." By a very slight blunder, he set the whole house to laughing. "Behold, I stand at the door and *peck*," said he; and he could not command silence until he discovered and corrected his mistake, and added a pointed reproof. This man persevered, however, until he became very useful in word and teaching.

Peter Shick also became an able preacher among us, and at the first dawning of the Reformation became one of its most powerful supporters. I remember, on a certain occasion, he got into a controversy with one of our old brethren, who, in opposing our reformatory movement, boasted that he had not changed a whit for twenty years. Shick quoted the passage in Malachi, "Ye shall grow up as calves of the stall," and said: "If I had a calf, and should put it in a good stall, and feed it for a whole year on nourishing food, and at the end of that time it had undergone no change, I should turn it out, and say, 'Go, you runt; you are not worth your food.'"

The following fall and winter, I attended several Conferences which had been recently organized by the Christian brethren of Ohio. Our people conducted them

rather awkwardly, owing to the fact that, having set out
with Brother Stone to take the Bible as the only rule of
faith and practice, they had nothing in their creed to
guide them in such a meeting, there being no such organized body known in the word of God. They made
many attempts to transact business, but, owing to the di-
versity of opinions entertained, accomplished very little.
Hughes, Dooley and myself were anti-conference men,
and were so recognized by our brethren generally. Having fully investigated the subject, we were unwilling to
regard the decrees of any such ecclesiastical body as
authoritative. At one of those meetings, a very zealous
Conference advocate offered a resolution in substance
like the following:

" *Resolved*, That our Conference shall decide as to the
validity of the call and qualifications of all preachers
among us; and that those who are not licensed by these
Conferences shall not be recognized among us as authorized preachers."

This resolution, offered by Guss Richards, would have
excluded Hughes, Dooley and myself, which all knew;
and, as we had been successful recruiters, the brethren
were not willing to sacrifice us, seeing that they had no
divine warrant for so doing. So the calf was strangled
before it was old enough to have horns. At another
meeting, almost the entire time of the Conference was
taken up in the discussion of the subject of the call to
the ministry. In this discussion I took a deep interest,
for this had been to my mind a most perplexing question. Many of us believed that we were the successors
of the Apostles, and, therefore, that we had a right to
expect the same signs that attended their ministry, and
to have all their functions and powers. True, we were
quite sensible of the fact that, as yet, the signs of our
apostleship had not been given; that we had not yet
been able to demonstrate our call by the exercise of
miraculous powers; but we believed that, when the
Church should have come to a certain degree of per-
fection, which we anticipated, then these powers would

4

attend its ministry. Meanwhile, we contented ourselves with dreams and strong impressions, in the absence of higher evidences of our divine call. Some even attempted to work miracles, and one of the most earnest and zealous among us apostatized from the faith on the ground of his repeated failures to work miracles, alleging that, if called of God, as he had believed himself to be, he should have had the signs following his call.

I was deeply concerned myself, and, at times, almost driven to despair on this very account. On one occasion, I met a lunatic wading through the mud, and, having neither silver nor gold to give her, I prayed God to heal her. She looked up at me, and said, "It's very muddy." I suppose that I was like the man that prayed to have a mountain removed, and who, after prayer, seeing the mountain as it had always been, said, " I knew it would not be removed." Upon failing to get the desired answer to this prayer, my only refuge from skepticism was, that the weakness of my faith and the imperfection of the Church were the causes of this failure.

During the discussion of this question, one preacher, Job Combs, desired to know how to distinguish between impressions made by the Lord and those made by Satan. He stated that, on a certain occasion, when traveling on the highway, as he approached a large new dwelling, he became powerfully impressed that the Lord had called him to preach the gospel to the inmates, and warn them of the ruin that would certainly overtake them if they did not speedily repent. Accordingly, he approached and called several times, but received no answer. Borne on by this irresistible impression, he alighted from his horse, and knocked at every door, but found not a single inmate. It turned out that the house had not a single occupant in it. " Now," said he, " I suppose this was from the devil, for the purpose of shaking my faith ; for this false impression was as strong as the one which I construed as the call of God to the ministry." Though almost every member of the Conference relied either

upon a dream or an impression as evidence of their call
to preach, yet not one could answer satisfactorily the
brother's question.

The present generation may laugh at our folly, call us
idiots, crazy, or what they please; but what better could
have been expected of those who made no distinction
between the extraordinary and miraculous dispensations
granted in the establishment of the Church, and the ordinary procedure of the Church and ministry after its
establishment? There are multitudes at the present time,
with the accumulated light of the nineteenth century,
who prefer a dream, a feeling, or an impression, as evidence of their acceptance with God, to the word of the
Lord. There are respectable preachers in our midst
who yet claim to have heard a voice calling them to the
ministry, and who claim to speak as the Holy Spirit
gives them utterance. It is true, they do not deny the
fact that the day of miracles is past; but they still claim
that every conversion is a miracle, and as direct a result
of the power of God as the creation of a world would be.

CHAPTER XIV.

Call to Virginia.—Counter-call to Missouri.—Doubts and perplexities.
—Hamrick, Hughes and Dooley.—At Indianapolis.—Horses escape.
—The pursuit.—They give up the tour and return home.—Moss
saddles.—Backgirths and stirrups.—Sad disappointment.—Faith
shaken as to the call to the ministry.—The visit of the Muse.—The
poetical effusion.—The ministering angel-wife.

The following Spring I arranged my affairs, with the
view of visiting the land of my nativity — Charlotte
county, in Old Virginia. For some time this matter
had occupied my thoughts, and now so impressed my
mind, that I concluded that God had really called me to
the Old Dominion. Just on the eve of starting, I received a letter from James Hughes, requesting me to be
at home at a certain time, nearly at hand, when he expected to be at my home with a message from God for
me. This somewhat puzzled me; for I had made up my
mind that God had called me to Virginia, and now a
man of God requests me to await his coming, with another, and, perhaps, an adverse message.

Soon Hughes arrived, in company with his son, John
H. Hughes, and brother Lewis Hamrick — all in high
glee for a summer campaign through Indiana, Illinois
and Missouri, and declaring that they had been impressed so deeply that it was the will of God that they
should go and take me with them, that they had called
for me, not doubting my readiness to accompany them.
Now, my difficulties were insuperable. Three men in
whom I had implicit confidence, and whom I believed
God had certainly called to the ministry, were opposing
their impressions to mine. Up to this time I had been
directed mainly, as to my course, by my impressions —
impressions similar to those which now determined me
to go to Old Virginia. If all of these impressions are
from God, I reasoned, how is it that they are contra-

dictory? I must either ignore them altogether, and be turned adrift, or conclude that either the Hugheses and Hamrick, or myself, must be mistaken in this instance. Of the two evils I chose the lesser, and tried to persuade myself that my recent impressions had not been as deep as usual, and so I yielded to Hughes and Hamrick. My wife saw my difficulty, and accounted for my inclination to go to Virginia upon natural principles. They said it was reasonable to suppose that I would be drawn towards my native land, where so many of my relatives dwelt, and that I should have a strong desire to break to them the bread of life. I determined, notwithstanding, to spend one night in solemn prayer to God, and the next day to shape my course from all the premises before me. I can not say that prayer, on this occasion, relieved me in the least from my embarassment; but I determined my course, and was now prepared to go with my friends. I can not say that I went with them "nothing doubting;" for doubts and perplexities clung to me like a loathsome leprosy, giving me little rest until, by the providence of God, the light of the present reformation broke in upon my way — then I found peace; and since then not a single doubt has disturbed my thoughts regarding the call to the ministry, or the way in which I should direct my steps.

The next day we set out upon our journey, and, after traveling only a few miles, brother Hamrick was taken quite ill. After a short rest we went on to Lebanon. The next day we started on our way, Hamrick being yet quite unwell, and by eleven o'clock he became much worse. We hurried on, however, and got to Hamilton, where we were compelled to put up at a hotel, and call in a doctor. That night we almost despaired of his life. The next morning we held a council, in which it was determined that John Hughes should hurry back to Kentucky, for sister Hamrick; that James Hughes should remain with Hamrick until his wife arrived; that I should go on West and fill our appointments. In the meanwhile, Hughes was to follow on and overtake me, provided he could leave Hamrick in time. Proceeding on my way, I spent the following night with Thomas Dooley, whom I enlisted to go with me on my journey.

Dooley was soon ready for the tour, and our first night out we staid with Dooley's brother-in-law. He and his Christian wife entertained us well, and the next morning bid us God-speed, as we set out for Indianapolis, which was our next station. The seat of government had been recently located there, though, at the time, the country around appeared to be almost a boundless wilderness. We were kindly received by brother Morrison Morris and his Christian wife, who were early emigrants to this place from Concord church, Nicholas county, Ky. Here we were quite at home. After having preached a few discourses, we attempted to cross White river; but it had been raining for several days, until the river had overflowed its banks, and the current had become so rapid that Dooley, being no swimmer, was afraid to venture across. So we determined to go down the river about ten miles, to a small settlement that we knew of, and there hold a meeting until the tide should recede.

We put up at the house of sister Potinger, who immediately sent out runners to tell the glad tidings, that two preachers had arrived and would begin a meeting that night at her house. As our horses had been stabled for some time, we thought best to place them in a lot, until night, supposing that they would be perfectly safe. Up to this time my horse had never left me. In a few hours the horses began to play, and directly they bounded over the fence, and were soon out of sight. Dooley and I seized our bridles without ceremony, and pursued in haste. Soon we came in sight of them, but they again bounded away and disappeared in the deep forest. We tracked them through the slashes until we lost their trail. By this time it was growing late; we turned to retrace our steps to the place of meeting. The earth was covered with water, night was fast approaching, and the wolves began to howl dole-

fully around. Dooley became alarmed, especially when
we were unable to avoid the deep waters that were before us. Being a good swimmer, I went before, and
more than once fell into pools of water over my head.
Dooley, being behind, was able to shun these deep
places. After plashing through the swamps for some
hours, we came to high ground, and were soon in a
road; but which end of it to take, we knew not. Fortunately, we took the right direction, and, late at night,
were back at the place of meeting. The people had
been there, waited until a late hour, and then returned
to their homes.

The next morning we took our bridles and saddle-
bags, and started again on the track of our horses. We
traveled all day through the slashes, and late in the
evening came to a cabin on Sugar Creek, where we
found that our horses had been secured by the gentleman who lived there. We were now far on the way to
Jackson's, where we had lodged as we came out, and, believing that God had called us home in his providence,
by the events of the last two days, we determined to
heed the call. We gathered moss, which we used instead of saddles, by fastening it on our horses with
girths of bark, of which material we also made stirrups;
then we mounted and hurried homeward. We arrived
that night at Jackson's, where I changed my moss for a
real saddle, thankful that I had not been taken up for a
horse-thief while on my moss. The next day Dooley
obtained a saddle, and the following night we arrived at
his house, and found all well. This made me more un-
easy than ever; for I felt almost certain, that after our
misfortune at White River, something serious had happened, either to Dooley's family or mine, or the Lord
would not have so hedged up our way. Now, since we
had found all well at Dooley's, I expected to find some
of my family sick or dead.

I had fifty long miles between me and my home, and
I determined not to rest until the mystery of this providence should be reached, for, that it was a special provi-

dence to turn me homeward, I had scarcely a doubt. I started early in the morning, and by, or before, sunset, I got in sight of my little home. As I approached it, the fear and dread I experienced, and all along the way the anxiety I felt, can not be described. Dark visions arose before me along the way. At one time it seemed to be a sick or dying child—at another, a dying wife, who, with last accents of affection, was leaving directions in regard to the little ones. I expected, in all probability, to see the neighbors' horses hitched around my house, as I should approach, and to meet some kind one at the door who would break the sad news to me with a tearful face, etc. Now the worst was to be known in a few, brief moments, and I could almost hear the throbbings of my aching heart, when the cabin and meadow beyond were in full view. But no neighbors' horses were there —no funeral procession in view—but wife and children, who had been spending the day at a neighbor's, were crossing the meadow on their return, all well, or apparently so. The children were skipping and chatting by the mother's side, and all seemed happy. Notwithstanding my great disappointment, I was more than happy to find every one in good health and better spirits than usual. What now could I make of all this? I could not doubt the goodness of the Lord; but I could not see into, or explain, this mysterious providence. What would now become of Hughes' and Hamrick's impressions? What would become of my own impressions?

I was now ready to learn and embrace the truth. Certainly, I had been going on, heretofore, chiefly by the direction of blind impulse. Reason, judgment, and the Word of God, had been thrown into the background. Dreams, visions, feelings, impulses and vain imaginings, had been consulted and chiefly relied on, even in the most important undertakings. This I began to realize, and I panted for a clearer light.

The fatigue of the journey, together with the perplexity of my mind, consequent upon the recent events,

were more than a match for my robust constitution. I
fell sick, very sick, both in body and mind. As I began to recover, I went over the whole ground again, in
reference to my conversion and call to the ministry. I
could not doubt the truth of the Christian religion, nor
could I question the wisdom and goodness of God. I
gave myself up to the contemplation of God, both in
the dispensation of nature and of grace. But what,
thought I, avails all the glory of the heavens above, or
the beauty of the earth beneath, without the love of
God in the soul, or without the hope of redemption,
through Jesus, from sin, death, and the grave? I was
not so much concerned about anything on earth, as the
questions—"Is Jesus mine? has he recognized me as
his child? has he, as I have fondly hoped, called me to
work in his vineyard? have I evidence sufficient to
prove that he has called me to preach the gospel?" O,
wretched man that I was! groping my way in darkness,
and the light of truth so nigh.

In the midst of these reflections, my muse came to
my relief. I called for pen, ink and paper. I know
nothing of the laws of poetry, and may not know even
what true poetry is, unless it be the spontaneous music
of the soul. Yet I have, at intervals during my life,
felt an irresistible impulse to write what I felt in my
soul—whether it be poetry or a jingle of words. The
following is a short specimen:

> Could I, with Herschel's piercing eye,
> Among the planets soar on high—
> What then? Of all that I might gain,
> Without religion 'twould be vain.
> Were I possessed of Newton's mind,
> And all his talents in me shined—
> The world to thunder its applause,
> And fix my name above the stars:
> With Newton's skill and Herschel's eye,
> And all their deep philosophy,
> If love be absent from my breast,
> I am accursed with all the rest.

4*

Could I fathom Nature — vast, profound,
And with the comets take my round,
And gaze on every sun that burns,
And every globe that round them turns
And after all my journey round,
Could tell the wonders I had found:
Not all the glories of the sky
The want of love could e'er supply.

As I began to recover, my faithful wife, with ever
vigilant eye, discovered my despondency, and administered to my poor heart the very consolations that I
had ministered to others. Said she: " Why should we
be cast down? Has not the Lord done great things for
us whereof we should be glad? Has not his gospel
been powerful to our salvation? Have not multitudes
been brought to repentance by your preaching? What
more should you expect from the Lord than what he has
done? Suppose you have been deceived as to your impressions; what of that? Are not all men'liable to be
deceived? The Lord has not deceived you. Man may
have done so, or you may have done so yourself. You
know that the promises of God are yea and amen. Has
any promise failed you? Besides," said she, "you
are not your own, but are bought, even with the precious blood of Christ; and therefore you are to serve
Him. You are called to be a doer of good; to let your
light shine; to improve your talents, whether one or
five; to teach; to warn; to exhort. This much, in his
Word, God calls on you to do, and, on the great day, he
may ask you, should you now give up your work,
' Why have you been all the day idle?' " After listening in silence to such gentle words as these, I felt again
the inspiration of the cause, confessed my weakness, and
renewed my vows.

CHAPTER XV.

Preaches in Highland county.—Baptism of a cripple.—Treatment
by a preacher.—Attack by a ruffian.—The ruffian flies.—Does not
accept fully the doctrine of non-resistance.

I had sent an appointment to Brother William Stewart's, in Highland county, where Lynchburg now stands.
I attended the meeting at the appointed time, and enjoyed my usual freedom in addressing the people. A
young lady was brought to the meeting who had not
walked from her birth, and who, on hearing the discourse, seemed deeply affected. I requested Sister Stewart
to ask her the cause of her weeping. The young lady
answered that she wished to be a Christian, and to be
baptized; but she was a cripple, and was not able to
obey the Lord in that institution. I approached her
myself, and informed her that she might be of good
comfort; she should have the accomplishment of her
desire, if she loved the Lord Jesus Christ with all her
heart. After the meeting, I carried her in my arms into
deep water, repeated the ceremony, and immersed her
without difficulty. As she came out of the water, she
clapped her hands and rejoiced with exceeding joy. I
represented to her that she would be healed by and by,
if faithful; that, in her baptism, she had represented
the resurrection, in which she should come forth free
from her infirmities, enabled to leap, and walk, and
praise God. We were all very happy in sympathizing
with the rejoicing girl.

After a short circuit among the brethren in neighboring regions, to see how they were doing, I returned and
held a meeting of some days here, which resulted in
much good; indeed we had additions in those days at
almost every meeting. During the meeting, I related a
circumstance that had occurred at Williamsburg between
a Methodist preacher and myself, as follows:

I had an appointment at Williamsburg, at the court house, at eleven o'clock, and the Methodist preacher had an appointment an hour later at the same place. I was at the place in time, but found the door locked. I did not inquire as to who was responsible for this; but, as I was a stranger in the place, I did not think it very good treatment, especially as the house was public property. We searched in vain for the sheriff, who had gone away with the key. We waited patiently until twelve o'clock, when the sheriff and the other preacher came up together. The door was unlocked, and we all entered, I following close upon the heels of the minister. After we went into the judge's stand, I informed him of my appointment, and requested the privilege of speaking when he should be through. He said he had some church matters to attend to, after which I might speak. When he had completed his work, I arose with a song, after which I exhorted with much freedom, and, as I became quite animated toward the close, several Methodists began to shout. Up to this time they did not know who I was, or of what religious complexion. I thought it a good time to let in a little distinctive truth; so I told them that I claimed to be simply a Christian, and that I recognized no other name. The shouting ceased instantaneously upon the announcement of my name, and all was as still as death, and apparently as cold. The preacher arose to catechise me about my creed. I handed him my Bible. He remarked:

" That is not a creed; that is a Bible."

Said I: " Is not that enough? Does not that contain all truth? and is it not enough for 'doctrine, for reproof, for correction, for instruction in righteousness, that the man of God may be perfect, and thoroughly furnished unto every good work'?"

" Oh," said he, " I understand who you are now. You are one of the followers of Barton W. Stone—a New-Light."

I answered: " No, sir; I claim to be a follower of Jesus Christ, as my name imports."

The preacher at once dismissed the people, and closed the controversy without ceremony.

As I related this incident in about the substance of the above, a young man present, who was a nephew of the preacher alluded to, became very angry, and threatened me with violence. I heard his threats, but disregarded them. On my way home from this meeting, in company with my wife and Brother Daniel Combs, this fellow watched his opportunity, when Combs was some distance ahead, stepped out into the road, took my horse by the bridle, and broke the unpleasant news to me that he intended to give me a "sound thrashing." It had been several years since I had had any experience in this sort of argument, but I was by no means alarmed, only for my wife, who was greatly excited, and cried out: "Whip your horse; give him the whip!"

"No," said I; "not until I shall have whipped this cowardly miscreant;" and, suiting the action to the word, I dismounted, and the fellow fled like a coward, and was heard from no more. I knew that he was a coward, and would run the moment I should dismount, for no one but a coward will attack a gentleman in company with his wife. The place where this occurred has borne ever since the name of Preacher's Pinch. Perhaps this was neither the safest nor the most scriptural way of treating the case; but, as the tactics which I had studied in early life had no rules laid down, either for flight or retreat, I did not know very well, upon the spur of the moment, how to do either; and, at this very writing, it is difficult for me to adopt the doctrine of non-resistance without reluctance and a degree of mental reservation, to which those trained under different circumstances are strangers. I was taught, from my youth up to mature manhood, to be prudent; to keep out of harm's way; to lead a quiet and peaceable life, if possible; but I was also taught that, as God had armed his creatures with weapons of defense, He meant thereby that, when driven to the wall, it was not wrong to strike. I know very well that vengeance belongs to God; and

that He will repay; that, therefore, we dare not to
avenge ourselves: but I consider that defending oneself,
and taking vengeance, are very different things.

We can not overlook the fact that God only promises
to help us when we can not help ourselves. That this
principle holds good both in the kingdom of Nature
and in the kingdom of Grace, I think, is not to be
questioned. If, therefore, I have all the means of protection from bodily injury, shall I refuse to use them
altogether, trusting in God for deliverance? To my
mind, it is in more complete accord with His economy
that I should do what I can to help myself, and call on
him to prosper me in the proper use of the means. It
must be admitted, however, that an abuse of the means
is often confounded with their proper use. This does
not more frequently occur in Nature than in the economy
of Grace, and can not be brought forward as an argument against the use of physical means, any more than
it can be as an argument against the use of moral and
spiritual means.

With the example of Christ before us, we are forced
to conclude that the cases are few and far between in
which it may become our duty to use physical force
in maintaining our rights and defending our persons.
It is unquestionably wrong to use such means for the
purpose of gratifying our passions, or repelling an insult. But men are more ready to use carnal weapons
in repelling insults and in punishing enemies, than in
merely protecting themselves from bodily harm. No
man can possibly state the doctrine upon this whole
subject with anything like the force and beauty of the
following passages in the twelfth chapter of Paul's letter
to the Romans:

"Recompense to no man evil for evil."

"If it be possible, as much as lieth in you, live peace-
ably with all men."

"Dearly beloved, avenge not yourselves, but rather
give place to the wrath of God: for it is written, Vengeance is mine; I will repay, saith the Lord."

"Therefore, if thine enemy hunger, feed him; if he thirst, give him drink: for in so doing thou shalt heap coals of fire on his head."

"Be not overcome of evil, but overcome evil with good."

If we enter fully into the spirit of this teaching, we will not have frequent occasion for the use of carnal weapons, if we have any such occasion whatever. My observation during a long life has satisfied me that, in ninety-nine out of every one hundred cases, physical force has been used to gratify feelings of hate and resentment, rather than for purposes of protection from harm.

CHAPTER XVI.

Still despondent.—Advice to young soldiers.—Tour to Missouri with
his brother John.—Lexington.—Dover.—Mixing things.—The rattlesnake.—Howard county.—Fall from his horse.—Raccoons.—Safe
at home.—Lungs involved.—No lions in those days.—All praise
to God.—Why not?

As stated in a previous chapter, my wife, who has
ever been to me an angel of light, by her gentleness
and courage had lifted me out of my despondency and
gloom; but my deliverance was not complete. I was
relieved, comforted, and strengthened, but not altogether
cured. The real cause of my trouble had not been removed. In spite of all efforts to the contrary, doubts,
despondency and gloom, at intervals, overcast my mind,
oppressed my spirits, and almost drove me to despair. I
found myself moving on to my work in a sort of me-
chanical way, laboring as one oppressed with a burden
too grievous to be borne, ready to cry out, "O, wretched
man that I am! who shall deliver me from the body of
this death?" I knew not then that, in the volume of
God's inspiration, I might find a ready solution of every
difficulty, if I would only examine it with an unpreju-
diced mind, reading it as I would read any other book,
taking it for granted that its most obvious meaning was
the true one. I was like the idiot who went about with a
thorn sticking in his flesh, agonizing with the sufferings
it produced, but without common sense enough to remove it.

In looking back upon those days, and remembering
how I suffered, and agonized, and prayed over my
troubles, when the cure was so near, so convenient, and
so simple, how I sympathize with the thousands of poor
deluded souls who, from one cause or another, are wandering in the mist and fog of Babylon, and know not
the way to Jerusalem, and have no one to show them

the way. I now wonder, that with the Bible before me, I did not see the truth sooner. I can not account for the fact that one in search of the truth should pass over it so frequently without finding it. I was like the old lady who was all day searching for her spectacles, and never found them until a friend showed them to her on her own forehead. The young preachers of this generation can never fully appreciate their privileges and opportunities. They were free born, and know not how much trouble they have been saved from ; they can never know how hateful a thing it is to be a bondman in Mystery Babylon. Old as I am, the remembrance of the days of my bondage stirs my blood, and animates me with the desire to renew the conflict against error, superstition and mysticism, that, happily, I might set some prisoners free who have been bound in affliction and iron, and lead them into the glorious liberty of the sons of God. Young Soldier of the Cross, see that you make no compromises with error and sectarianism. Unsheathe your sword, and never return it to the scabbard until the last captive to superstition and mysticism has been set free.

I suppose it was partly to attempt an escape from the sad reflections that had been haunting me, and partly to see again the country and people, and especially the mother that I loved, that, in the summer of 1822, I made another journey to Missouri. My brother, John Rogers, accompanied me on this tour. We had arranged our appointments at proper stages along the route, so as to have preaching almost every day or night on our journey. The greatest distance between settlements now being but a moderate day's journey, we were not under the necessity of camping out, as I had often done on former occasions. We still carried some provisions with us in case of necessity, and often dined upon our cold bread and dried beef. Though we held no protracted meeting on the way, yet we had many joyful seasons. It was not unusual, after a hard day's journey, to meet at night a crowd of anxious people waiting for the bread of life. Sometimes we were detained in exhortation, singing, praying, and talking to anxious inquirers after the way of salvation, until midnight.

I believe the first protracted meeting we held in Missouri was in Lexington, then an inconsiderable village, not much like the Lexington of to-day. We were permitted to hold our meetings in the court-house, which was a rude log structure, of which the present proud inhabitants would be ashamed. The log court-house was in keeping with the houses generally, and compared quite well with all the surroundings. The people were, in the main, a rough-looking class, though they treated us as kindly, and heard the word as gladly, and listened as patiently, as the most refined and cultivated could have done. We had our mourners' benches in those days, and proceeded in our meetings much like the Methodists do now. We had a great many mourners to come forward at this meeting. We prayed for them as usual, and quite a number professed religion, as we used to say. During the meeting, we sojourned with an old sister who lived in the edge of the town, as she was better prepared to entertain us and take care of our horses than anyone else. This dear old lady, having learned that I was very fond of tea, and never having used the article herself, sent off and purchased some for my special benefit. At supper she asked me how I enjoyed my tea. I told her that it did quite well, but I thought it would have been better if it had been allowed to draw longer. The next evening, when we sat down to supper, she congratulated me upon the prospect of my having a better cup of tea than that of the previous evening: "For," said she, "I have had it on boiling all the evening." This occurred in the house of one of the best families in that country. I suppose their descendants could do better now in the way of tea-making, but I very much doubt if they know any better how to use real Christian hospitality than did their ancestors.

Our next meeting was at the house of Brother Solomon Cox, where the town of Dover now stands. Here the emigrant found as rich a country as any in America. At least, such was my opinion from the luxuriant growth of walnut, linden, hackberry, box-elder and spicewood, that, with the immense grape vines, made a shade so dense as to almost exclude the rays of the sun from the earth. I have no very distinct recollection of the result of our meeting, or how long we remained. I have, however, a vivid recollection of an adventure that I am tempted to relate. I have often been in the habit of mixing up a little recreation, such as fishing and hunting, with my preaching, especially when a favorable opportunity offered. Being naturally fond of the deep forest, I was in the habit of taking a daily stroll through it for reflection and quiet meditation. At different times, I had seen squirrels sporting in the trees around me in such a manner as to put me in the notion of carrying a rifle. So the next stroll I made to the forest, I carried a rifle with me. Having pursued my accustomed path for some time, until I came to a large vine, which had grown in such shape as to afford an inviting seat, I sat down, and bent my gaze upon a neighboring tree, where I discovered a large fox-squirrel about half concealed. The wind was blowing briskly, swaying the branches of the tree, so that I concluded to watch and wait for the wind to subside a little before discharging the contents of my rifle at my game.

Meanwhile, I heard a suspicious crackling of the dry leaves near by, and though reluctant to withdraw my gaze, at length I turned, and looking down, saw, to my astonishment and dismay, a huge rattlesnake, with head erect and tongue playing like forked lightning, moving slowly towards me, and almost within touching distance. At a single bound I was out of his reach, and in a moment had discharged the contents of my rifle with deadly aim. He was a monster in size, and venerable with age, having no less than sixteen rattles attached, which I carried home as a trophy. If the old serpent in the garden had resembled him in shape and in appearance, I am not disposed to believe that our mother Eve could have been

greatly charmed.   It was a long time before I recovered
from my fright; so, you may imagine, my sermon for
that day was completely spoiled, it being impossible for
me to so concentrate my thoughts upon the subject as to
exclude the horrid vision from my mind.   We may learn
that in all the walks of life the old serpent is watching
his opportunity to strike us, and that it becomes us to
watch with unceasing vigilance his every avenue of approach.   He is apt to surprise us, too, in the midst of
pleasure — more liable to approach us then than at any
other time, because, being off our guard, we afford him
the most favorable opportunity to do us injury.   Notwithstanding my pleasure-seeking and unwatchfulness,
the Lord graciously preserved me, and I praise Him
for it.

From this place we went into Howard county, having
crossed the Missouri at the mouth of Chariton River.
Our road led us through a large tract of prairie, which,
at that season of the year, was infested with green horse-
flies, which were so thirsty for blood that they made
our horses unmanageable.   We alighted to obtain some
brushwood with which to drive away the flies, and I
unfortunately selected a brush from the sumac tree.   The
leaves of this tree are green and purple on one side, and
of a milky whiteness on the other.   When, therefore, I
attempted to mount my horse, he took fright at the bush
of many colors, and threw me on the ground so violently that for some time I was quite insensible.

When I had measurably recovered from the shock,
my brother assisted me into the saddle, and, riding by
my side, supported me for seven tedious miles before we
were able to find a resting-place for the night.   I have
called them tedious miles, and so they were: for every
step of my horse pierced me with pain, and almost sick-
ened me unto death.   I wanted to lie down on the
ground, and rest, or die, but my brother encouraged me
to endure the pain, and urged me on until we arrived at
a house where we were made welcome for the night.
Providentially, we found a traveler there who was fur-

ished with a lancet, and, being an expert at blood-let-
ng, he bled me copiously, which gave me great relief
nd enabled me to rest for the night with some degree
f comfort.

The next morning, I had sufficiently recovered to ride
n, by very short stages, to our appointment, but my
rother had to do all the preaching. From this place
e went on to Franklin county, where I spent several
ays with my kindred and friends, but was still not able
o preach. It was now agreed that my brother should
ll all our appointments, and that I should return home
nd recruit my health. Accordingly, I turned my face
owards home, and, after a long and tiresome journey, I
rrived there in safety, but not by any means with a
ound body. By close examination, it was found that a
ib had been so fractured as to involve my lungs quite
eriously. Hemorrhages had set in, from which I was
ot relieved for many months. For a long time, I ap-
eared to be going into a decline, and at one time, my
riends despaired of my recovery; but, by the goodness
f a kind Father, I was able in less than a year to take
he field again.

On my arrival at home, my friends gathered in to see
ie, as was their custom, to welcome me back, and to
ear the news. They did not come in to lionize or to
lolize me on account of my successes. Far from it.
'here were not many lions in those days. They would
ave thought of praising the man in the moon as soon
s me, for the work of the Lord which I, as an humble
istrument, had accomplished. In those days, men
ere left pretty much out of view. We trusted God
or everything; we gave Him all the honor and all the
raise.

It was customary, upon my arrival home from a
reaching tour, to detail minutely to my family and
riends every incident and circumstance of my jour-
ey, with a particular account of my meetings; and
ll looked and listened with interest, not to hear or
ee me in all this, but to hear the footsteps of God, and

to see the work of His hand in all these things. If a great revival had occurred, we praised God for it with one heart and one voice. If affliction had befallen me, we saw, or thought we saw, in it, the workings of a kind though mysterious providential hand. We saw God in everything; we saw Him everywhere ; we saw Him in prosperity and in adversity, in sickness and in health, in life and in death. I would not say that my kind-hearted and loving wife did not allow herself to utter a word of regret at my affliction; but she, and all my friends together, saw, or thought they saw, the hand of God in the whole affair.

Though I will not say that we did not go to great extremes sometimes in our attempts to trace the hand of the Lord, yet I believe we were nearer right then than the majority of professors of religion are now in their attempts to ascribe everything to natural causes. Indeed, if natural causes do produce the effects that we see, why should we exclude God from them, seeing that nature works by His almighty power? I do not see why we may not as readily see God in the ordinary and every-day workings of His mighty power, as in the extraordinary and miraculous demonstrations of His power. I know that old men are disposed to magnify the virtues of the past, and I will not say that I form an exception to the rule. But, with all our faults and foibles in those days, there was that commendable un-selfishness that all the godly must admire, which gave God all the honor and all the praise, however successful an instrumentality might be. We heard then of what God had done for the soul, not what man had done. We are now almost afraid to say, God has done this, or God has done that, simply because we understand by what means and instrumentalities it has been accomplished. Because we understand that faith comes by hearing, and hearing by the word of God, and because we un-derstand what the conditions of salvation are, is no reason why we should leave God out of the question. Does not God give day by day our daily bread? Does

He not feed the young ravens when they cry? Is it not true that the gospel is the power of God unto salvation to every one that believeth? Vain and silly men would have us believe that God has only done a few days' work from all eternity. They say He worked in Nature six days, and ceased forever from all care of the physical world. Then they would have us believe that He worked a little while in the establishment of the Church, and ceased from His labors in that respect. But the truth is, that in Him we live, and move, and have our being, both temporally and spiritually. He numbers the very hairs of our head, and not a sparrow falls to the ground without His notice.

CHAPTER XVII.

Starts in company with John Rogers for Virginia.—Churches visited
by the way.—Need of caring for weak churches.—Visit to their
uncle, John Williamson.—Parson Mitchell's attempt to immerse.—
A Calvinistic argument.—Great awakening in Pittsylvania county.
—The O'Kellyites.

By the blessing of God, having so recovered my
strength as to be able to endure the fatigue of another
journey, I arranged for another visit to the Old Dominion, in company with my brother, John Rogers.

We left home in the latter part of the month of May;
passed through Eastern Kentucky, along the Little
Sandy; then over to the Kanawha, and up New River
into Giles county, Virginia. We found several congregations on the way, but I regret to say, that many of
them had a name to live, while in reality they were
dead. If a dead body is a stench in the nostrils of men,
what must a dead church be, in the nostrils of Him who
gave His Son to redeem it, and purify and sanctify it?
We had our plans so arranged that we could not stop
with these churches long enough to do them much good.
I believe, however, that the passing words we gave
them was not labor lost, for many whom we communed
with expressed not only a strong desire, but a firm determination, to do better.

In Giles county we found the churches in need of
much encouragement. With some of them, the light
seemed to have been altogether extinguished. None of
them were living up to their privileges, and all needed
much instruction and encouragement. Here we remained long enough to see the drooping spirits of the
people much revived. We reorganized a few congregations; reclaimed many backsliders, and witnessed the
conversion of many souls to God. The little that we
did here for the Lord, was signally blessed to the up-

building of the drooping cause throughout the county. I have reason to believe that our visit to this part of the country was just in time to save many from a hopeless state of apostasy. There is a critical period in the history of every backslider, when a little encouragement and instruction may save from irrecoverable ruin. I am disposed to think that in the providence of God our mission in Giles county, Virginia, was at the very time to save them.

It would be a great thing for the cause of Christianity, if we could have a few experienced men in every district, who were willing to devote themselves to the work of visiting the weak congregations, not only to see how they do, but to tarry with them long enough to get them on their feet, and make them self-sustaining. God never intended that his evangelists should build up congregations and then leave them to perish in helpless infancy; but that they should nourish and cherish them until they have strength to stand and walk alone. All extremes ought to be avoided. After a child is born, it would be an extreme measure to keep a nurse by its side perpetually, and on, during the entire period of its life. This would be a destructive measure, calculated to rob the child of its independence. So I would not have the church nursed to death, and nursed forever, by the preacher. But there ought to be such nursing in the beginning, and then, such watch-care to the end, as would promote the health, growth and strength of the church, and prevent the backslidings and disbandings that are of so frequent occurrence.

But then we are such sticklers for plans and schemes, that nobody can go and do God's appointed work without having his commission made out, signed and countersigned, and sealed and delivered, according to the latest decision of the wise and prudent. So, while all this is being done, souls die, and churches dissolve. I care very little about plans, and shall never fight against them, nor shall I fight for them. I have worked by or under plans, and have worked without them. I have la-

5

bored as the servant of a single congregation, and as the
servant of a county co-operation, and as the sent of the
State Board, and I have sent myself out; and have been
blessed equally in all these ways, and have had no conscientious scruples about the matter at any time. This
only has concerned me: Am I doing God's work, and
am I preaching by his authority? Where there is desti-
tution and suffering, there I have made it my business
to go and carry relief; instead of letting souls perish
while I was preparing to carry life to them by special
rule. Let every preacher of the gospel resolve, when
he first devotes himself to God's cause, that he will do
all the work in his power, whether sent and sustained
by a National Board, a County Board, or by himself; and
if I know anything about the gospel of God's grace,
prosperity will follow him. To the young preacher I
will say, while it is in my mind to say it: Preach on, and
go out preaching, and continue preaching, situation or
no situation. You must not think that, if you go out
preaching without a situation, you will starve or want
for clothing. If you want a situation, go to work
with such trust in God as will make you worthy of a
place. I fear a great many look more to men for a
position, than they do to God; and hence, neither God
nor men care to give them situations. Do not forget
that God is the great Disposer. I would also say to our
older preachers, who are literally nursing many of the
large and strong churches to death, that if they would
leave the home church to take care of itself about one
Sunday in every month, giving that day to some weak
point in the country, many dying churches might be
saved, the home church benefited by being thrown upon
its own resources, and the preacher himself recreated.
But the churches will not allow this. They are like
spoiled babies, that cry and fret if the mother leaves
them only long enough to make up a bed or sweep the
house. If the preacher desires ever so much to go and
work a little for the destitute, there is so much grumb-
ling and fretting by his spoiled and cross members, that

he becomes discouraged, and abandons his purpose. We found two godly men in Giles county, who, at their own charges, were giving a portion of their time to the work of the Lord. I allude to brethren Duncan and Adams. But for their watchfulness, I doubt if many witnesses for Jesus had been left in all that region of country.

From here we crossed over the Allegheny Mountains, into Botetourt county, spending only a few days there, on a visit to our uncle, John Williamson. Thence, crossing the Blue Ridge, we entered Bedford county, preaching in the neighborhood of the Mitchells, who were relatives of my wife. Notwithstanding they were Presbyterians of the straitest sect, they heard us patiently. The young people seemed to be pleased with the doctrine of free grace, and expressed a desire to hear us further upon our peculiar views of the Christian religion. The old people, however, though treating us courteously, informed us candidly that they had no use for the doctrine of free grace; which, had they known it, was equivalent to saying that they had no use for grace at all, seeing that all grace must be free.

Parson James Mitchell, uncle to my wife, was a prominent preacher and teacher of theology among his people, and had everything pretty much his own way. A certain Baptist preacher had been very recently among them, as I was informed, and gave the old Parson considerable trouble. Many of his recent converts demanded immersion of him, which annoyed him very much. He told me an amusing story about a servant of one of his neighbors, who had been so urgent in his request for immersion, that he consented, at length, to gratify him, though he had never done the like before. Accordingly, he prepared a platform, leading into the water about neck-deep, so that he could take the man into the water and baptize him, the administrator himself keeping perfectly dry in the operation. But, in attempting to put the head of the subject under water, he lost his balance, and, plunging headlong into the flood, was completely immersed himself. This, he said, should be his last attempt at immersion; the rest he would leave for the Baptist preacher to do. He would not say, positively, that immersion was not apostolic; but he insisted that the mode was unimportant, and therefore he followed the practice of the fathers of his church. He expressed deep concern for his sister — my mother-in-law, who had abandoned the Presbyterian faith in 1801, and had gone with B. W. Stone in the great movement of that day. I told him that I was rather astonished to hear him speak in that manner about his sister; that if, according to his theory, she was only filling out the destiny marked out for her in the counsels of eternity, he ought to be content to let God's will be done. Or, if she had been reprobated or passed by, her remaining in the Presbyterian Church could not save her — that no faith or good works could save her. His answer was, that though it was true that the destiny of all had been fixed in the counsels of eternity, yet it was our duty to do all we could to reclaim men from error, and establish them in the right way; that the doctrine of election and reprobation did not justify indifference or neglect on our part. Of course, this was the only answer that he or any other Calvinist could make in such case. They set out with a doctrine that, carried out to its legitimate results, makes all our efforts fruitless, and makes everything that occurs but the fulfillment of God's will. But, as common sense and reason revolt at such results, they are compelled to say, at last, that which contradicts the doctrine — i. e., that we are to be praised for doing this, or blamed for doing that; that we are free, and must choose or refuse. This is the plaster that they put upon the loathsome cancer that is eating the life out of the church of God; that is paralyzing all our efforts, and, without doubt, sending thousands of souls to perdition, who have vainly waited for God to do what he has told them to do.

After leaving Bedford, my brother and I parted for a season — he to go over into Charlotte, and I into Pittsylvania county, on the border of North Carolina. I

stopped and held a meeting in the neighborhood of the
Terrills and Dejarnettes. People came to this meeting a
great distance, and from every direction. We had, as
we used to say, a great awakening, or a great outpour-
ing of the Holy Ghost. Our language would have been
more scriptural, if we had said that we witnessed a
great manifestation of the Spirit; for, certainly, the
Spirit did manifest itself at that meeting. I believe
that I manifested the Spirit in preaching; that the saints
prayed, praised and rejoiced, in the manifestation of the
Spirit; and that the Spirit converted many souls at that
meeting, through the gospel, which is the power of God
to salvation unto every one that believeth.

After closing this meeting, I rejoined my brother at
the Red House, in Charlotte, where my uncle Williamson resided, of whom I have spoken. This was the old
homestead of my people. My people used to attend the
old Rough Creek Church, which stood not far from
this place, where, in my infancy, I was christened by
Bishop Asbury, after the fashion of the Methodist
Church. The people of this section were mostly either
Methodists or O'Kelleyites. These O'Kelleyites were a
very liberal people, and in full sympathy with us.
O'Kelley broke off from Coke and Asbury, in the beginning of the present century, and traveled extensively
with Rice Haggard and Joseph Thomas, the White
Pilgrim, all of them preaching the same views, in the
main, with Barton W. Stone. I do not remember that
O'Kelley ever visited the West; but Haggard and
Thomas did. Haggard first suggested to Stone the
propriety of wearing the name Christian, as that given
by divine authority to the disciples at Antioch.

CHAPTER XVIII.

Meeting at Charlotte Court-House.—Clopton and Alexander Campbell.—Conflicting views about Alexander Campbell in Virginia.—Meeting at Fredericksburg.—Brother Fife.—Visit to Washington's tomb.—Baltimore and Harford county.—Judge Norris and wife.—A model family.—Reflections on Female Education.—The Creed question.—Salem and Hanoverton, Ohio.—John Secrist and John Whitacre.—Home again.—Reflections on the support of preachers.

At Charlotte Court-house, we were kindly received by our kinsman, John Roach, and by a Brother Clopton. These men were Baptist preachers of considerable influence, and of advanced religious views. They had begun to see men as trees walking. Our meeting here lasted for two weeks, and many professed faith in Jesus. There was evidently a hungering and thirsting after the bread and water of life among the people. We might have organized a church here, but our Baptist brethren held such liberal views of Christianity that we thought proper to advise all our converts to join them. This turned out very well; for in a very short time they all, with a few exceptions, came into the Reformation.

Brother Clopton informed me that he had met Alexander Campbell, and was delighted with him. As a scholar and gentleman, he esteemed him to be equal, if not superior, to any man he had ever met. He gave us a glowing account of his efforts in Spottsylvania county, in Fredericksburg, and in Richmond, among the Baptists. Yet, he said, there were many of his brethren who were shy of him, lest he should lead the people away from some of the old Baptist landmarks. As for himself, he stated that, while he felt himself unable to controvert his teaching, yet he was evidently striking out new lines of religious thought, which might work disastrously to the Baptist cause, without the exercise of much wisdom and prudence. He expressed his determination, however, to hear him fully before passing final judgment in the premises. My brother and I listened with eager interest to everything we could hear about Alexander Campbell, for already we had been catching glimpses of light sufficient to stimulate our desire for more. My brother left me here again, for the purpose of going directly through Lynchburg on to Bethany, Brooke county, Va., with the intention of spending a few days with Brother Campbell, that he might get from his own lips what were his views upon certain questions that had recently disturbed and bewildered his mind. I took my route through Fredericksburg, Washington City and Pennsylvania. Before leaving Brother Clopton, he kindly furnished us with letters of introduction to various Baptist churches and Baptist preachers along our respective routes.

On my way to Fredericksburg, it was my good fortune to meet several intelligent persons, preachers and laymen, who could tell me a great deal that I wanted to know about Alexander Campbell. I found their judgments considerably divided. Some of them endorsed all his teaching, and looked upon him as a great apostle of truth. Others appeared to be as greatly alarmed as Belshazzar was when he saw the handwriting on the wall, which forboded his doom. Others there were who had just light enough to bewilder them, and not enough to enable them to form any definite ideas respecting him or his teaching. From all I could gather, I was inspired with a good degree of hope that he might be the man, under God, to dissolve my doubts and fears, and to dissipate the dark clouds which had so often overcast my sky. This I determined to do, whatever might be the consequences: I determined to give him a fair and full hearing, and, if he had any new light, to follow it unhesitatingly wherever it might lead me.

At Fredericksburg, I remained and preached several days, forming, meanwhile, many acquaintances. Among these, I may mention my dear friend and Christian brother Fife, a most intelligent and warm-hearted gentleman. He was loud in the praise of Brother Campbell, having heard him preach on several occasions, and was better able to give me a full, clear and unbiased account of his teaching than any man I had met. I then held it as an opinion, from all the premises before me, that he was a great teacher, raised up in the providence of God to enlighten the world. What was then only an opinion has long since ripened into a clear conviction, which has never since been changed. This was also the conviction of my good Brother Fife at that time. Years after this, Brother Fife moved to St. Louis, married the widowed mother of Dr. Winthrop H. Hopson, and, as an elder and teacher in the city of St. Louis, did much to advance our cause. Many years ago I met him, and sojourned with him while holding a meeting in St. Louis. I found him here the same calm, clear-headed, conscientious and .faithful man of God I had taken him to be at our first meeting. Well may I say many years ago, for, at that meeting, we baptized our converts in Chouteau's Pond, which was then a large and beautiful basin of water, but is now covered with some of the proudest structures of that city.

From Fredericksburg, I passed through Dumfries to visit the tomb and home of Washington, on the Potomac. Though I had but little time to spare, I could not pass hastily the tomb of America's greatest chieftain and statesman. While standing by that tomb, my mind took in at a single glance the eventful period of the Revolution, when, on account of the weakness of the colonies, the division of counsels, and the jealousies of rival interests, all the noble traits in the character of this great chieftain were tried as gold in the fire, and, like gold, shone all the brighter for the trial. I thanked God devoutly that the grave I looked upon was not the grave of American liberty, but simply the tomb of him whom men called the Father of American liberty. These were some of the reflections of that silent, solemn hour.

I have not now the same veneration for great men that I then had, however great their achievements.

Washington was an instrument in God's hands, and only an instrument. God could have used any other instrumentality as well. I am not now willing to say that Washington was either the father of American liberty or of his country. In this I do not mean to abate one iota of his goodness or his greatness. But, looking beyond instrumentalities, I count God as the Father of our liberty and of our country, so far as there is any liberty or goodness among us.

I pursued my journey, by way of Alexandria and Washington City, to Bladensburg, where I remained several days. I next visited the brethren in Baltimore, preaching for them several discourses. We had at that time no house of worship worthy the name. If I recollect rightly, we had a school-house or a sort of academy to worship in. Notwithstanding we had a good meeting in Baltimore, I left them with some misgivings in regard to the future of the little congregation, on account of seeds of dissension that had been sown there a little before by a corrupt and designing man, who claimed to be a pattern of piety, but who was evidently a pattern of deceit and treachery. Long since, that trouble has been healed, and I am glad to learn that the congregation in Baltimore is in a flourishing condition. As my labors had been signally blessed in Harford county on the occasion of a former visit, I determined to visit again that field and hold a few meetings. My old friends were happy to see me, and were much encouraged and comforted during my stay with them. We had joyful seasons together. I have strong confidence of meeting many of those good people when I get home.

For several days I sojourned at the house of Judge Norris, a real gentleman, whose wife was certainly a model of Christianity. I do not remember to have met in all my life a more amiable, intelligent and pious Christian woman. She appeared to be highly educated and refined, using in her ordinary conversation the most beautiful language I ever listened to. She was perfectly natural and easy in her manner, making every one feel

5*

at home in her presence. But what I noted particularly was the fact, that all her children had copied her language and manners completely, and all that were old enough had copied her religion too. Who can estimate the worth of a refined Christian mother to a family of children?

I left the bosom of this model family with the firm resolve that, if I could do nothing more for my daughters, I would give them a liberal education and as thorough instruction in the way of the Christian life as I was capable of doing. I am impressed more and more with the importance of proper and thorough female culture, as I observe to what extent the mother's influence shapes the character of her children. It is not stating it in language too strong to say that the world is, in a great measure, what the mothers have made it. I would not relieve the father from his share of responsibility, but the experience of a long life has taught me to look hopefully upon those children who have a pious and intelligent mother to instruct them; and to look with distrust upon those children whose mothers are wanting in religious intelligence and Christian deportment. No matter how accomplished, how religious, the father may be; this can not compensate for the defects of the mother. If either boys or girls must be neglected in their training and education, we say, by all means let the boys suffer, and not the girls, if we have any care for the welfare of future generations. As God has committed to the mother the responsible work of molding the character of the child, we should spare no pains in qualifying her for the faithful discharge of that responsible duty. We should remember that the effects of a mother's training and influence are not felt alone in the limits of her own household, but also far and wide in society, and extend to all generations, and into boundless eternity.

I had a large family of children, about equally divided between boys and girls; and, not being able to give them all such an education as I desired, I turned the boys out to shift for themselves, but educated my daughters to the utmost of my ability. This course, by God's blessing, turned out well for both boys and girls. If I had a thousand families to rear, I think I should act upon the principle of doing all I could for the girls, and as little as the nature of the case would admit of for the boys. Before dismissing this subject, I must be permitted to enter my protest against that sort of female education that pampers the young lady for frivolous employments and fashionable life, making her a pleasure-seeking butterfly, instead of an angel of mercy. No education or training is worth the name, which does not prepare the child for the stern realities and serious duties of life. I have ever looked upon my sojourn at Judge Norris's, in Harford county, as a providential circumstance, suggesting to me proper ideas upon the subject of female education.

My next appointment was at Harrisburg, Pa. Very little occurred here worthy of note. I fell in at this place with a Brother Winebrenner, who informed me that he was acquainted with Brother Campbell, and could find but little fault with his teaching. This man was far in advance of most of his brethren, both in religious knowledge and Christian liberality. I was surprised to hear him say, however, that he thought it would be a good thing for every church to have written out a small creed, containing simply the essentials of Christianity. Though not altogether out of the smoke of the old city, I was far in advance of Brother Winebrenner on the creed question, and, of course, I took issue with him there. I told him I was afraid of these essences. They had divided the Church of God; they were the wine of Babylon that had made the people drunk, and had sent them reeling and staggering towards every point of the religious compass. He answered, however, that he did not want a regular creed, but a few of the essentials written out for the purpose of securing uniformity. Again I answered him that the principle was what I opposed; that, with me, it was not a question of quantity, but of quality; that the small creeds had grown into large ones;

that, admitting that the small creed could never be developed into the larger one, yet it was equally as poisonous and destructive as the large one to the extent that it was received by the Church; that we wanted no extracts of the truth, but the gospel as God had given it. The gospel, as God had given it, was the power of God to salvation to every one that believeth.

I argued that, as wheat and corn, as God had given them, were the staff of life; so the word of God, as He had given it to men, was the bread and water of life, of which we may eat and drink without stint, and find spiritual vigor and health. And as the extracts of the natural grain, after men have distilled it, are poisonous, and will destroy both body and soul in hell; so, when God's word has been put into the theological distilleries of men, and the essentials have been extracted, woe to the man who imbibes! As sure as history repeats itself, so sure will follow alienation, division, strife, spiritual delirium tremens and death. But Brother'Winebrenner was not to be diverted from his course; for, having prepared his essential articles of faith, he sat down about midway between Jerusalem and Babylon, and died. The best feature in his creed was the name which he adopted for his church, i. e., Church of God.

From Harrisburg I went to Bedford county, where I remained two weeks. This was, perhaps, the happiest meeting of the campaign. From Bedford I passed into Ohio, by way of Pittsburg. At Salem and Hanoverton I had pleasant and profitable meetings, and fell into company with John Secrist and John Whitacre, men of considerable ability, who had embraced the views of Brother Campbell as far as they understood them, and were making quite a stir among the Quakers, who were very numerous in that part of the country. Stopping a short time at Carlisle, on' the Hockhocking, and at Williamsport, on Deer Creek, I reached home the latter part of August, after an absence of three months.

Though, as the result of these three months' labors, many scores were converted to God, and many luke-

warm Christians revived, yet, from all the contributions
I had received, I had not enough money left, after pay-
ing expenses, to pay for a pair of boots. This was no
new experience for us. I never knew more than two or
three of the preachers in our ranks, at that day, who
supported themselves by preaching exclusively. Yet no
class of men ever labored more faithfully or constantly
than they for the salvation of souls. They claimed to be
called by the Holy Spirit to preach the gospel, and they
had confidence that God would see to it that their families should not suffer. Both among our preachers and
people, there was prevalent a sense of foolish timidity
upon the matter of taking up contributions of money for
the ambassador of God, lest the world might conclude
that he cared more for the fleece than he did for the
flock. The little that we did receive was collected and
given to us in a manner so sly and so secret, that the
giver often appeared more like a felon than like God's
cheerful giver. And we, who were the recipients of those
small favors, were ready to jump out of our boots if anyone should hear the money jingle in our pockets. Well
do I remember how I used to receive those small pit-
tances from my brethren. When a brother or sister, in
telling you good-bye, took hold of your hand in a clumsy
sort of way, with their hand half shut and half opened,
you might look out for a quarter, or a few cut nine-
pences. You may imagine that our hands became very
sensitive to those clumsy touches. I have had money
slipped into my vest pocket, into my pants pocket, and
once I found a piece of money in my sack, which had
been deposited there while I was asleep. All this was
done that the ministry might not be blamed, and for the
purpose of keeping that tell-tale left hand in blissful ignorance of what the right hand had done. The people
were not nearly so scrupulous about giving anything else
as they were about giving money. They acted as if they
really thought money was the root of all evil, whose
very touch would contaminate the fingers of the man of
God. Some persons may take this to be an attempt at

burlesque on my part; but I am writing the history of facts, and have not drawn an extravagant picture of the case, by any means.

I must add that, though we suffered and sacrificed much more for the cause we were advocating than our children can ever appreciate, yet there was one compensating feature that is worthy of note. Our families were not left to starve in our absence by any means. It is true, they did not enjoy the luxuries in which the families of preachers now indulge, but they were supplied by the benevolent of the neighborhood with the ordinary comforts of life. There was no regular agreement to this effect, but, by common consent, it was understood that the preacher's family must not suffer while he was publishing the gospel to the world without promise of earthly gain. The brethren, in sending to the mill, generally put in an extra bushel or two of corn, or of wheat, for the preacher's family. At hog-killing there was also remembrance made of the preacher. At sugar-making there was an extra stirring-off for the benefit of the preacher. In preparing the web for the loom there was often an extra yard or two of linsey put on for this girl or that, and the same of jeans for the little boy; so that in the long run we got along bravely, considering all the circumstances.

CHAPTER XIX.

A desire to see and hear for himself.—He hears Alexander Campbell for himself.—His opinion of him.—Reflections.—Attempt at schism. —The church had rest.—Walter Scott.—Aylett Raines.—The Mahoning Association.

During my three months' tour through Virginia, Pennsylvania and Ohio, I had learned enough concerning the teachings of Alexander Campbell, together with what I had gleaned from his debates, and his writings in the *Christian Baptist,* to excite in me a burning desire to see him, and hear him for myself. From what I had heard and read, I believed that he could solve all my difficult religious problems.

You may imagine, therefore, the joy that filled my heart, upon the reception of the news, that I should at last have the coveted opportunity of seeing and hearing Brother Campbell for myself. I believe it was in the year 1825 that, in passing through Ohio, he made it in his way to visit Wilmington. It was my privilege to hear him in a discourse of two hours' length, and I regretted that he could not continue his discourse for two hours more. I believe the whole audience would have listened patiently until sunset. As he spoke, cloud after cloud rolled away from my mind, letting in upon my soul, light and joy and hope, that no tongue can express. After the sermon I was invited to accompany him to the house of Brother Jacob Strickle, where it was my good fortune to have a free and full conversation with him, which gave me more light, and afforded me more comfort, than any conversation I had ever enjoyed. The evening was spent, chiefly, in asking and answering questions. At the close of this protracted interview, I felt that my fondest desire was satisfied — that my most sanguine hopes, in reference to this meeting, had been more than realized.

For years I had been tossed upon the billows of doubt and perplexity, narrowly escaping, in more than one instance, the whirlpool of skepticism, if not infidelity. But now, thank God, I was resting calmly in the harbor of peace. I looked upon him as the sent of God to restore the law to Israel.

Some of my friends asked me what I thought of him, now that I had heard him for myself. I told them that I looked upon him as the modern Ezra, whom God had sent to restore the lost law to his people. And so I yet believe. Of course, I do not believe that any man, in these latter times, is inspired to speak as Paul and Peter were, but I shall die believing that God raised up Alexander Campbell to accomplish the very work which he has done. Indeed, he seemed to be sensible of this very fact, for he spoke as one having authority. He did not speculate or dogmatize, but he pleaded, with all the earnestness and confidence of an inspired man, for the restoration of the ancient order of' things—for Apostolic doctrine and discipline. With facts and documents completely overwhelming, he demonstrated the fact that the Church had apostatized from primitive faith and practice, and that the only remedy left us was, in going back to the days of divinely-inspired teachers, and in adopting their doctrine and practice as our infallible guide. He showed that human standards might be good, or they might be bad; that human teachers might be right or wrong; but that the holy men of God, who spake as they were moved by the Holy Spirit, could not by any possibility be wrong; and that, therefore, we were absolutely safe in teaching what they taught, and in practicing what they practiced.

Long before I became acquainted with the views of Brother Campbell, I had an impression which at times amounted to a conviction, that beyond my horizon there were fields of truth, clearer and brighter far, than any I had ever yet explored. The wish might have been in some measure the father of the thought. I did certainly sigh, day by day, for a better understanding of the truth, and could not for a moment admit that God had originally intended that his creatures should be satisfied with anything short of the assurance of faith. Yet I did not know how to become the recipient of such faith. Guided, mainly, by feelings and impressions which were fluctuating and deceptive, I felt that there must be some sure guide — some better way; but how to find it, I knew not.

Though my ideas were not so exact, yet, I presume, they were of the same nature with those of Christopher Columbus, who came to the conclusion that there must be another continent, because the lands he knew of did not complement his ideas of the world which a perfect Creator would make. Upon being led to the discovery of the gospel in its ancient simplicity and beauty, which was the consummation of all my fondest dreams and hopes, satisfying all my longings after a better way, I doubt not my joy far exceeded that of Columbus and his crew, when the land of their dreams first burst upon their vision. It has been said, that the times make the man; but it is my belief that God sends the man for the times.

I was not alone in waiting and sighing for the day of clearer light. Expectation was on tip-toe in thousands of hearts, when Alexander made his appearance upon the stage, and began to write and speak upon those great questions that have since almost revolutionized the religious world.

It will ever be a cherished belief of mine, that Alexander Campbell's coming to America was by the direction of a gracious providence of God. He found here, as he could not have found in the old world, a people looking, longing, and waiting for him; or, if not exactly for him, they were waiting for that day of religious reformation which he was instrumental in bringing about.

Most of the members of Antioch church, where I had my membership, now betook themselves to a careful and prayerful study of the word of God, such as I had never witnessed before. The result was, that with a few exceptions, they were in a short time willing to adopt the apostolic order of things, as to church government and worship. There were a few brethren who could not see their way clear to observe the ordinance of the Lord's Supper upon every first day of the week. They, however, with a spirit of becoming liberality, were not inclined to put any obstacle in the way of the majority who felt it to be their duty to so observe it. We, with the same liberal spirit, allowed them the exercise of their own choice upon this question. For some time, only a portion of the church observed the ordinance of the Lord's Supper; but at the end of a little more than a year we were completely organized, as we thought, according to the divine model, and the church, with the exception of two or three disaffected spirits, was walking in all the ordinances of the Lord, blameless. About this time, one Thomas Campbell, who claimed to be specially called of God to put down heretics, came among us, and by his mad endeavors, aroused the two or three discontented ones who had refused to adopt the apostolic order with us. The end of it was, that they attempted to close the house against us, upon the ground that we had departed from our original foundation.

Campbell was a man of a low order of talents—of more than ordinary cunning — had a stentorian voice, and an address calculated to inspire awe in the minds of the ignorant. Brother William M. Irvin and I, with Bible in hand, met this bold intruder, in regard to the question of our having departed from the faith, or from the original ground upon which we had been constituted. We proved that we had originally taken the Word of God as our only rule of faith and practice, and we challenged him to show wherein we had departed from it. We argued that, though our practice was different from what it was formerly, yet every change which we had made only brought us into stricter conformity with the letter of our creed. Our adversaries, after making a few feeble attempts to answer us, retired from the field, and thenceforward we had no more trouble with them. In former days, I had constituted a number of churches in the surrounding country, all of which, in a short time, came into the Reformation, with the exception of a few individuals whose religion had more to do with feeling than faith. Some of these abandoned the faith; the rest came into their respective churches, so that we had peace in all our borders.

The Reformation had an easy conquest over all our churches, for the reason, that they were right, constitutionally, i. e., they had taken originally the Bible alone for their only rule in faith and practice. It was not necessary, therefore, that they should change their ground; but all they needed was a better understanding of it. This explains the fact of the early triumph of the Reformation in Kentucky, and especially of its having so deep a hold in the Blue Grass Region. Brother Stone, and those laboring with him, had constituted churches throughout the central and northern portion of Kentucky, upon the Bible, and the Bible alone, and all these, without exception, came early into the Reformation. The very first churches, both in Ohio and Kentucky, which embraced the views of Brother Campbell, were those which had been planted by Brother Stone and his fellow-laborers, so that it appears that Stone's Reformation was the seed-bed of the Reformation produced by Brother Campbell. It is true that the formal union in Kentucky, between the friends of Stone and Campbell, did not occur until the year 1832; but a large proportion of the friends of Stone received the teachings of Brother Campbell almost from the very beginning of his writings in the *Christian Baptist*, which commenced July 4, 1823.

In the year 1827, Walter Scott was appointed Evangelist for the Western Reserve, in the northeastern portion of Ohio, where his labors were signally blest in turning men from darkness to light, and from the power of Satan, unto God. He was among the first who had immersed believing penitents for the remission of sins.

The news of his triumphs having spread over the whole
country, his work became the subject of comment and
criticism, in the most distant parts of the State. For a
time, little else was talked of in the religious circles of
our part of the country, save the work of Walter Scott,
the great apostle of the Western Reserve. In the
Autumn of that year I determined to go into those parts
where the truth had triumphed so gloriously, for the
purpose of seeing the men who were engaged in this
work, and hearing for myself. So, mounting my horse,
I rode more than two hundred miles, to the town of
Warren, in Trumbull county, Ohio, where the Mahoning Association was to be held. (I believe this Association never had another meeting.) There I met Thomas
Campbell, and his illustrious son, Alexander, Walter
Scott, Adamson Bentley, Jacob Osborne, A. Raines, Syd-
ney Rigdon (who afterwards abandoned the faith and joined the Mormons), besides I know not how many others.
The meeting was largely attended, and the business
transacted was of vital importance to the interests of
primitive Christianity.

The most important and exciting item of business,
and one which had much to do in shaping the future
course of our churches upon questions of Christian fellowship, was the reception of Brother Raines into communion. He had been a great light among the Restorationists — had traveled extensively among them, confirming them, and reviving their drooping cause in many
parts of the country. They looked upon him as the great
champion of their cause. Having been thrown into the
field of Scott's labors, he took occasion to hear him, and
being so well pleased, he heard him again, and I know
not how often. Being a clear-headed and conscientious
listener, he was not long in coming to the conclusion, that
upon the subject of conversion, Scott's preaching was in
complete harmony with the teaching of Scripture. So, in
a short time, he presented himself for baptism, and immediately after his own immersion, he went among his
brethren, baptizing many of them for the remission of

their sins. He also united with Scott, and others, aiding them in their meetings, and giving abundant proof of his ability, faithfulness and efficiency, as a proclaimer of the gospel. Notwithstanding this, he still held, as an opinion, his old speculation upon the subject of Restoration. He attended the meeting at Warren, where he was cordially welcomed by most of the brethren, and especially by Scott and Elder Thomas Campbell, who had been laboring with him heretofore. Brother Osborne, having discovered him in the congregation, raised the question of receiving him into fellowship, and inviting him to participate in the deliberations of the Association. Some favored his being received, while others thought the motion premature. After the subject had been discussed on both sides, at some length, Elder Thomas Campbell arose and addressed the Association, in favor of Brother Raines's reception into fellowship.

I have regretted ever since, that an exact copy of his speech had not been preserved. In my opinion, that speech sounded the key-note upon the subject of Christian union and communion.

He contended that they might as well exclude him as Brother Raines; because he had spent the prime of his life in preaching the doctrine of Calvinism, and, though he did not now preach it, yet, philosophically, he was still a Calvinist, holding his speculations upon this subject as private property, just as Brother Raines holds his speculations upon the subject of the final restoration of all men to the favor of God. He drew the distinction between the matters of faith, which are enjoined upon all in order to the enjoyment of Christian fellowship, and those opinions or speculations which are our private property. I regret that I can not recall his main arguments and illustrations, and the exact language that he used; but I distinctly remember that I left that Association with the impression that the speech of Thomas Campbell was of more practical value to me, than all I had heard at the Association beside. I must not omit to state, that he added, in the conclusion of his speech, that he had no hope of ever getting entirely clear of his Calvinistic speculations, unless it should be by the slow process of perspiration; for, said he, if I should attempt to vomit them up all at once, they would choke me.

It was finally agreed by the Association, that we have nothing to do with the opinions of men — that they are private property, and as long as they are held as such, are not a bar to fellowship. On this ground Brother Raines was received, and invited to take part in the deliberations of the Association. This was a bold step for the times; but certainly it was a safe and correct one. On that ground, and on that alone, can we ever hope to see the Christian world united. Men can never agree on opinions — they have no binding authority, and should not have. But in matters of faith, tens of thousands have been united, and millions more may be. All that is needed for the accomplishment of this end, is a high regard for the plain teachings of God's Word. On matters of faith, there would be but one mind and one voice, to-day, but for the fact that men have made void the Word of God by their traditions. Of course, so long as men cling to tradition, and boldly set at defiance God's holy Word, there can be no hope of union. But if the day should ever come, when the whole Christian world shall hold God's Word in greater reverence than they do human traditions and speculations, then the whole Christian world will be one. I may be charged with a want of Christian charity; but I shall die in the opinion, that nothing but a criminal contempt for God's Word is at the bottom of all our divisions. I may have attached undue importance to the case of Brother Raines, but to my mind nothing more important to the interests of Christianity has occurred, since the great apostasy. From the days of the apostasy, until the present day, opinions have been held with as much tenacity as matters of faith. Indeed, in many instances, the plainest teachings of God's Word have been treated as things indifferent, while mere human deductions have been set up as sacred standards of Christian fellowship.

Standing only second in importance to this case, was that of the six men who wrote the last Will and Testament of the Springfield Presbytery, in the year 1804. These great men proposed a union with all Christians upon the Bible alone, as the rule of faith and practice. But for want of the distinction between faith and opinion, which the two Campbells made upon the occasion of the reception of Brother Raines, they were embarrassed, and were not able to carry out practically the principles which they had adopted. The consequence was, that instead of contending earnestly for the faith, they often contended only for opinion, and neglected the matter of faith. For instance, they were often more zealous in attempting to enforce their opinions in regard to the mode of the Divine existence, than they were to enjoin it upon all as a duty to be baptized. They were sometimes more tolerant towards the unbaptized professor than they were towards the man who, in popular parlance, was a trinitarian. They committed two errors. The first was, in their zealous attempts to propagate mere opinions; and the second, in their violent contentions against the opinions of others. Had they contended only for the faith once delivered to the saints, and paid less attention to speculations, the faith would have triumphed, and these conflicting opinions of men would have died of being let alone. By letting opinions and philosophical speculations alone, men are apt to lose all interest in them, as in the case of Bro. Raines. And they will also forget the arguments by which they attempted to support them.

After Brother Raines had been received into fellowship, I sought and obtained an interview with him, which impressed me so favorably, that I invited him to visit us in Clinton county at his earliest convenience. Before we separated he accepted my invitation, stating that he had long desired to visit our part of the country, and now that he was instructed in the way of the Lord more perfectly, it would afford him great pleasure to do so. He was not slow in fulfilling his promise; for in a few weeks his voice was raised in our midst, in advocacy of ancient Apostolic Christianity. At first some of the old brethren and sisters were a little shy of him, not only on account of his having been so recently a preacher among the Restorationists, but because he came among us wearing green spectacles—a thing that was made odious because, a short time before, a vile pretender had been among us wearing green glasses. His first meeting was largely attended, some coming out of mere curiosity, some to find fault, and others simply to hear the truth.

Before he had proceeded a half hour in his discourse, any one could see that the whole house was completely captivated. They were leaning forward, and some almost upon their feet, in their eager endeavor to catch every word that fell from his lips.

He was a young man of medium hight, standing very erect, with a clear, penetrating gray eye, and an unimpassioned face. But in the midst of his discourse, he seemed to be a head and shoulders taller than other men; and that face, before so calm and unimpassioned, was now in every lineament and feature, wonderfully expressive of holy indignation, or divine beneficence, according to the sentiment of his subject. When treating of the love of God, his soul seemed to melt within him, and his whole nature seemed to be completely subdued. But when exposing sin, his entire being was fired with holy indignation.

At his first meeting several persons made the confession and were baptized, and among the number was my eldest daughter, who afterwards became the wife of Elder James Vandevort, a faithful servant of God, who lived and died an ornament to the Church of Christ, whose praise was among all that knew him. Soon after this meeting our brethren held a consultation meeting, which resulted in the employment of Brother Raines as county Evangelist; and well and faithfully did he perform the work assigned him. Wherever he went, he

planted the standard of the apostolic gospel, and defended it with the courage of a hero, carrying dismay
into the camps of the enemy, which almost completely
demoralized all opposing forces. He spent much of his
leisure time at my house, and, as my wife used to say,
gave the family less trouble than any preacher she had
ever attempted to entertain. I am inclined to think
that he was partial to my house, because my wife understood better than most women the kind of entertainment a young preacher ought to have. Most persons
feel that when a preacher is about the house, he must
not be allowed to stay alone for a single moment, but
must be either kept busy talking or listening, from
morning to night; whereas nothing is so agreeable to the
preacher as being left alone, especially if he should be
as great a student and as fond of his books as brother
Raines was.

I would not convey the idea that Brother Raines was
either grim or tactiturn. On the contrary, he was really
fond of conversation when the subject was one of any
interest, and but few men were more gifted in conversation than he, when the theme or the subject inspired
him. He had no taste, however, for frivolous or light
conversation, and studiously avoided the company of
young ladies. In all my acquaintance with men, I have
never known a more modest and prudent young preacher
than Aylett Raines was. He was, in all his intercourse
with society, without reproach and above suspicion.

He used to say, that when ready to marry, he would
make a business of it, and search until he found a Christian woman who would make a wife suitable for a
preacher, and if they could agree upon the terms, he would
marry without much courting, and without ceremony or
parade. In due time he accomplished his object, and in
the manner proposed. Having become acquainted with
the daughter of William Cole, an eminent lawyer of
Wilmington, Ohio, he married her, and a better selec-
tion of a woman for a preacher's wife could not have
been made. I knew her when she was a girl, and have

6

known her well as the wife of Brother Raines; and take pleasure in saying that she was true to her Saviour, faithful to the best interests of her family, practical in her domestic affairs, and, taken all in all, was such a woman as few preachers have either the good sense or the good fortune to find.

During the labors of Brother Raines in Clinton, he received two or three challenges for debate; but I think among all his adversaries, but one ever met him, and he became so completely demoralized after the first round, that he left the field in a most ridiculous and disgraceful manner. Raines was a moral hero — a soldier of no mean metal, ever ready to hurl the arrows of truth with fierceness and unerring precision against the citadel of his Master's foes. Yet he was a dignified and polite antagonist, never condescending to use vulgar means to obtain the victory over his adversary.

After his marriage, it was not long before he moved to Paris, Kentucky, since which time his name, as a sound and able expounder of God's Word, has stood at the head of the list of gospel preachers in this Reformation. I will conclude by saying, that he had fewer foibles, and more strong points, as a gospel preacher, than one out of a hundred of the pioneer preachers of the Reformation. I shall soon go home, and shall expect to see among the first comers, at the gate, my dear brother Aylett; and when we have shaken hands, we will sit down together and talk over the toils and the victories of the olden times.

CHAPTER XX.

Our worship then and now.—The contrast.—In bondage.—Sighing for freedom.—The bait of the enslaver.—Had the right creed.— Our advantage.—Rebaptism.

In those days we were emphatically a Bible people. The Scriptures were our daily study; we attempted to do nothing, either as a church or as individuals, without the divine warrant. As we were assembled together to worship on the Lord's day, we resembled more a school of children, with text-books in hand, than a modern congregation of worshipers. In fact, between the religious worship of that day and this, there appears to me to be almost no resemblance at all. We occupied the time then chiefly in reading and expounding the Scriptures, and in the breaking of the loaf. Now the sermon is the main source of attraction; and, in too many instances, that is but a string of sickly sentiments, poorly calculated to impart vigor to the soul, or to edify the body of Christ. We then delighted in the law of the Lord; now, we delight in the eloquence of the preacher. Then the chief object of our worship was to please God; now, it is to please the multitude.

When I speak of these things, I am told that the times change, and we must keep up with the times; that such old-time service would drive the people away, and leave us nothing but empty pews. I answer, that it would be better to have a few empty pews than to have the pews filled with so many empty heads and hearts. We had better fall behind the times than to go beyond the bounds of Apostolic doctrine. I am now, and have always been, afraid to follow the times, lest they lead me clear out of sight of Christ and the Apostles. I had rather have a few hearers and Jesus in the midst, than to have ever so many hearers, and be without Him.

Having been in the bondage of Egypt, and having felt the scorpion lash of sectarianism, I know, as those who were free-born can never know, how sweet a thing it is to enjoy the light and liberty of the gospel of truth, both as to faith and practice. Our children think us in our dotage, and that we see ghosts and hobgoblins where no real danger exists. But I know what I am talking about, and would warn them against any, even the slightest, departure from the plain teaching of the word of God. I am willing to be liberal, and will be as far as it is lawful; but I must not be liberal at the expense of the truth. We may be as liberal as we please with our own things, such as our opinions and speculations, for they are private property; but let us be careful how we touch the Ark of God. When the devil wants to make us slaves, he baits his traps with sentiments of extreme liberality and a show of all-abounding love. When he wants to enslave men, he is not so silly as to let them see the prisons he has prepared, or the chains he has forged for them. When he comes to us with purposes of hate, he often covers himself with a cloak of charity, and many are weak enough to take the bait, and lose their liberty forever. We must remember that divine precepts and practices can not be set aside for any consideration. God's word must be the measure of our charity, our liberality, of everything pertaining to doctrine or practice. "When it speaks, we may speak; when it is silent, we must be silent."

It may be of some benefit to others for me to give in this connection a brief chapter of my own experience. For many years before the Reformation day, I had taken my Bible as my only guide in all religious matters. I read it as constantly and as prayerfully as I have ever done since; my desire to know the truth was as sincere then as it ever was; yet I did not come to a proper knowledge of it, with all my endeavors. Seeing that I had then the same Bible open before me which I have now, I am astonished that I did not sooner come into the light of its teachings. I can only account for this fact upon the ground that my mind was preoccupied with certain mystical and deluding notions, the correctness of which I never thought of doubting or questioning, as they had the sanction of all the pious with whom I held intercourse. It is true that I was troubled with doubts, and often felt there was a wrong somewhere, and was, by no means, satisfied with my religious situation. I was earnestly and hopefully looking for light; but I was not looking for it in the right direction, nor did I suppose for a moment that it would dissipate my errors if I should come to the light, for I did not allow myself to think that I had any errors. I knew that I was ignorant, and did not fully understand the Scriptures; for I saw that my views were not in harmony with their literal meaning. But I supposed that this want of harmony between my views and those apparently conflicting Scriptures, was owing to the fact that I had not appre-- hended the true meaning of those Scriptures, and not that I was holding false views of Christianity. I was expecting such light upon the Bible as would bring it into harmony with my mystical and erroneous views, and not a light that would dissipate them altogether. Like many others, I failed, because I was always trying to bring the Bible to my theory, instead of trying to square my theory with the Bible. It never occurred to me that I ought to read the book of God to learn the truth for the truth's sake. All this may sound strange to one who has never been bewildered in the smoky precincts of Babylon; but I do not exaggerate the truth when I say that we never thought of testing our theories by the Word of God. It is true that we tried to prove them by the Bible for the sake of those who heard us, but not to confirm our own faith.

We always gave our theories the benefit of every doubt. For instance, I believed that the happy feelings I once enjoyed were the highest evidence of my acceptance with God; but when I read the following: "He that believeth and is baptized shall be saved;" "Repent, and be baptized every one of you in the name of Jesus Christ for the remission of sins, and you shall receive the gift of the Holy Spirit;" the only impression made upon my mind was that I did not understand those Scriptures, or they would harmonize with my religious experience; or I might turn to the Scriptures in the third chapter of John and read: "The wind bloweth where it listeth," and, wrapping myself in that mantle of mystery, retire to rest. So God's truth, sinking into my error, was neutralized, and subsided.

When I undertook to preach, I selected my subject, or theme — we were theme-preachers in those days — and went to the Bible to find proper texts and illustrations. If my subject was Grace, Gospel, or Love, I quoted the Scriptures that contained these respective terms, and then launched forth upon the subject according to my own experience or theory. Perhaps, after speaking in general terms of the grace of God, or the love of God, I would occupy my time in giving an account of my own conversion, or of the conversion of some one else, setting up human models, instead of the divine ones which were before my eyes. I never dreamed of giving a scriptural definition of the gospel, for I did not know that such a definition could be found between the lids of the Bible. I did not know the meaning of grace, or faith, or how either grace or faith came. We were not encouraged to learn the truth. If anyone should ask, Why? What? How? he was reproved for attempting to pry into the deep things of God. O, what slaves we were to superstition! We were slaves to our religious experiences. Of all the things in the world of which we felt most certain, the experience of pardon at the mourners' bench, or somewhere else, was that thing. For a thing of absolute certainty, we were willing to put our feelings against the world.

With all our errors, however, we were far in advance of our religious neighbors, and had this decided advantage, that, from the beginning, we had taken as our creed the Bible alone. As Paul, at Athens, had only to declare the God whom the people ignorantly worshiped, without

exciting any undue prejudices or opposition; so, when
Brother Campbell took up the Bible, and unfolded its
truths with such power and simplicity, many of us, with
a ready mind, received his teachings and rejoiced in the
light. In our case it was only advancing on our own
ground to follow the light of his instruction. The Reformation was the legitimate issue of our creed. It was
far different with those who had adopted human creeds.
Reformation was all that we needed. Revolution was
what they needed. In other words, reformation in our
case was revolution in theirs; hence, but few of them
came into the light and liberty of Apostolic doctrine.

Most of my old brethren, in coming into the Reformation, differed from me in one particular. They were
quite satisfied with their baptism; I was not satisfied. I
heard with a disquiet conscience the command, "Be
baptized for the remission of sins." It was urged by my
brethren that the highest and purest motive had actuated
me in my baptism; that is, a desire out of a pure heart
to obey God; that it would be unreasonable to believe
that, because His loving children did not understand
all that was in store for them in their obedience, therefore, He would withhold any good thing from them.
They argued that no earthly parent would be so hard
with his child as to withhold what he had promised
upon condition of obedience, on the ground that the
child did not understand the nature and full meaning
of what had been promised. I was not, however, satisfied with this sort of reasoning; first, because it was a
false mode of reasoning—because we can not, by first
finding out what man would do under certain circumstances, take that as a basis for what God would do. In
the next place, I insisted that I had not obeyed the
command, "Be baptized for the remission of sins." I
had tried to get remission in some other way, and had
then been baptized. I had, therefore, only half-way
obeyed the command. I had been baptized, but my faith
was defective. God had said plainly, "I give remission
of sins;" but by my act I had said, "I do not want par-

don in baptism; I found that long ago, at the mourners'
bench, or by agonizing in the lone woods."

"Well, then," said my friends, "are you willing to
say that, in your baptism, God did not perform his
promise in your case, and that, hence, you are an unpar-
doned man?"

I answered that I had nothing to do with that question, but this one thing I knew I had not done : I had
not fulfilled all righteousness before the world in declaring in baptism that, to the believing penitent, God, for
Christ's sake, does forgive sins. And thus ended the
argument.

In a few days after this, I settled the question by being baptized for the remission of sins, and since then my
conscience has been at rest. And I now believe I did
right, though I do not fall out with those who believe
differently. To my mind, an unintelligent baptism is
little better than no baptism at all. I have given this
subject much study, and the more I think of it, the less
I am inclined to take anything for baptism except an intelligent submission to the institution, both in manner
and design. Christian baptism is not simply an act, else
an immersed infidel could claim the blessing of remission. Faith must precede it, all admit. But are the
antecedents more important to make it baptism than its
consequents? Certainly not. Scriptural baptism is
immersion, with its antecedents and consequents. I
claim that the antecedents are defective, necessarily, if
they do not embrace the consequents. There can be no
intelligent faith that does not embrace the promises con-
nected with any act of obedience which we are required
to perform.

CHAPTER XXI.

Brother Campbell misunderstood.—Compelled to seek a new home in the West.—Stars falling, description of.—The journey.—The safe arrival.

The war waged by Brother Campbell upon the kingdom of the clergy, which, in the beginning of the current Reformation, was carried on with such telling power, was greatly misunderstood by friends and foes. In his earnest efforts to correct prevailing abuses, for which a venal clergy were largely responsible, should we admit that some of his utterances were extreme, and susceptible of misconstruction, we would only admit what has been true of all great and good men who have undertaken to reform a corrupt church. It is perfectly natural that the greater the effort to draw men from extremes of one sort, the more imminent the danger of falling into extremes of an opposite character. However much we may differ concerning the meaning of Brother Campbell's teaching upon the subject, it is clear that he did not intend to put an end to preaching, or to encourage a penurious people in " muzzling the ox that treadeth out the corn;" for he taught, emphatically, that " the laborer is worthy of his hire," and that " the Lord loves a cheerful giver," and that " those who preach the gospel should live of the gospel." There can be no doubt that he aimed at nothing short of the annihilation of the proud and mercenary priesthood that claimed the right to " lord it over God's heritage "—" to care more for the fleece than the flock "—" to open and shut the kingdom of heaven at pleasure;" all because they belonged to that exclusive class called the clergy. Besides, it is equally clear that he believed every well organized congregation should be able to edify itself; that its elders should be capable of feeding the flock of God, over whom the Lord had made them overseers; that

6*

every man, to the extent of his ability, should preach,
teach and exhort; not because he belonged to a distinct
class like the clergy, but because of his being a disciple
of the Lord Jesus Christ.

Unfortunately, there were some who, desiring an excuse for their avarice, seized upon and tortured some of
the sayings of the great Reformer, so as to find justifi-
cation in their withholding of support from the faithful
minister of the gospel, who, having forsaken all, had
gone forth to preach to a perishing world the unsearch-
able riches of Christ.

Preaching had never been a profitable business to me,
pecuniarily; but it had now become, I may say fairly, a
starving business. The result was not altogether from
the cause alluded to above, but was, no doubt, partly
brought about by the revolutionary effects of the Reformation. Many churches which, before I preached this
apostolic doctrine, were friendly to me, and ready to
lend me a helping hand, now turned from me; while
others were so engaged with their home troubles, and so
discouraged, that they were powerless to do anything towards sending the gospel to the world—or, at least,
they felt themselves so to be. So, from these causes, I
was compelled, for a time, to draw my support chiefly
from secular employments, notwithstanding it was contrary to my wishes. I applied myself very closely to
my business, for a short time, preaching only on the
Lord's day; but my soul was not satisfied.

Having received the ancient and apostolic doctrine in
its fullness and simplicity, it was to me a pleasure to
preach it. The story was plain and easy to tell; there
was nothing to do but open my Bible and let it tell to a
perishing world the way of salvation. It was not necessary, as it was of old, to warp or twist a single word or
sentence, to make it harmonize with my religious theory.
Now, my theory was, of necessity, in complete harmony
with my text; I having adopted the faith that the Bible,
in its plainest and most obvious meaning, is the Christian's sole guide—feelings, impulses, dreams and vague

impressions, all being counted as naught. Having been a religious enthusiast by nature, as well as by practice, it was not an easy matter for me to hold my breath for six days out of the week, having the old gospel at my tongue's end, and a breast panting for the salvation of souls and the enlightenment of my friends who had not yet received the ancient gospel, while the richest harvest that ever waved before husbandman was now all ripe for the sickle, waiting to be gathered in. I imagine that Saul of Tarsus was not more ardent and zealous in disposition than I was; and that after he saw the true light, he was not more anxious to convert his brethren, and by faithful service, redeem the time, than I; yet I was bound fast in the stocks. My supplies having been cut off—my family more needful of my attention than ever before — what was I to do? This question became the subject of my most earnest prayers. No man ever toiled, day after day, under greater embarrassment, than I did, for more than a year. The physical exertion demanded, was nothing. I was willing to work in the field; to work in the shop; to work anywhere, if I might only be relieved of the weight of responsibility that seemed to rest upon me on account of being hindered from gathering in the ripe harvest that was waving before me. In all my life I had not, in the same length of time, had so many and such urgent calls to preach the gospel, nor had I ever before felt one-half so competent to do good. There was not a lingering doubt in my mind but that I had the apostolic gospel, the whole gospel, and nothing but the gospel — the power of God for salvation to every one that believed it. With this assurance, how could I be contented with anything short of devoting my whole time to telling abroad the glad tidings? At length I determined to get out of the old ruts — to change my location — to go further West, if, happily, the Lord might open to me a more effectual door. My purpose was to obtain more land, and, by the aid of my boys, who were getting large enough to work on a farm, make a living for my family without devoting so much

of my time to secular employments. I trusted that I
might be, in the end, so fortunate as to be able to devote my whole time to the work of the Lord. At any
rate, I felt that I could scarcely do worse than I was
then doing, and the chances were favorable for doing
better. The thought of this gave me relief.

Accordingly, in the year 1833, and in the early
Autumn of that year, I visited the middle portion of
the State of Indiana, in company with my old and tried
friend and brother, Joseph Rulon. Attracted by the
beauty of the country, and its fertility, as well as by the
fact that some friends and brethren had already settled
there, we located in the western portion of Henry
county, on the waters of Fall Creek. Brother Rulon,
having considerable means, bought a fine farm, tolerably
well improved for that day; but as my means were quite
limited, the best that I could do was to buy two hundred acres of Government land, at one dollar and
twenty-five cents per acre. This land was very fertile
and well watered, but it was covered with a heavy
growth of timber, which made it a laborious business to
prepare it for the plow. Our purchases made, we returned home early in the month of October. I at once
sold my little farm in the neighborhood of Antioch, and,
having disposed of what stock and stuff I could not
take with me, on the 13th of November, 1833, I was
ready to start upon the journey for our new home in the
West.

Nothing short of a firm conviction of duty could have
induced me to make the sacrifices I made in leaving this
memorable field of my early labors, where I might number hundreds of firmest friends, who, by a thousand ties,
were bound to me — ties never to be broken. I look
back through the dim years to that day of tears and
farewells with feelings of mingled joy and sadness. I
had been an instrument of much blessing to that people,
and they looked upon me as their father in the gospel,
which I really was. I had found them a people without
God and without hope, except one here and there among

them. From the beginning to the end the Lord had, in a remarkable measure, blessed my humble labors. My home church, Antioch, was a large and spiritually-minded church, exerting a powerful influence upon the surrounding country ; but, when I first came into their midst, a child could number all of the professors of religion in the country. There was not a highway or a by-path that I had not traversed, in all the country, on missions, either of joy or sadness. I had baptized the people ; had married their children ; had comforted their dying hours ; had preached their funerals ; or, I would rather say, had preached their resurrection — for I never believed in funerals — they are a relic of popery ; but I do believe in preaching the resurrection. I repeat, that nothing but a sense of duty to my Lord, whom I delight to honor, could have induced me to leave those hallowed grounds.

On the evening of the twelfth, many of our dear friends came in to bid us adieu, and they remained until a very late hour, when, after a prayer, the most of them returned to their homes — a few remaining to see us off in the morning.

We had but little rest that night, for, before three o'clock in the morning, we were all aroused from our slumbers, making preparation for an early start. Some one, on looking out of the window, observed that it was almost broad daylight. "That can not be," another answered, "For it is scarcely three o'clock." "I can't help what the clock says," replied the first speaker, "my eyes can not deceive me ; it is almost broad daylight — look for yourselves." After this little altercation, some one went to the door for the purpose of settling the question. Fortunately, there was not a cloud in the heavens ; so by a glance, all was settled. I heard one of the children cry out, in a voice expressive of alarm: "Come to the door, father, the world is surely coming to an end." Another exclaimed: "See! the whole heavens are on fire! all the stars are falling!" These cries brought us all into the open yard, to gaze upon the grandest and most beautiful scene my eyes have ever beheld. It did appear as if every star had left its moorings, and was drifting rapidly in a westerly direction, leaving behind a track of light which remained visible for several seconds. Some of those wandering stars seemed as large as the full moon, or nearly so, and in some cases they appeared to dash at a rapid rate across the general course of the main body of meteors, leaving in their track a bluish light, which gathered into a thin cloud not unlike a puff of smoke from a tobacco-pipe. Some of the meteors were so bright that they were visible for some time after day had fairly dawned. Imagine large snowflakes drifting over your head, so near you that you can distinguish them, one from the other, and yet so thick in the air as to almost obscure the sky; then imagine each snowflake to be a meteor, leaving behind it a tail like a little comet; these meteors of all sizes, from that of a drop of water to that of a great star, having the size of the full moon in appearance: and you may then have some faint idea of this wonderful scene.

It must be remembered that, in the Western States, at that day, there was not much knowledge among the masses upon the subject of meteorology. Not one in a thousand could give any rational account of this wonderful phenomenon; so it will not appear strange that there was widespread alarm at this "star-shooting," so called. Some really thought that the Judgment Day was at hand, and they fell upon their knees in penitence, confessing all the sins of their past lives, and calling upon God to have mercy. On our journey we heard little talked of but the "falling of the stars." All sorts of conjectures were made by all sorts of people, excepting there were but few, if any, wise conjectures, and very few wise people to make them along the way we traveled. Not a few thought it an evidence of God's displeasure, and believed that fearful calamities would probably speedily follow. There were those who believed the Judgment Day was near at hand, and undertook to prove out of the Scriptures that this was one of the signs of the coming of the Son of Man. One old lady was emphatic in the statement that it was certainly a "token of some sign." Statements made even by good-meaning people were often quite erroneous. Some men declared that they saw great balls of fire fall into the water, and heard the sizzling noise, like that made when a red-hot iron is thrown into a slake-tub. Others thought they saw these great balls of fire bursting among the tree-tops. We may learn from this that, when men are in a high state of excitement, their testimony must be taken with many grains of allowance. I heard of a few who professed religion under the influence of these lights. In that day, for the sinner under conviction to be able to say that he had seen a light, whether he had heard a voice or not, furnished a ready passport into almost any church in the land. I suppose the reformation produced by these meteors was like the appearance of the meteors themselves — of very short duration. I have no faith in any repentance grounded upon objects of sense. The gospel only is the power of God unto salvation. Love to God and hatred for sin, only can work a permanent change in the life of a man; and nothing short of this can be trusted as permanent in its effects.

The journey to our new home was a rough one, not only because the road we traveled was new and poorly bridged, when bridged at all, but because cold weather set in soon after we started, and prevailed with more than ordinary severity to the end of our way. Moving in 1833 was not much like moving is now. Indiana had not then a railroad, turnpike, or anything like a well-constructed highway of any considerable length. There were large districts of country that had not a single inhabitant. Around the towns and older settlements, the traveler could get along very well, but he had, even in 1833, to pass over many miles together of road so poorly worked that he could have done about as well, and in many cases better, to have cut his own way through the forest altogether.

Thirty-two years before this, I had passed through this State, then a Territory; but it was under very different circumstances. I was a boy, ten years old or more, with an elasticity of body that defied hardship and laughed at the wilderness-way. That journey was made earlier in the autumn, when the streams were dry and the ground was solid. Now I had a large family of children to undergo their first experience of travel through rain, and snow, and ice, to a home among strangers. It required no little nerve to struggle along against the difficulties, without occasionally giving way to feelings of despondency and expressing words of complaint. I could have borne the hardships myself, but I could not bear with patience the exposure and suffering of my wife and children. Nevertheless, the inhospitality of roads and weather was more than made up to us by the hospitality of the settlers along the way —be this spoken to the praise of new settlers generally all the world over. I regret to say that, with the growth of the country in material wealth and internal improvements, there has not been the same improvement upon the hospitality of these people. It is a poor compliment to civilization and refinement, that selfishness has, in so large a measure, absorbed that generosity which the traveler of forty or fifty years ago met so often in the rude cabin of the woods. The home of the new settler was approached with a freedom and confidence indicative of the hospitality that reigned within. Then the latch-string always hung out. It may be, however, that the same generous people of the wilderness, had they been placed in circumstances of independence, might have lost a large measure of their generosity in parting with their dependence and poverty.

On our journey, we had a rich experience with these people, and, though our bodies may have been chilled by the blasts of winter, our hearts were warmed by their kindness. On one occasion we found night coming upon us, and no stopping place near, save a little shanty in the edge of a deep forest. We knew that we must find

shelter here, or else take the shelter of our wagons for
the night, and that promised anything but a pleasant
picture before us. I approached the cabin and called.
A man of rough exterior and with no very agreeable-
looking face, came out, and walked directly to where our
teams were, without listening, as I thought, to my
inquiry for lodging. He said in a gruff voice : "A bad
night—a bad night! This is bad business—bad business! Drive in, drive in," said he; "the cabin is small,
but it is better than the wagons, I suppose. You are
welcome to share our shelter and fire; we will do the
best we can for you. Come in, come in." We were not
long in making the change from the wagons to the cabin;
and warmer hearts or richer hospitality we have never
met. There may be standing now, on the same spot
where stood that cabin, a splendid mansion, erected by
the descendants of that man ; but I doubt if there is as
much room in that great mansion for the stranger as
there was in the cabin. What a great world this would
be if generosity would increase with riches! but this is
rarely, if ever, the case. On the contrary, the larger
our earthly mansions and storehouses are, the less they
contain for the poor wayfaring man.

After hindrances of various kinds, which kept us on
the road beyond the time calculated upon, we arrived
without any serious casualty safe in the neighborhood of
our new home. As Brother Rulon did not propose
moving for some time, we were permitted to occupy his
house until we could build one on our own land. By
late planting time, we were in our own cabin, and had a
garden spot and a small field ready for the plow.
There being no school in the neighborhood, and no one
better qualified to teach than myself, and having been
urgently solicited to undertake the work, I, promising to
do what I could, and to give way at any time that a better teacher might be obtained, taught three months,
which was about the length of time that I had gone to
school myself, all put together. My son John I., then
about fourteen years old, and pretty well advanced for

one of his age, assisted me at night in preparing for the
labors of the coming day; so that, by hard work and
close application, I was able to keep well ahead of my
pupils, with only a few exceptions.

Brother Joseph Franklin, my near neighbor, and the
father of Ben Franklin, had a large family of boys—
six in all. Ben had just married; the remaining five attended my school, and but for them I would have experienced no difficulty in keeping ahead of my scholars.
They learned rapidly, and pushed me on in a way not
altogether comfortable. They were addicted, too, to the
habit of asking questions—so much for their Rhode
Island blood. Sometimes they puzzled me sorely, but I
would put on a bold front, and, what with my own assurance, and the polite disposition of the boys not to
push their questions into unpleasant territory, I closed
my school with some degree of satisfaction to myself,
and I hope not without profit to the young people of
the neighborhood.

The school-house was large enough to hold a moderate
congregation; so I commenced preaching there at the
same time that I began to teach the school. In a short
time, we had gathered together a little band of disciples,
and organized them into a congregation. Though few
in numbers, we were strong in faith; and I then believed
that the day was not in the far distance when we would
begin to reap in earnest, for the harvest was inviting indeed. But, alas! how soon a cloud can settle upon us,
darken our way, and disappoint our hopes.

I suppose there has never been a congregation, however small, without the necessity, arising now and then,
for the exercise of discipline. Our little band was not
an exception to the rule. The case which came up was
a very delicate one, and of such a nature that, without
the exercise of much wisdom and forbearance, it was liable to give considerable trouble. We would have very
little difficulty in settling any case of discipline if all
parties were willing to be guided strictly by the letter
and spirit of the Law of Christ; but, when a case arises

involving the honor or good name of a party, passion is likely to take the place of reason, the law of the "old man" to be substituted for the "new man," resentment and hate to take the place of long suffering and love; so that the eye is closed, and the ear stopped, and all means of pacification are set at naught. After many attempts to bring the parties of our trouble to a proper understanding, and having utterly failed, we were compelled to resort to the last remedy ; so, in the fear of God, we pronounced the sentence of expulsion.

As I was the most active officer in the congregation, of course the shafts of hate were aimed chiefly at me; and, as the result of the whole matter, such a flood of persecution poured in upon me as to overwhelm me altogether. And, for some little time, though I struggled against the tide in the fear of the Lord and with all the power of my soul, it did appear that all my fond hopes of promoting the honor of my Master's cause, and of being more useful in His vineyard than I had ever been, were about to be swept away in the wild storm of passion that had been raised against me for having simply done my duty. The house of worship was closed against us, and everything was said and done that could have a tendency to hedge up the way of truth. By the help of God, however the storm might rage, we were resolved to work on, pray on, and trust the Lord for results. Though I tried to put on a bold front, anyone might have seen that I had the appearance of a disappointed man. I can now see that my faith was, for a season, defective, or I would have said to my troubled soul, "All this may end well, and, certainly, if we love God, it 'will work together for good.'" And so it turned out, even sooner than the most hopeful expected. Our troubles were an advertisement that brought us into notice more than our preaching had done.

New hearers appeared in our audiences — men who had never heard, and who, perhaps, might never have heard us under other circumstances. But we were turned out of doors, and had to find shelter in the woods, or in such barns or houses as a generous people would furnish. This excited sympathy, and brought out large audiences to hear us; and I think it operated not only upon the public favorably, but it brought all nearer to God, and, of course, it made us more humble. In our weakness we became strong. "Man's extremity is God's opportunity." Looking back over the past, I realize with great force the truth of the Apostle's remark: "That the trial of your faith, more precious than of gold that perisheth, though proved by fire, may be found to praise and honor and glory at the revelation of Jesus Christ."

CHAPTER XXII.

Joseph Franklin's family.—A happy union.—How to treat our adversaries.—Conversions and the extension of the gospel.

Among those whom our troubles had interested were Joseph Franklin and his Christian wife. They had never taken any interest in our preaching before. Even then, I do not suppose they came out of any sympathy they felt for the doctrine I preached; but to hear a man for whom a kindly feeling had been awakened on account of the bad treatment he had received. In one particular, they agreed with us religiously: they believed in immersion, and were immersed Methodists. I wish all Methodists were immersionists; they are a liberal-minded people, and could be easily approached if their baptism did not stop their ears. A strong attachment was soon formed between Joseph Franklin and wife and myself and wife. I think the desire was mutual that we might be bound together, not only in bonds of friendship, but also in the holier bond of Christian union and communion. This desire was intensified from the consideration that our union might result in the conversion of our children, who were on the broad road to destruction.

To this end, we made an agreement to meet together at the house of one or the other of us, regularly upon every Saturday afternoon, and employ the time in reading the New Testament, marking all passages as we proceeded upon which we could not so agree as to fellowship each other. In this attempt to see and believe alike, we agreed to sacrifice our prejudices and opinions, and to be guided only by the infallible Word of the Lord. All of our meetings were opened by prayer, sometimes by song and prayer. It was not long until we had finished the book.

"Now," said I, "let us examine the marked passages, and see how far we are apart."

How many were there? Not one. Why? Because we read this book with the true spirit; with an intense desire to be guided by it alone, and were thus brought together. If all men would so read the Scriptures, they might so be agreed as to its meaning, I doubt not. During our investigation, we avoided every question or expression that might arouse prejudice and obstruct our union. We sat down to our readings, not as partisans, but as if we had no opinion of our own on the matters we were considering. And when our work was done, and a complete union on the Bible, and the Bible alone, effected, no one claimed the victory, or uttered a word of triumph; but we rejoiced in that gospel which is so simple that a child can understand it, and that foundation that is broad enough for all that believe and obey the gospel of our Lord and Saviour.

If we could keep *self* out of the way in all our attempts to build upon the one foundation, and make those whom we would enlighten feel that we have no selfish end in view; but, on the contrary, that it is God's cause we are laboring to defend, and His truth alone we are laboring to maintain; we would be far more successful in our efforts to effect that unity of the spirit contemplated in the gospel. In all my attempts to preach the Apostolic gospel, I have endeavored to make my hearers realize that the whole controversy was between themselves and God. I endeavored to keep the Bible between myself and the people, so that their controversy should be, of necessity, not with men, or the words or systems of men, but with the Word of God, which is the only infallible rule of faith and practice. When constrained to make allusion to the men who stand at the head of the great religious parties of the day, such as Wesley, Luther and Calvin, it is wise to do so with becoming respect; to allude to them as men who attempted a great work, and who were great reformers in their day, to whom we owe, at the present time, a large debt of gratitude.

In my Indiana work, I found that this course of procedure told with good effect upon my hearers, who were from almost every point of the religious compass. To the day of his death, Joseph Franklin contended with his son Benjamin that, in our meetings upon the Bible, if any one had changed, I had, and not he. Quite satisfied to see him standing upon the true platform, we were all willing that he should hold this opinion. Whenever we ask men to come to *us*, to join *our* church, or when we in any way mix *ourselves* in the matter, we prejudice the cause of Christ. We must say : " Here is Christ! What think you of Him? Are you willing to believe Him, obey Him, trust Him? This is not my church, but the Church of Christ. This is not my gospel, but the Gospel of Christ, which is the power of God to salvation."

I never *made* a fine sermon in my life; but I have preached a great many very fine sermons ; yea, as powerful sermons as were ever uttered on earth. But all of these fine sermons were borrowed. I borrowed them from Christ and the Apostles. They contained the most sublime facts in the universe to be believed, the grandest commands to be obeyed, and the most precious promises to be enjoyed. From the bottom of my heart do I pity any poor upstart who preaches as if he thinks that he can improve upon the models of eighteen hundred years ago ; who is ready to turn up his nose at the grand preacher of the Pentecost; who looks upon Peter as an old fogy, knowing more of law than of liberty — too unprogressive altogether. But I must get back to my narrative.

After we were denied the use of the school-house, as I have before stated, we preached in the woods when the weather would permit, and at other times we met in such houses as were opened to us. One of those houses, where we often met, was Brother Jóseph Rulon's. One night I was preaching there, when it seemed to me that the realization of our former hopes was about to be accomplished. I was preaching one of my borrowed sermons, that had faith, repentance and baptism in it. Having closed, we called for recruits, and several of the leading spirits of the young men of the neighborhood came forward to enlist in the army of the Lord. Among them were Benjamin Franklin and his brother Daniel. The effect of this meeting was felt with power through the whole neighborhood; for these young men began at once to work. They had enlisted in the Lord's army to fight manfully against sin and superstition, and everything in opposition to their Master's cause. They began at once the study of the Scriptures in good earnest. They assisted us with prayers and exhortations, both in public and private, on the Lord's day, and on every other day; so that the glorious work moved right on from that day, with no check or abatement, until scores had been brought into the kingdom, and the whole neighborhood had been entirely revolutionized.

Brother Joseph Franklin's house being quite commodious, we held many of our meetings there; and happier meetings than those were I have never enjoyed. It was soul-cheering, indeed, to see parents and children mingling together in song, and prayer, and exhortation; extending the hand of congratulation, or "shaking hands," as it was called; and, with tearful eyes, all praising God.

Old Brother Franklin was not the best balanced man in the world; he was too much like myself in disposition. With a quick and impulsive nature, he was easily exasperated, easily excited. He suddenly became very happy, and as suddenly very unhappy. Sometimes he was lifted to the third heaven in transports of joy, and would then relapse into a state of despondency and gloom almost bordering on despair. We used to say he either lived in the garret or the cellar. Withal, however, he was a good and pure man; earnest in the advocacy of the truth, and as far from making compromises with error as any living man. He stood upon principle; was ever ready to sacrifice personal interest and the praise of men for what he believed to be the truth.

His wife was of a different disposition. She was always cheerful, and hoping for the best. While he was apt to look on the dark side of things, she was always

looking on the bright side; her sky was a cloudless one.
Indeed, she was no ordinary woman. There were very
few women in her day who had a better acquaintance
with the Bible than she, or who had so bright an intel-
lect. Her husband was sensible of this, and, when hard-
pressed in a controversy, had a happy way of getting out
of trouble by calling to his aid his wife, who, with wonderful skill, could turn the shafts of any common adversary. When in a desponding mood, he used to call upon
his wife to lead the worship. This she did with such fer-
vor that, by the time the "Amen" was uttered, Brother
Franklin was a new man. There was a depth and pathos
in her prayers and exhortations that at once solemnly
impressed all present. Prayer with her was no mere
form of words; it was literally a pouring out of the
soul to God in love, joy and praise, and in such a warm
tide as to touch every heart and suffuse every eye with
tears. When we consider the character of this woman
of God, we are not surprised that four of her six sons
became ministers of the Gospel of Christ. It would be
interesting to know how many preachers in the world
are indebted to their mothers for all they have been as
preachers, and for all they have accomplished. Hundreds of preachers have had wicked fathers; some, like
myself, have had to confess that their fathers were infidels; but can any preacher say that his mother was an
ungodly woman? Let me say to the mothers in Israel,
that the hope of the world and the prosperity of the
Church rest upon you. Talk of woman's rights and
privileges! all other rights and privileges sink into
nothingness when compared with that of rearing war-
riors for the army of the Lord. Had Sister Franklin
and my own dear wife gone out into the world to occupy
the public pulpit, the chances are that the six preachers
whom they reared would never have been heard of. My
sisters, be content to stay at home and guide the house;
and think not that you are in any mean business when
you are only bringing up your children in the fear of the
Lord. No: this is the noblest work in the world; and

7

a mission a thousand times nobler than any known by those who are continually croaking about woman's rights.

We were now in the midst of a glorious revival; the spirit of inquiry was abroad; men, old and young, carried their Bibles with them, and undertook to establish the truth of their faith and practice from that book alone. Brother Benjamin Franklin's father-in-law and mother-in-law yielded to the gospel, and so did the greater portion of their children; several of them inclined to Universalism. A brother of Sister F., a man of strong mind and of considerable general information, gave me no little trouble upon the question of universal salvation. Whenever he succeeded in decoying me out into the regions of speculation, I felt that he had the advantage of me. So long as he kept me outside of the Bible, he made out a very respectable case. I soon learned what his tactics were, and never afterwards ventured beyond the limits of Revelation. I continued my thrusts with the sword of the Spirit until he cried "Enough," and acknowledged that there was no foundation for his theory in the Bible. The conversion of this man had a considerable influence in his neighborhood, and extended our opportunities for doing good.

CHAPTER XXIII.

Confession and baptism of John I. Rogers.—Results of the revival. Benjamin Franklin as a preacher.—Valuable counsel to preachers and young converts.

My son John, who had been attending school in Kentucky, now returned to find his old associates, with a few exceptions, in the church, and full of the Spirit of the Lord. He seemed to be completely lost. He could not turn away from his old associates, and yet he felt embarrassed in their presence. No effort was spared by his young friends to induce him to become a Christian. They prayed for him; exhorted and counseled him; reasoned and pleaded with him — all apparently in vain, for, as yet, he seemed unmoved. When he was preparing to leave home again, quite a number of anxious young men came in to see him, not only for the purpose of bidding him adieu, but, likewise, to make a last and determined effort to induce him to turn to God. They talked with him up to a late hour of the night, but seemingly to no purpose. His mother and I put in a word now and then, but at last we were all inclined to give him up as a hopeless case.

Prayer being the Christian's last resort, I proposed that, before any of the company should leave, we bow together in prayer. That hour was to me one of peculiar solemnity. I felt that the soul of a dear child was suspended by a slender thread between heaven and hell. Indeed, I felt that the last-mentioned place had the better chance for him; though I could not give him up without telling my Father all about it, and asking His help in this our time of need.

At such times, when we are vibrating between hope and despair, we can all pray fervently, if not eloquently. Perhaps, I never in all my life prayed a better prayer than I did that night. I prayed with the weight of an immortal spirit upon my soul, and that spirit was my own child. Blessed be God, I did not pray in vain. My son, after it was all past, remarked to me that every word I spoke went to his heart like a barbed shaft. When we arose from our knees, John I. stood before me pale and trembling, as if struggling to unburden his soul; and, for a few moments, a silence ensued that was really painful. All eyes were turned upon him when he broke the silence, and thus addressed me:

"Father, I believe I am as well prepared to confess faith in Christ now as I may ever be."

I at once arose, grasped my boy's hand, and took his confession. I then asked when he desired to be immersed; and he answered: "At this very hour."

While this was transpiring, there was not a dry eye in the house. His loving mother even shouted aloud, praising God. Torches were soon prepared, and we went directly to the water, which was but a few steps from Brother Franklin's house. When we arrived at the place, and had aroused old Brother Franklin and wife, we had one of our old-fashioned songs, a prayer, then attended to the baptism; and in all we experienced great joy together. Brother F. said to me:

"Brother Rogers, you are a great man for the water; you come here by day and by night; yes, and at midnight. It seems," said he, "that it is never too light or too dark, too hot or too cold, for you."

"Yes," said I, "we go when the Master calls; and, as He is always calling, we are always going."

I have never been in favor of deferring baptism to suit the convenience of any one. The Lord's time is my time. "Now is the accepted time," has always been my motto.

The good work went bravely on until multitudes were rejoicing in the liberty of the glorious gospel of Christ. The effect of this revival spread far and wide. Seven preachers came out of it, and, as far as I know, have been earnest workers in the cause of the Lord. The four Franklins have done a great work in their own State. Ben Franklin's influence has been felt over the entire continent, and beyond it, both by his preaching and writing. Brother Adamson became an able preacher, and exerted a good influence in the East. My son John I. is well known in Kentucky; others may speak of his work. These men, the fruit of that revival, have extended their labors over the entire United States, and eternity alone can tell the good they have accomplished.

I have ever felt, in looking back over those times and considering that work, that, if I had done no more for my Master than to be instrumental in giving to the world Benjamin Franklin, I would have no reason to be ashamed; but would feel that I had by no means lived and labored in vain. Ben Franklin may, in common with his race, have faults and foibles: but, to my mind, he is one of the most direct and powerful gospel preachers and writers of this age. He indulges very little, if any, in speculation, but lays down his proposition, and proceeds with proofs that carry conviction to the mind almost irresistibly. He is emphatically a gospel preacher. Christ is his theme, first, midst and last. We may have scores of men among us more learned, in the popular sense, and more refined and elegant in manners and address; but it is my judgment that we have not a man among us who can preach the gospel with less admixture of philosophy and speculation, and with greater force, than Ben Franklin.

It may be said that I am partial to him, because he is my son in the gospel. It may be so; yet, when I compare the result of his labors with that of others, and find that no man has produced more fruit than he in the same length of time, I think that I am not mistaken in my judgment. He has never pretended to be learned or eloquent; yet he is learned in the religion of Jesus Christ, and overwhelmingly eloquent in presenting the love of God, and in drawing the picture of the grace of our

Lord Jesus Christ. Ben Franklin has one characteristic that ought to endear him to every Christian heart; that is, his profound reverence for the Word of God, and his abiding confidence in its truth. I ought not to glory in my own work, I know quite well; but, if an Apostle could rejoice that he had " not run in vain, neither labored in vain," so may I, without appearing vain-glorious. I do then rejoice that thousands upon thousands will chant the praises of God in heaven as the result, either immediately or remotely, of the glorious revival of which we have been speaking.

It may be proper for me to state, before closing this chapter, that if we desire large and lasting results from our conversions, every young disciple should be put to work speedily; should be impressed with the idea that he is especially called to labor, and that God will have no idlers in His vineyard. Idlers always have been mischief-makers, and will always be. They will do no good for themselves, but will do an incalculable amount of injury to others. On the other hand, the working Christian is peaceable and full of good fruits. He is himself blessed, and is a blessing to the Church. He is not rebellious or quarrelsome; is in no danger of going astray, and has neither disposition nor time to do mischief.

If any one were to ask me to give the cure for all the maladies to which young disciples are addicted, I would say, Keep them at work. These suggestions are especially useful for the young. The history of one young wanderer is the history of every one, in all its main features. They all die of inactivity. In the revival of which I have been speaking, I made it my business to encourage every young disciple to engage at once in active service. If he could do but little, that little was required at once. If he could do much, he was encouraged to begin immediately, because the duty of to-day, if neglected, makes the duty of to-morrow so difficult that we are apt to be discouraged. The result of this course was not only manifested in the bringing out into the evangelical field of so many useful preachers, but in the strength and efficiency of the converts generally. There was erected in almost every family an altar, from which ascended the incense of praise to God continually, and religious themes formed the staple of conversation; not of Lord's days only, but of every day. There was a steadfast continuance in the Apostles' doctrine, in fellowship, in breaking bread, and in prayer. Consequently, but few apostasies occurred among them.

CHAPTER XXIV.

Removal to Darke county, Ohio.—Visit to Antioch.—Success.—Again settled at my old home, among loving friends.

My mission in Indiana extended over a period of about five years; and I may say they were five checkered years. If I had those five years to live over again, I now see where I could make great improvement upon them. But they now belong to God, who has recorded their events, and those records I can never change. If we could keep in mind the fact that the deeds of every day are recorded, with all the circumstances, extenuating or aggravating, and that they will confront us in eternity, no doubt we would live better lives, and do far more for God and humanity than we do.

In the Autumn of 1838, I was offered what I thought was a good price for my Indiana farm, and was induced to sell out, and seek a new home and a new field of labor. Having been reared upon the frontier, I have always been of a roving disposition, and had the foolish notion, which has deluded countless thousands, that, by changing places, I might greatly change the current of my fortune for good. Whereas, I now believe that it would be better for us, in the long run, to remain among our friends, and to develop the fields we are occupying, than to seek fairer fields among strangers. It is an easy, but neither a brave nor a wise, way of treating difficulties to go round them. We ought bravely to meet and overcome them, and they will be forever out of the way; otherwise, we will be in the condition of an army that has flanked the enemy, leaving him strongly intrenched in the rear.

Having sold out my home place, I made a considerable tour over the States of Ohio and Indiana, and finally purchased a farm and settled in Darke county, Ohio. I flattered myself that I had now found the most promising fields for usefulness I had yet known. In this I was mistaken. It is true that the field was not altogether barren, nor were our labors in vain in the Lord. At first, I witnessed quite a revival of the drooping spirits of the disciples in the neighborhood, and the conversion of a goodly number of souls. But my work was of a spasmodic nature. Though we had among us a few noble spirits, yet the masses were wanting in firmness and Christian enterprise. My work wanted underpinning and bracing to keep it standing at all. I visited the districts around with the hope of doing good, but the results of my preaching were meager and unsatisfactory.

While here, I had a pleasant visit from two of my children, Benjamin and Daniel Franklin. We had a pleasant time together, and I think I was a little vain as I listened to those boys whom I had been instrumental in bringing into the fold of Christ. They had been born only two or three years before, and yet they had grown so rapidly that they were now larger than their father. It was almost enough to make one jealous of his own offspring, so rapidly had they advanced.

During the second year of my sojourning here, I made a tour to Antioch, the place which I had left in 1833. Antioch and the surrounding country were dear to me on account of the memories of former years. We protracted a meeting here of several days. Up to this time, there were two or three old brethren that had stood out against the Reformation. They would long since have yielded, but for the persistent efforts of a few mischief-making spirits, who made periodical visits to the neighborhood for the purpose of stirring up strife, and reviving the prejudices of the few remaining disaffected ones.

From long acquaintance and intimate association with the people, as might have been expected, almost the entire community came out to hear me, and among the rest were the three men who had never given up their old ways of opposition to the Reformation. The years

7*

of our separation had been to many of the people full of sorrow. The destroyer had been among them, and laid many a brave heart low in the grave. Fathers, mothers, brothers, sisters, husbands, wives, children and friends, who, when I left, were in the bloom of health, were now sleeping beneath the sod. Scarcely a household could number the same as when I was among them seven years before.

These things softened our hearts, and cemented bonds of Christian friendship that were well nigh broken, even in the case of those who were alienated on account of religious differences. My falling in among the people there at that particular time, in its effect reminded me of the gush of grief that breaks forth when an old familiar friend drops into the midst of a family when one of their number is coffined for the burial.

During the progress of my meeting I had a dream. I tell it as a dream, and not as the word of God. " The prophet that hath a dream, let him tell it as a dream; and he that hath my word, let him speak it faithfully; but what is the chaff to the wheat? saith the Lord " (Jer. xxiii. 28). The dream was as follows: I dreamed that, on my way to meeting, I met in the way three rattlesnakes, and, having in my hand a flail, such as we used in olden times in thrashing our grain, I dealt a blow upon the head of each one of these serpents, scattering their blood and brains in every direction; so that the ground was literally covered with blood and mangled portions of their bodies. This dream made very little impression on my mind, though I related it to my son-in-law and his family next morning at breakfast.

That day I preached to a large and solemn audience, and at the conclusion of the discourse those three alienated brethren came forward, and, confessing their errors, asked to be admitted to the fellowship of the church. This produced a profound impression upon the audience, melting every one to tears. After the meeting was over, my son-in-law, James Vandervort, approaching me, whispered in my ear that my prophetic vision had been realized. Upon this question of dreams, I will say neither yea nor nay, more than this: that dreams are not to be relied upon, however frequently they may come true. But I can speak confidently of the results of this meeting. Many sinners were converted, all alienations were healed, and new life was infused into the church.

When the meeting was fairly over, and the time of my departure was at hand, I began to realize that it would be a greater task to bid my old friends and neighbors adieu than I had anticipated. I was bound to them by a thousand ties; the happiest years of my life had been spent here. In this region there were many spots hallowed by sweet and blessed memories. The old meeting-house, the graveyard, the neighboring groves, the valleys and streams, were all made dear to me by the events of years that stretched away back into my earliest labors in the gospel. With feelings like these agitating my own breast, I was not prepared to reject the overtures of my old brethren, who came, with tears in their eyes, beseeching me to return to the old stamping-ground, and settle again among friends who were tried and true. Having consented that they might send teams and move my family, the thing was speedily accomplished.

One of the brethren, Barnet Bashore, with whom I had lived on most intimate terms for many years, came forward and proposed to be at the trouble of moving me without any charge; other brethren made proposals equally liberal touching my comfort and that of my family; until I felt fairly overwhelmed and subdued by their kindness. If my inmost thoughts and feelings had been carefully analyzed, I am inclined to think that an under-current of vanity might have been detected; though, if vanity there was, I am sure it did not arise from a sense of my own worthiness, but from the fact that these people were my children. I had educated them with a father's care, and, both by precept and example, had inculcated upon their minds principles of liberality; and

I was now enjoying for myself the fruits of that instruction and training which I had given for the benefit of others. That man who would himself be blessed, must teach his children sentiments of goodness, and loving kindness, and charity. Though he should not do this for the purpose of reaping any personal advantage himself, yet the reward will come; for it is my experience that, in the end, every man will reap where he sows, and reap, in a great measure, the kind he sows. The proverb that "a man who has friends must show himself friendly," has been verified in my experience over and over again; as well as that saying of the Saviour, "Whatsoever ye would that men should do to you, do ye even so to them."

The disciple is sure to imitate his teacher. A penurious and selfish teacher will make a penurious and selfish people. Should a preacher refuse to give liberally and cheerfully, even of his penury, when the occasion demands it, the people will likewise shut up the bowels of their compassion, becoming as miserly as the preacher. Soon or late, that preacher will feel the power of his example and teaching, in witnessing the cutting-off of his own supplies as the legitimate working of the very principles which he practiced for the purpose of improving h's circumstances.

There are three considerations that should lead us to the practice of liberality. 1. There are objects of want that demand it. 2. The world needs the example. 3. The giver's own spiritual life and health depend upon it. A triple blessing will follow every gift as infallibly as cause follows effect, viz.: The recipient is blessed; the world is blessed with the light of the act; the giver is blessed in the realization of the truth that "it is more blessed to give than to receive."

Let no preacher complain of a want of generosity among his people who does not himself live in the daily practice of principles of generosity. "Be not deceived; whatsoever a man soweth, that also shall he reap." By the liberality of my children, whom I had begotten by the gospel, I now saw, with feelings of grateful praise, my family safely housed in the homestead we had left in 1833. This place I paid for at about three times the amount I had realized for it eight years before. I gave only a part of my time to the congregation at Antioch, and the rest to surrounding churches; spending, in this way, about a year pleasantly, and profitably too. It would be supposed that, from my past experience, I should be satisfied to "let well enough alone," as I was doing a good work, and was happy in the society of friends whom I could trust. But it was not so determined.

CHAPTER XXV.

Third visit to Missouri.—Elder Lockhart at Belleville.—Terre Haute
and the Combses.—Great meeting in Franklin county, Missouri.—
Philip Miller.—Urged to make another visit.

As I learned at the close of the year, that my mother,
in Missouri, was becoming quite frail, I resolved to
make what I supposed would be my last visit to that
country. I doubt not, that in my determination to
make this tour, I was actuated as much by a missionary
spirit as by affection for my mother.

This was the third missionary tour I had made to
Missouri on horseback, through the States of Indiana
and Illinois. My first stopping place was in Preble
county, where lived two brothers by the name of Har-
land, who were pioneer preachers of considerable ability. They had built up a fine congregation in their
neighborhood, which I had the pleasure of laboring with
for several days. This meeting was not successful in the
way of making additions to the church. I trust and believe that my labor was not in vain in the Lord. Thence
I passed through the city of Indianapolis to Belleville,
where, in concert with my dear friend and brother,
Lockhart, who resided there, we conducted a meeting
which lasted several days, and resulted in many conversions. Brother Lockhart had moved to that country at
an early day, and had become a preacher in the school
of necessity. He had not enjoyed the advantages of
schools to any considerable extent, and, perhaps, had
never seen the inside of a college. Notwithstanding
this, being a man of prayerfulness and piety, he was
urged to take an active part in the neighborhood meetings which he attended. This he did for some time,
and became so useful to the cause, that a few wise brethren, after some consultation, urged him to submit to ordination, and give himself to the work of the ministry.

He had many misgivings upon this subject, as he informed me; but being so urgently solicited by the brethren, he submitted to their superior judgment, and, being ordained, found abundant work immediately, not only in his own neighborhood, but in the surrounding country.

I am told that his first efforts were quite feeble; but what they lacked in force of argument and eloquence, was made up by his piety and devotion to the cause of his Maker. No man, without experience, can fully estimate the power of the Christian life in connection with the proclamation of the gospel.

At the time of my visit, he was a strong advocate of the truth. He made no pretensions to eloquence or to · oratory, in the common acceptation of the terms. But he was both eloquent and an orator, in the best sense. He was instrumental in building up a number of congregations in his region, and, in fact, accomplished almost everything that was done in his part of the country.

I doubt not, that in heaven, hundreds whom he has converted will chant the praises of God with as clear a voice, and a soul as full of divine love, as if they had been converted by the most refined, eloquent, and learned preacher in the land. If you will visit, to-day, the neighborhood of his labors, you will hear him spoken of as the man to whom our cause in that district owes more than to any or all others together.

We see in this case what a devoted Christian can do, not under the manipulations of theological trainers, but under the influence of strong religious convictions and the pressure of circumstances.

From Belleville we passed on to Terre Haute, our next place of meeting. Here I met my old friends and brethren, Michael and Job Combs, with whom I had labored in days long gone. These men, like Brother Lockhart, had sown the good seed broadcast, without any plans or direction, save the plan that one who loves the truth will somehow devise, and the direction of a sense of duty. The Lord had raised up quite a number of faithful disciples in this part of the country, mainly by the instrumentality of a few noble examples. One consistent, Christian life, in a community, is worth more to the cause than many eloquent sermons. From Terre Haute I crossed the Wabash River, and passing through Paris, held a meeting near the State line, which was the most profitable meeting of my journey, if I may judge by the visible fruits. Many souls professed faith in the Lord Jesus Christ.

It being now midwinter, and fearing the breaking up of the hard weather, I hurried on to the place of my destination without much delay. Passing through St. Louis, where we tarried but a day or so, we were soon among our old friends in Franklin county. As I have stated before, this was my third missionary tour to this country. The first was in 1819, in company with my brother, John Rogers, who, but a short time before, had entered the ministry. We then belonged to the old Christian body, and were called, by our enemies, New-Lights, Arians, Schismatics, and I know not how many ugly names. The next visit was made in company with James Hughes, in 1825 or 1826, I am not sure as to the date. Hughes was one of the most successful men of the Stone Reformation. He was a native of Kentucky, early emigrated to Illinois, and traveled extensively with me through Ohio, Indiana, Illinois and Missouri.

I believe I was the second preacher who carried across the Mississippi the doctrine that the Bible, and the Bible alone, is a sufficient rule of faith and practice. As far as I am now informed, Brother Thomas McBride was the first to preach these views in Missouri. In the year 1813, he moved from Barren county, Kentucky, and was a lifelong advocate of the doctrine that the Bible is the Christian's only creed; that baptism is scripturally administered by immersion; and that the name Christian is the true name for the disciples of Christ.

My visit, of which I am speaking, was made in the year 1839 or 1840, and my first since I had fully received and avowed the doctrine of the current Reformation.

As before stated, I had, about the time of my last visit, glimpses of the truth, and was quite satisfied upon the subject of the call to the ministry; but as yet there had been no formal union of the old Christian people with the Baptists who had adopted Brother Campbell's views; nor was there any radical change in the organization of our congregations, especially in Missouri. But by this time all the congregations which I met with had been brought fully into the light of Apostolic Christianity, though in and around Franklin they were much discouraged, having but one preacher in the entire district, and he only preaching among them on Lord's days, being a merchant, and wholly dependent upon his business for a living. This was Jas. K. Rule, who, with his brother, professed Christianity in old Concord, while living at my house, in Nicholas county, Kentucky.

He moved to Missouri in an early day, and, being a faithful Christian, he went about doing good upon every favorable occasion. I give Brother Rule credit for doing all he could under the circumstances, notwithstanding some of the congregations in his region of country were almost extinct, and others were in a low state, spiritually. Here I found Philip Miller, a native of Nicholas county, Kentucky, who, at the time of his removal to Missouri, was a Baptist; but afterwards became a convert to the views of B. W. Stone, under the preaching of Elder Thomas McBride. Miller was a man of rare good sense, and exerted a happy influence in his neighborhood. James McBride, son of Thomas McBride, married Miller's daughter, and became a useful preacher, and until his removal to Springfield kept up quite a religious interest among the people in the neighborhood.

The removal of McBride was a great misfortune to the churches in the vicinity. After his departure many troubles arose, many apostasies occurred, and even Philip Miller, who had been an example to the flock, now was about ready to give up the ship. Knowing him to be a man of noble impulses, and capable of doing a great amount of good, it was my first object to revive his flagging spirits and put him to work.

My first meeting was held at his house, near the place where my mother then lived, and is now sleeping. The news of the meeting had been well circulated, and the people came out in great numbers to hear; some from the opposite side of the river, others from adjacent neighborhoods, in such numbers that we had not room for them in the house. We had a blessed revival in the church and in the world. Sinners came weeping, and weeping saints embraced them, and we all rejoiced together. Hands that had been hanging down were strengthened, and spirits that had been despondent were now revived. Philip Miller became almost wild with delight.

For a time sectarianism had been very quiet; but now that our cause had received a new impulse, and our people were aroused from their stupidity, and were at work in good earnest, the opposition became more violent, so that no means was spared, upon their part, to stop the onward progress of the gospel in its ancient simplicity, and to fortify themselves against our attacks.

I do not remember how long these meetings lasted, but if nothing more had been accomplished upon this tour than what was done here, we had great reason to rejoice in the fruit of our labors.

Philip Miller expressed his determination to live a more active and consistent Christian life, and well and faithfully did he keep these solemn vows. His son Samuel has since expressed it as his opinion, that this meeting saved his father from apostasy.

At the close of this memorable meeting, Brother Philip Miller and others insisted upon my giving them another appointment. This I could not do during my present visit to the State. It was then urged that I should return home, and arrange with my Antioch brethren to let me off for a few months, and come back as speedily as possible to this field of labor which seemed to be so promising. Brother Miller, to make assurance doubly sure, proposed to advance one hundred dollars towards my compensation. All that I could do in the case was to make them a conditional promise.

Upon my return home, I consulted my family first, and then laid the matter before the brethren, asking them to decide the whole question in the light of all the circumstances. The brethren consented to let me off for three months, believing that the circumstances of the case demanded it. A few of my friends criticised me for making so many changes. They thought me naturally fond of roving from place to place, in search of novelties, rather than in search of fields of greater usefulness. I am free to admit that the course of my past life gives some foundation for such a charge. But this fault of mine is the result of making a bad use of a true principle. I have always believed it to be my duty to go where I could do the most good, without for a moment consulting convenience, ease or pleasure. But my mistake lies in the fact, that I have often hastened to conclusions without weighing with sufficient care all the facts and circumstances of the case, and not in any love of change or novelties.

CHAPTER XXVI.

Fourth visit to Missouri.—Conversion of a skeptic.—Sermon on Election.—Total Depravity.—Being born in a potato-patch does not make you a potato.—Being shapen in the forest does not give you the nature of a tree.

Upon returning to my Missouri field of labor, I found the opposition to our cause intensified and systematized. The scattered ranks of our religious opposers had been suddenly brought together, and they were ready for a combined attack upon what they chose to call the soul-destroying heresy of Campbellism. I can not say that I liked this state of things; but I believe it was to my advantage, and in favor of our cause. It stimulated me to increased activity and boldness in preaching the ancient gospel in its simplicity, and in defining our distinctive plea with more precision. Their misrepresentations, meanwhile, were so glaring, that I had an easy conquest of it. They accused us of denying the Divinity of Christ; of casting aside, as useless, the Old Scriptures; of baptizing infidels; of teaching that water washed away sins; that if we could get people under the water we declared them safe for heaven; that we had no use for evangelical faith: and I can not say how many things they accused us of teaching, the like of which we had never dreamed of, and things that would shock the common sense of man. The result of this kind of opposition was, that we found ourselves well advertised, all over the country, and so many strange and absurd things had been said about us, that enemies as well as friends came to hear us, giving us generally large audiences everywhere, before whom we had a fine opportunity of repelling these slanders, and presenting primitive Christianity. Scores of enemies came to hear, believing these vile stories, who, after hearing for themselves, were compelled, as honest men, to confess that we had been slandered. Many of this class, upon hearing a few times, were so pleased with the doctrine which they heard, that they abandoned sectarianism, and became our fast friends.

If I were to give a detailed account of every meeting held during these months, it would be a repetition of almost the same thing. The field was indeed ripe for the harvest. The people were anxious, and came by hundreds to hear the gospel, and scores were converted. Many, also, were reclaimed who had forgotten their first love.

I shall never forget the conversion of a noble-minded man by the name of Davis, who had heard so much contradictory and false religion preached, that he became confused and disgusted with everything bearing the name of religion, and resolved never to have anything more to do with it. He informed me that he had allowed those absurd notions which he had heard from sectarian pulpits to drive him into downright skepticism.

While in this state of mind, he heard that a "Campbellite" was preaching strange things in the neighborhood, and he concluded to venture out, and hear what he had to say. He had heard of Campbellites as a sort of half infidels, who held to every absurd notion, almost, imaginable. He entered the house and took his seat, just as I was reading my text from I. Peter i., as follows: "Elect according to the foreknowledge of God the Father, through sanctification of the Spirit, unto obedience and sprinkling of the blood of Jesus Christ; grace unto you and peace be multiplied." I endeavored to show, that according to Macknight and others, whose learning and wisdom qualified them to speak with authority upon the subject, the apostles meant to convey the idea, that the election of believers was according to an arrangement which God had previously made known — that God had made known long before the coming of Christ, how men were to be elected to the salvation he had devised. I showed that elections in the State are carried on according to the law and the Constitution of said State, previously arranged and made known, viz.: according to the foreknowledge of the framers of the Constitution—that every man elected at all, must be elected according to that previous arrangement which had been made and promulgated. I showed that, however men might have been elected before the adoption of the Constitution, it is certain that since that time, the demands of the law regulating elections must be met, to make an election valid; and that the law clearly defined, first, the character of the person to be elected to office, and, secondly, the mode and manner of holding said election. I then applied my illustration by showing that God had made and promulgated the law concerning the election of men to a place in his kingdom; and however, and to whatever men had been elected before the promulgation of this law of pardon, or election to the favor of God under the reign of King Jesus, it was absolutely certain, that since its promulgation, men must be elected according to the divine law regulating the case.

I then proceeded to show that the kingdom was set up on the day of Pentecost, proving it by the fact that, up to that time, its setting up was referred to as an event yet to take place, and that after that time it was referred to as an event which had already taken place. I also proved that Peter was the proper person to publish the law of election, and that Jerusalem was the place from which it was to go forth, and that the day of Pentecost was the proper time. And I proved that this proper person, at the proper time and place, did open the polls, laying down the rules regulating the election, and that three thousand men were elected, according to this previous arrangement of God the Father, through sanctification of the Spirit, unto obedience and sprinkling of the blood of Jesus Christ. Now, said I, the same law is in force to-day for you; and the same commission is in force now that was given to the apostles, to preach the gospel to every nation; and that law is, "He that be-

lieveth and is baptized, shall be saved." I then declared
the polls open, and asked all to come forward who desired to be elected. This man Davis was the first to
arise and come forward. Being something of a politician, he understood my illustrations, and as he came
forward, he cried out, "I am a candidate for election, and
had I understood the subject as I now do, I should have
been elected long ago."

Sixteen more followed him upon the same invitation,
and a glorious victory was won that day for the truth.
Close akin to this doctrine of election, is that of total
hereditary depravity, which is one of the main pillars of
sectarianism. The people had been taught to believe
that they were so completely depraved, that they could
not think a good thought, nor perform a good action;
and they had willingly accepted the doctrine that they
were incapable of doing anything whatever, in order to
the enjoyment of salvation. They wanted to know my
opinion of certain texts bearing upon this subject, one
of which was the following: "Behold, I was shapen in
iniquity, and in sin did my mother conceive me." I told
them that this text might establish the fact that the
parent was depraved; but it certainly did not follow,
from anything it taught, that the children were depraved, much less did it teach the doctrine of total and
hereditary depravity. Said I, suppose David had said,
"Behold, I was shapen in the woods, and in the forest
did my mother conceive me; would that prove that he
was a tree, or even that he partook of the nature of
trees? Or if any one should declare that he was born
in a potato-patch, would that prove that he was a potato, or anything of the kind? I admit that my illustrations were homely, and they might now be called vulgar,
but they had the effect to silence the batteries of the
enemy, as far as I know. But it must remembered that
I was among a plain-spoken, pioneer people, who did not
stand upon the elegancies and niceties of things. They
were satisfied with language which conveyed the idea of
the speaker clearly, whether it was according to the

latest rules of rhetoric, or not. They were offended at me for charging them with digging up the dry bones of this doctrine, which had been buried nearly three thousand years ago by Ezekiel the prophet, who preached its funeral and laid it away to sleep in the grave forever, never dreaming that in these last days any prophet would become so fond of the relics of the dark ages, as to dig up these bones and endeavor to infuse into them life again. I read to them a part of this ancient funeral discourse: "What mean ye by using this proverb concerning the land of Israel, saying, The fathers have eaten sour grapes, and the children's teeth are set on edge? As I live, saith the Lord God, ye shall have occasion no more to use this proverb in Israel. The soul that sinneth it shall die. The son shall not bear the iniquity of the father, neither shall the father bear the iniquity of the son. The righteousness of the righteous shall be upon him, and the wickedness of the wicked shall be upon him." I rejoice to believe that our religious neighbors are, in these latter days, becoming ashamed of their speculations, both upon the subject of Calvinism, and total hereditary depravity. I judge that they are ashamed of them, from the fact that they rarely refer to them in their sermons.

When I began this second missionary tour of labor, I supposed that at the close of the allotted time, the churches and the cause in this district would be upon a footing so firm that I might leave the field without detriment to the cause of truth. In this I was mistaken. Every day the field became wider and more inviting, and the opposition became more violent and concentrated. If there was reason for my returning before, there was much greater reason now. The Macedonian cry was coming up from every part of the country — "Come and help us." I received petitions from various churches and from individuals, urging me to remain a little longer, or, if I could not do so, to return again by all means, and spend a few more months in the field. The enemies of truth had become so hostile, that the strongest and best brethren in the district feared that the result of my leaving them now might turn out disastrously. I knew not what to do; for I felt the force of their arguments, and appreciated their plea. But my family was large, and needed my presence every day, and my poor wife had lived almost like a widow more than half her life. The fact that she had always been willing for me to go where the Lord called, did not relieve me, for I felt that I was imposing upon good nature. It was also true, on the other hand, that my family were among friends tried and true, who were ready to give any assistance needed, and that my wife, with the help of the older children, managed affairs about as well as I could have done; yet I was needed at home, and I felt much inclined to commit to the brethren and the Lord the keeping of the cause in this country, and return to the bosom of my family, and give up what appeared to be too much of a roving life, for repose in the bosom of a family now anxiously awaiting my return.

But when I thought of abandoning this people, and leaving them as sheep without a shepherd, I was in a strait betwixt two. At the close of my work, and while preparing for my journey, entreaty after entreaty was made, both by individuals and congregations, to return at my earliest possible convenience, if it were only to stay for a very short time.

So, upon leaving them, I promised that after consulting with my family and friends, if I felt it to be the will of the Lord — and that was saying simply that if I felt it to be my duty — I would return. Upon my arrival at home I found all well, and everything prospering beyond my expectations. My son-in-law was preaching to the church with great acceptability, and the cause was prospering generally. Upon presenting the case of the cause in Missouri to my wife, she answered very calmly, that she had long since determined to leave all those matters at the bar of my own conscience; that if I felt it to be my duty to go, she should put no

8

obstacle in my way; but if I felt that I could serve my Master as well at home, she would be happy. We prayed and talked much, however, upon the subject, until I think my wife began to feel that I ought to go back for a season, and help those people whom I had left in an almost helpless condition.

CHAPTER XXVII.

Fourth trip to Missouri.—Tricks of opposers. — Owens. — Bowman baptizes face-foremost.—His converts leave him.—An earnest call to return to Missouri.

When I started again upon the journey, she said to me, " Go now, and the Lord be with you; but I hope you may, upon your return, be able to say, ' I have come home to stay.' But," she added, " the will of the Lord be done." To make a long story short, my work so increased upon my hands that, from week to week, as I proceeded, instead of seeing an end of it, it seemed to be but fairly beginning. Multitudes had yielded obedience to the faith; multitudes more were almost persuaded. The country had undergone a complete religious revolution. Our success had only added fuel to the flames of opposition; so that there was now as great need as ever of bold and fearless defenders of the faith. Unfortunately, the young men who had begun preaching had not sufficient experience to conduct a successful campaign against their opposers. Some of them were young men of promise; but, being modest and timid, as well as inexperienced, I felt that it would work disastrously to commit to them alone the entire work of this large district.

For the sake of decency, saying nothing of the effect upon the cause of Christianity, I would be ashamed to mention all the low and vulgar tricks resorted to for the purpose of bringing our cause into disrepute. No politician could stoop much lower for the purpose of destroying the reputation, and overthrowing the cause, of an adversary, than some of the opposition did in their attempts to stay the tide of success that followed the proclamation of the Apostolic gospel in this country. We will not disguise the fact that these things were calculated to betray us into the use of much harsher language towards our opposers than we can now appróve. On one occasion, as I was reading from John Wesley's doctrinal tracts, to prove that he made as much of baptism as we did, and that he believed immersion to have been the ancient mode of baptism, a Class-leader by the name of Owens arose, and declared before a large audience that what I was professing to read was all a lie of my own getting-up. After I showed him the texts I was reading, though he had to admit that the words were there, still he contended that it was a forgery; that John Wesley never held such sentiments.

Soon after this, I met Mr. Owens in company with his Presiding Elder, Mr. Compton, to whom I referred the question in dispute; and, though his Presiding Elder agreed with me, still Mr. Owens insisted that what I had read upon the subject of baptism was a forgery, introduced for the purpose of sustaining our cause.

I had been preaching in the town of Pinckney, on the Missouri River, in the house of one Colonel Griswold, a man of high position in the neighborhood, who had generously opened his house to all who desired to use it for religious worship. But when our opposers discovered that we were getting the ears of the people and baptizing many of them, they petitioned Colonel Griswold to close the doors against us. They told him that I was a vile heretic, not to be tolerated; that I denied the divinity of Christ; that I did not believe in the work of the Spirit; that I had no use for saving faith; that I substituted water in the place of the blood of Christ; and I know not how many vile slanders they circulated of the same sort. Mr. Griswold, however, informed my accusers that the house was his own, and he claimed the privilege of opening it to whomsoever he pleased.

These foul slanders, which were circulated for the purpose of prejudicing our cause, had the very opposite effect; for the people came to hear us in still greater numbers, and, becoming convinced from what they heard that we were a much abused people, their sympathies

were enlisted in our favor, and multitudes were induced
to bow to the authority of the Prince of Peace. Among
the number was Colonel Griswold and his entire family,
of whom we shall have more to say hereafter. It was not
long before our opposers abandoned this house, assigning
as a reason that they could not conscientiously occupy
the same house with such vile heretics. So this fruitful
field was left to me altogether. It was a school-boy saying
in the olden times, that "Cheating luck can never thrive;"
and it is true now that the more unreasonable and violent the opposition of our foes, the more assured will be
our success, if we are found in the faithful discharge of
duty. The last meeting held there by our opposers was
conducted by a Mr. Bowman, whose converts refused to
take sprinkling for baptism. He then proposed to immerse them, but, with the exception of one youth, they
all came to me, and requested baptism at my hands, saying that they would not consent to be immersed by one
who did not believe in immersion himself.

Bowman undertook to immerse one youth only. This
boy he took down into the water, made him kneel, and
then attempted to put him under face foremost. The
boy, never having seen anything of this sort, resisted
Bowman's attempt to thrust his head under the water,
broke away from him, and ran home. This youth also
came to me, and I baptized him in a decent manner. I
then sent the circuit-rider word to send all his converts
to me, and I would take pleasure in baptizing them according to the ancient mode. Bowman returned the
answer that I, in baptizing, introduced the candidate to
his Master back foremost, and that he, with becoming respect, always introduced him face foremost. I could not
help answering him again, that I did not doubt the fact
that he held his master in very high esteem, and, from
the fact that he always introduced persons to him face
downwards, I must conclude that his master was from
beneath; that my Master being in the heavens, I was
disposed to baptize with face upturned. This man,
soon after the disgraceful affair with the boy, was

taken down with a severe attack of chills, which he ascribed to going into the water. I told him that he deserved to be severely shaken for attempting to scandalize a sacred ordinance in such a manner; that I hoped he might be shaken until thorough repentance was produced. I record these facts simply for the sake of giving some faint idea of the times of which I am speaking, and without endorsing altogether my own conduct in the premises.

The meeting which I held in Griswold's house resulted in more than forty additions, many of them being heads of families and leaders in society. After this, I was sent for to hold a meeting in a place called Sieter's Island, twelve miles above Pinckney. This was a very wealthy and godless neighborhood. There were a few honorable exceptions, but, as a rule, they were regular worshipers of mammon. This was in the neighborhood of an influential family by the name of Shobe, relations of the Griswolds. This family received me with marked kindness, and attended to the things which they had heard. I conducted my meetings in a house belonging to the Baptists, and had the privilege of receiving an entire Baptist family into the church. Their name was Finney. Some time before, they had offered themselves for the purpose of joining the Baptist church, but objection was made to Mr. Finney, because, in relating his experience, he was not willing to say that he believed himself to be the greatest sinner in the world. This he said he could not do without telling a falsehood.

My next meeting was at the house of a sister by the name of Ray. At the conclusion of my first discourse, her daughter, who was confined to her bed with an attack of chills, made the confession, and desired to be immersed. I suggested to her that it might be proper to wait a few days; but she insisted upon being immersed immediately. We, therefore, conveyed her to the water, and immersed her, after which I learned that she never had another chill. I have no doubt but the treatment was the best that could have been practiced in her case.

There is much foolish timidity indulged in by people of little experience in regard to going into water. Among all the thousands that I have seen baptized, I have never known one injured.

During this missionary tour, I constituted several new congregations according to the Apostolic doctrine, the largest among them being the one on Burbois River, a tributary of the Merrimac. Philip Miller assisted me much in establishing this church. The people there very justly hold him in grateful remembrance. Our first appearance in that neighborhood was under very unfavorable circumstances, judging according to human judgment. Reports had gone out before us that we were coming to make war upon the Methodists, with the purpose of breaking up their churches, as it was reported I had done in Warren county. Of course, the object in circulating these stories was to forestall public opinion, and prevent us from getting a hearing. The devil is often caught in his own trap, and this was one of the instances. The effort made to keep people from hearing excited their curiosity, and brought them out by scores to hear. The most of them were disappointed, for they had expected to hear me abuse other people, and to use bitter epithets towards them. But, having heard nothing but the presentation, in a plain and simple style, of what I called the Gospel of Christ, they went away satisfied that we had been misrepresented. The consequence was that the gospel swept over that country like fire in stubble, and we left a large and flourishing church there. A remarkable incident occurred there, which is worth relating.

A Methodist preacher by the name of Shockley, having become highly exasperated at us, came forward on one occasion, and opposed us in terms so harsh and unreasonable that his talk sounded more like the ravings of a madman than the discourse of a preacher of the gospel. In the midst of his ravings, he was seized with convulsions, and fell to the floor as suddenly as if he had been shot. His friends were alarmed for him, as he lay like a dead man. He soon recovered, however, and, after giving us a patient hearing, acknowledged his error, embraced those views which he had so violently opposed, and went forward, preaching the Apostolic doctrine with as much zeal as he had before opposed it. As far as I know, he continued faithful. I do not relate this for the purpose of conveying the idea that God struck this man down in this manner because he was opposing the truth. I suppose that his madness brought on convulsions, and that these convulsions brought him to his reason, and then reason owned the truth.

I had here a little discussion with another preacher, whose name I have forgotten, but whose foolish objection to immersion I remember well. It is strange how an objection so flimsy and groundless as the one he used should gain currency, and be considered of such importance as it is by the advocates of a bad cause. That is, if baptism is a condition of salvation, then the interest of the soul is suspended upon what might, in certain cases, become an impossibility; as, for instance, in dry countries, when there is not enough water to immerse in, or, in cold countries, when the water is all frozen. I answered him that no people had ever inhabited a country where water could not be found in sufficient quantities for purposes of immersion. They might pass through such a country, but, in the nature of things, it would be impossible for them to live there as permanent inhabitants; and that, if it were possible for people to inhabit such countries, then they would be dealt with in the judgment on the principle that will govern the cases of deaf persons, who can not obey the command to hear; and as blind persons, who are commanded to look; or idiots, who are commanded to believe; or dumb persons, who are commanded to sing, etc.: according to the rule that when much is given, much will be required; and that when little is given, little will be required. I added that my faith in God was such that, if it should become the duty of any one to live in a country where it was either so cold and frozen, or so dry and parched, that enough water could not be obtained for purposes of immersion, and that if the command was absolute, then I believed that God would dig a pool with his own hand, rather than allow his word to fail.

Instead of spending three months on this mission, I saw no end to it until six months had expired. My last meeting was amongst the most successful. It was in St. John's meeting-house, in Franklin county. Several promising young men came in at that meeting who became very useful to the Church. Among them were the two Valentines. One of them I ordained, and he became a good teacher of Christianity.

My labors having closed, I was ready and anxious to return to the bosom of my family once more. As I was about to start, petitions came in from various quarters urging me either to remain a little longer, or else return again and hold a few more meetings. Under all the circumstances of the case, I was peculiarly embarrassed. I knew how important it was to the cause that some one of experience should be here a while longer. Being familiar with the field, I could appreciate the feelings of the brethren and the demands of the case. To a man who really fears God, and appreciates the value of an immortal soul, it is no little thing to turn a deaf ear to the cries of men who are ready to perish. I have been criticised for remaining so much away from home, as if I had a right to control my time and strength in any way that might suit my pleasure. But, in my case, the question stood thus: hundreds around me are perishing for the bread of life, which I have it in my power to supply without peril to either the souls or bodies of my own children. They are supplied with what is needful for the body, and have the blessed influences of religion pressing upon them on every side. They are in the midst of religious people; they have a godly mother, whose counsel and example is all that could be desired; who prays with them, talks to them, and lives Christ before them. Now, if I turn my back upon these starving souls, at whose door will the responsibility rest in

8*

the day of God, when they shall be driven away into outer darkness? Will none of them say to me, "You did it"?

From considerations like these, I determined to say positively neither yea nor nay upon the subject, but to leave it an open question, to be decided by the best lights before me upon my arrival at home. This, however, I determined: that, if I should return, it would be to stay at least a year, and that my family must be with me; and so I stated to the brethren. This inspired them with some degree of hope, and, therefore, they prepared a petition, setting forth in a preamble the necessities of the case, asking, by almost every consideration that could move us to decide favorably, that we consent to come and spend at least a year with them. They proposed to pay all the expenses of moving back and forth, and to compensate us reasonably for all the sacrifices we were called upon to make. With this petition, I returned home, and was almost ashamed to show it to my wife, or to intimate that I thought we ought to consider it favorably, so gracefully and cheerfully had she heretofore yielded to every demand of a like nature. In due time, however, I handed her the petition, and, after a most solemn and prayerful consideration of it, shall I say she decided it to be our duty to go? Yes, to the praise of that woman, be it said; that woman whose first and highest aim always was to have the smiles and approbation of her God; that woman to whom I owe more than to all others; that woman to whom the world is indebted more than can ever be repaid. Her comfort, her convenience, her pleasure, she was never known to bring into the account against her duty to God. When but a young bride, I was called to my country's service, and, with a bright face and tearful eye, she said, "Go, and the Lord keep you." And since the first day that God called me to fight in the army of King Jesus, she said, "Go." The only change she made in the premises was, that we should stay two years, and by that time I might have my work in shape to leave it.

CHAPTER XXVIII.

Fifth tour to Missouri.—Baptism of a dying girl.—Revival in Gasconade Valley.—A house built and the cause permanent.—Young
Hopson shaving shingles.—He rises above suspicion.—A traveling
companion for two years.—His politeness and humility.—One
makes the log-heap, the other fires it.—The teacher sits at the
feet of the pupil.—Ham's text; foolish preaching.—Thomas M.
Allen.

I rented out my little farm in the month of September, and, having put my affairs in shape for the journey,
started for Missouri. About the first of October, we
landed at South Point, and took up our abode at Griswold City, a village near by, where we had our head-
quarters for about a year.

I reaped the first important fruits of this mission in a
rich and beautiful valley of the Gasconade River, in
Gasconade county. In this grand valley lived a number
of wealthy families, who had moved from the south
branch of the Potomac, Virginia, and among whom the
most prominent names were: the Parsons, Shobes, Hulls,
Atkinses, Perines. These people had brought with them
not only much wealth, but a large amount of worldly
wisdom and pride. The men of the valley were mainly
unbelievers, and some were almost scoffers at religion.

The circumstance that led to the introduction of the
gospel into this valley, and to the conversion of this
carnal-minded people, was as follows: The eldest
daughter of James Parsons, being in a state of declining
health, had been staying at her aunt Griswold's, under
the treatment of a physician. During this sojourn, having availed herself of the opportunity to hear me preach,
she became convinced of the truth, and demanded baptism at my hands. But her physician prevented the
accomplishment of her desire. Meanwhile, the poor
girl ·returned home, and, finding that her days upon

earth were about numbered, she desired her father, who
was an unconverted man, to baptize her. He declined,
saying, that he was not worthy to perform so sacred a
rite. But his daughter still urged him to baptize her,
saying, that she understood me to teach that the validity
of an ordinance does not depend upon the administrator.
The family, and all of the friends, were deeply moved
by the entreaties of the dying girl; but they felt themselves helpless in her presence. They sent far and near
for a preacher, but none could be found. The hour of
her dissolution was rapidly approaching, and the family
were suffering the most painful suspense, lest the girl
should die without an opportunity of consummating the
desire of her believing heart. In the midst of this suspense the dear child solved the problem, and was consequently relieved. She remembered that the old colored
" mammy " of the family, was a pious, God-fearing
woman; she called her and demanded baptism at her
hands. The poor old servant could not deny her young
mistress anything that would make her happy, and, more
especially, when she was in so much distress; so she consented, and, a bath-tub being provided, Sarah, the believing girl, was baptized by the old nurse, and was
happy from that hour to the time of her death. This
was eloquent preaching to that worldly-minded people; it was the opening of the iron doors of many hearts
to the reception of the gospel.

The dying girl, having learned that it was expected
that I would soon arrive at Griswold, sent word to her
aunt, that if, upon my arrival, she was still living, I
must come immediately to see her; but, if she should die
before my coming, it was her request that I should
preach her funeral. A few days after we landed, the
news came that the dear child of faith was dead, and I
hastened to fulfill her dying request. The funeral was
preached at her father's house, where were assembled
those worldly-minded men, whose hearts had never yet
been touched by gospel truth. Judging by what I then
saw — and afterwards learned — very few of those proud

men left the house as they had come into it. The story of the conversion, baptism, and happy death of Sarah Parsons, was the wedge that opened their minds and hearts. All knew her and loved her. I had then only to preach to them Jesus, and the work was done. Eternity alone can tell the result of that day's work.

I continued preaching in that valley, more or less, for months, which resulted in the conversion of a large majority of the people, and the erection of a house of worship which, I believe, is standing yet, though only occupied once or twice a year, owing to the fact that the organization removed to a new church, which they built at Chamois, a short distance, only, away.

The work which I accomplished, as an humble instrument under God, in Gasconade Valley, has been the source of great joy, not only to myself, but also to hundreds who date their conversion from that revival. More than thirty years after that time, I met a German preacher by the name of Stirwig, who told me that the truth first broke in upon his mind at one of my Gasconade meetings. He moved to Texas; was there baptized by one of our brethren, and since that time has devoted his talents and money to the gospel. I also, last year, met an old colored preacher, who was converted at the same time, and who is now a pious, humble, intelligent proclaimer of the ancient gospel.

About this time I was approached by a tall, spare youth of about eighteen summers, neat in his attire; graceful, gentle and dignified in his bearing; with an intelligent eye and charming voice — altogether, such a one as would at once command respect, and, at the same time, excite the suspicion of the beholder that he might be a scion of the stock of F. F. V.'s, of old colony times. He bore letters from Abram Miller, of Millersburg, Calloway county, recommending him to me as a pious youth, who desired to devote his life to the work of the ministry, and who wished to place himself under my care. He also brought letters highly commendatory to Philip Miller, then of Franklin county. Philip

Miller was a man of great goodness of heart, but very plain-spoken, and sometimes blunt—almost offensively so. When the young man approached Miller, Miller was busy shaving shingles, and, as if to test him, asked the very blunt question: "Young man, do you think you are of any account? Can you shave shingles?" "I suppose I can," was the reply. "Well," said Miller, "take off your coat and try." The youth, nothing daunted, threw off his coat, took hold of the drawing knife with his white, tender hands, and went to work as if he had served an apprenticeship at the business of shingle-making.

A few minutes satisfied Miller that the handsome youth was no humbug; so he urged him to resign the knife, saying, "That will do, sir." This, to us, appears a trifling incident; but it was enough to endear the young man to Philip Miller for life; it was the beginning of a lasting friendship. Years afterwards I heard Philip Miller tell how his admiration had been excited by the simple determination expressed on this occasion by the youth, and how his sympathies had been aroused by the discovery of great blisters, which the knife had raised on the delicate hands.

This young man placed himself at once under my care, for the purpose of training himself to the hardships of the Christian warfare; and I take pleasure in bearing witness that this young Timothy served his father for two years, as faithfully and lovingly as any Timothy could serve. At first I put him to blowing and striking for me—to use a blacksmith's phrase—but, finding him a young man of great promise, I put him in the lead, requiring him to deliver the opening discourses, generally, while I followed with exhortation. I have had a long and a varied experience in helping young men into usefulness; but have never been better satisfied with the progress of any man with whom I have been associated, than the young man, Winthrop Hopson.

His discourses were finely arranged; quite logical, clear and forcible. They were always delivered in the finest language, yet presented in a manner so simple that a child could comprehend them. On this account I generally put him forward to preach the sermons, and I followed with exhortations. In this way we labored together to great profit; for his forte was preaching; mine, exhortation. We always traveled together, and in the circuit of four or five counties, accomplished a grand and glorious work, which eternity alone can fully reveal.

The old men to this day dwell with animation upon the transactions of those primitive times, when I did the grubbing, and Winthrop piled the brush; or, when Winthrop made the log-heaps, and I fired them. Or, in a different phrase, they speak of his shooting with a rest, always hitting the mark; and of my shooting off-hand, taking the game on the wing. These phrases, homely though they be, very aptly describe the manner of our work. This very difference in manner and method, gave efficiency to our labors, and made each more useful to the other. Our union was sweet, and our harmony complete throughout the campaign. Winthrop sat at my feet, like a little child, to receive, both by precept and example, all I had to give that would make him useful in the vineyard of his Master; and I sometimes found it profitable to reverse the order and become his pupil. Him I found to be an accomplished scholar; and I knew myself to be very defective, even in the King's English; so I requested him to criticise and correct me, when there should be necessity for it, and to do this without hesitation. This he did; but with a manner so humble and gracious, as to almost make me feel that my fault was a virtue. Dear boy, how I loved him!

I have said that he was always neat in his dress, and dignified in his bearing. Owing to this fact, many poor people appeared a little shy of him on first acquaintance. To dwell in log cabins and dress in homespun, was the style in those days in that country. Upon entering the cabins of these lowly people, Winthrop was quick to detect the cause of shyness upon the part of the inmates, and always ready to remove it by his easy, gentle way of making himself perfectly at home, and appearing as if he had been used to nothing better in all his life. He was a very magnet to little children, and possessed that rare faculty of remembering their names, so that, meet them where he might, he would address them by their proper names, and make them feel easy in his presence. He was never vulgarly familiar with any one, old or young, and was never guilty of the use of slang phrases, and could not be tempted to approach even the precincts of a conversation vulgar or smutty. When he entered a house, it seemed to be his first study to avoid giving trouble to any one. Winthrop H. Hopson had then, and now has, the appearance of being stiff and proud; but this is only the man as he appears to the stranger. Let him come near to you, and all this appearance of haughtiness and pride will vanish; for, it is like beauty, only skin deep. To know him and to love him, your acquaintance must extend beneath the surface. I wish the young men of this day, who have not one-half so much to puff them up with pride as he had, were as humble and teachable as he. Being handsome and accomplished, and belonging to a family which took rank among the best of that country, or any other country, it is not strange that he should have been greatly loved and honored by the young and old of all classes. But it is passing strange that his head should not have been a little turned by the attentions and compliments he received.

I never knew him to compromise his dignity in any manner; what is better, he maintained a pure and spotless character.

Winthrop prudently avoided the meshes of matrimony, as well as every appearance of the kind, until after our separation; then he married a charming Christian girl, whom I had baptized — Rebecca Parsons, the fourth daughter of Col. James Parsons, before alluded to.

We found many of the preachers in the bounds of our circuit to be shamefully ignorant and conceited. I give below a specimen which may suffice: On a certain occasion, as Winthrop and I were on our way to Gasconade, we came to a school-house, and, halting, learned that a meeting was in progress there. Winthrop proposed that we should hitch our horses, and hear a sermon. Accordingly, we entered, took our seats near the door, so as to create as little disturbance as possible. We found that the pulpit was occupied by the Rev. Mr. Ham, a Baptist preacher, who was in the midst of a discourse, in which he was attempting to establish his call to the ministry. Among other proofs, he quoted from I. Cor. i. 21: "For after that, in the wisdom of God, the world by wisdom knew not God, it pleased God, by the foolishness of preaching, to save them that believe." Either in haste or ignorance, or both, he quoted the passage: "It pleased God, by foolish preaching, to save," etc. Now, my tongue has always been an unruly member, but that day it was especially unruly, so that, before I had time to bridle it, I cried out: "Thank God, if foolish preaching will save Missouri, she is indeed safe." Poor, modest Winthrop could not stand his ground, but bolted in an instant. Not so with Ham. He seemed delighted with my compliment, having failed entirely to catch my idea. When I rejoined Winthrop, and rehearsed the outcome of the matter, he seemed to be as much relieved as he was amused at the man's ignorance.

There are those, perhaps, who may think that I should not have said so much about my Timothy. But such persons must know that what I have said is specially for the benefit of young preachers, who, when they read this, may take my boy-preacher for a pattern. I do not know that what I am writing will ever see the light; lest it should, I must add a few more words upon the same subject, and for the same purpose.

No loving son could ever be more attentive to the wants of a father, than was Winthrop Hopson to mine. On stopping for the night, his first and increasing care was my comfort. I must be first seated, must have the best chair, and have it in the best place. If there were two beds offered us, I must have choice; or, if we had to occupy the same bed, I must have choice of sides. In those days money was scarce, and came to us in small installments. When money was offered to him, he was in the habit of refusing it, as I learned, by saying, "I am young and have no family, I can get along without it; give it to Uncle Sam; he has a large family to support, and needs all he can get." Thus he was ever regarding my welfare, and in his unselfishness forgetting his own comfort and convenience.

On one occasion, as we were going to an appointment on the head waters of the Burbois River, we came to a tributary that was so swollen by a recent rain, that we were unable to ford it, and our embarrassment was increased by the fact that the canoe was on the other side. Winthrop, without a word, stripped himself, plunged into the turbid stream, and brought the canoe over, so that we were enabled to get across in good plight, and to meet our engagement promptly. How all this contrasts with that class of coarse, ill-bred young men, who act as if they suppose people will not hold them in honor, unless they are very peevish, fretful, fault-finding, and troublesome, in general.

Thirty years full of import, full of change and disappointment, have been numbered with those beyond the flood, since Winthrop and I traversed the Missouri hills and valleys together, bearing the joyful tidings of peace and love to the listening multitudes. But the results of the work begun by us will never pass away. At this distance from the scene, it were vain for me to attempt a description in detail, of the work which was accomplished. Whole communities, almost, were turned from the service of sin unto the service of God. Where only the songs of the reveler had been heard before, you could now hear the songs of praises to our God. Family after family was completely transformed. I have reason to think that, when Winthrop and I get home, we will find a blessed congregation of those dear souls who were brought to Christ under our preaching, waiting for us at the gate.

It was with a heavy heart that I began to realize the near approach of the end of my missionary work in this country. Yet I had the consolation to know that God had raised up men in this district, in whose hands the cause of truth would not suffer. If there had been no other, I could have entrusted the work to the hands of my Timothy with utmost confidence. But then there were others coming into usefulness. I can not name them all, but will speak of Jas. K. Rule, Ira and Levi Valentine, young men of promise; also Brother Shockley, who bid very fair to become useful as a proclaimer. Besides, our beloved brother, T. M. Allen, was now extending his labors to this district of country. These noble young men, with the wise counsels of Brother Allen, I felt assured would be quite able to carry on the begun work without my assistance. T. M. Allen was Missouri's model evangelist and pioneer preacher. Having talents of a high order, a liberal education, refined manners, and a commanding appearance, with the gospel at his tongue's end, it is not strange that he became at once the model and teacher of so many young men of that region. I have heard it said that he could put more Bible truth into a single sermon than any man west of the Mississippi. It was fortunate for the young preachers of the State of Missouri, and for the cause they advocated, that they had such a model. I have heard this fact given as the main reason why the Missouri preachers of the present generation have taken such high rank, not only in their own State, but wherever they have lived and labored. I have fancied that I could see something of T. M. Allen in most of those with whom I am acquainted.

CHAPTER XXIX.

Leaves Missouri and sojourns awhile in Guernsey county, Indiana. —No rest for him who is called to save souls.—Settles in Carlisle, Ky.—Preaches at Indian Creek, Carlisle, and in Jessamine county.—Elkhorn Mission to the mountains.—William Rogers, with one wife and twenty-two children.—How he talked to the mountaineers about guns.—Crying babes.—William Jarrott.

At the close of my two years' mission in Missouri, I had not at my command money sufficient to defray our expenses back to our old home. I was looking forward to the "enduring substance," which was being laid up during those years of toil and care, where moth and rust can not corrupt. Thank God that, in the world to come, we will get all our back-pay, with interest compounded. Having borrowed money sufficient for our expenses, we moved late in the autumn of 1843 as far on our way as Guernsey county, Indiana, where my son-in-law, William Utler, then lived. Here we sojourned for the winter and part of the summer following. After the incessant work and anxiety of the past three years, I had now for a season comparative rest, though all the time busy in doing what I could in confirming saints and turning the minds of the unconverted to God.

I am now a very old man, and very nearly worn out in my Master's cause, yet I have never been in a field so barren that some fruit might not be gathered for Christ; nor have I ever been so tired that I did not feel myself able to do some work in the Lord's vineyard. Preachers of the gospel, if called to seek and to save the lost by a conviction of duty deep down in the heart, will accept no furlough here; nor can they be contented in idleness for a single day. If, however, they are working for money, or praise from men, they will become tired and quit the field when these motives are withdrawn. In the olden times, we were often puzzled to determine as to the genuineness of our call to the ministry. I have, however, no difficulty now in settling that question. If the preacher's call is genuine, he will never tire; he will "not fail, nor be discouraged."

The beloved Johnson used to say that he wanted no rest; that he would not receive a furlough. Said he: "If my Lord and Master were to come to me from the skies, and were to say, 'You have been toiling hard for many years, and have endured many hardships for my name's sake, now take your rest; you have done enough;' I would say to him, 'Please, Master, let me work a little longer in this glorious cause; it is so delightful to work for you. Do not, Lord, deprive me of the exquisite pleasure of serving thee.'"

During my sojourn in Indiana, I found plenty to do, though the field was not so inviting as I could desire. I visited many sick persons, and gave relief to many. Some there were, however, who, in spite of any words of comfort I had to offer, passed into the shades of death in hopeless despair. It is a fearful sight to behold a man die in despair who has been in sight of life and in easy reach of salvation all his days.

Early in the summer of 1844, leaving my family with my son-in-law in Indiana, I visited my old neighborhood in Ohio, having been absent for more than two years. I found things greatly changed in many respects. I still had many warm friends there, but, in my absence, certain sentiments had obtained a footing among them which I had reason to believe might antagonize my usefulness to such an extent as to make it expedient for me to seek some other field. So, upon rejoining my family, it was determined that we should settle in Carlisle, Ky., the home of my brother, John Rogers, and the neighborhood of many dear and tried friends. My brother John Rogers and my son John assisted us in moving, and, by their aid, I was enabled to obtain a comfortable home in Carlisle. Though my brother had been preaching for this church more than a quarter of a century, yet, in his unselfishness, he induced the brethren to employ me one-fourth of my time, and to otherwise assist me in securing a support for my family. Though my brother John was a very frugal man, and a model economist, and thus prospered in the world, yet, in acts of Christian benevolence, there were few, if any, preachers in Kentucky who surpassed him. He fulfilled the Scriptures in this, that he did not look on his own things only, but also on the things of others. He contributed much to my comfort during my stay in Carlisle, not only by securing me in employment at home, but also by getting employment for me abroad.

There was a small church, about midway between Millersburg and Cynthiana, called Indicutts, or Indian Creek. Several prominent members of this church were old friends and acquaintances of mine; so soon, therefore, as they heard of my arrival in the community, they invited me to preach one Lord's day in each month there. This I consented to do for about fifty dollars a year, which was equivalent to two hundred dollars for my whole time. This was about one-third less than ordinary country salaries at that time. The balance of my time was taken up in evangelizing in Jessamine county, in conjunction with my brother John Rogers. Our work was distributed chiefly between the congregations of Keene, Liberty, Old Jessamine and Bethlehem; though we preached a few times during the year at other points. I do not remember the exact number gathered into these congregations by our joint labors that season; I only remember that we had many very successful meetings, and that there was a general awakening throughout the county on the subject of religion.

While preaching at Keene, I was sent for to baptize a Mr. Davis, who had been so reduced by a spell of protracted sickness that his physician thought he could not recover. On my arrival at the house of the sick man, I learned that his physician, or rather his physicians, father and son, who were known by the name of Young, had peremptorily forbidden his being baptized. Believing, from a long experience in such cases, that it could do the man no harm, but might be of great advantage to him, I immersed him in spite of the physicians' protest. Not long after this, in passing on to an appointment, my brother and I stopped on the way at the house of old Father Symmes, in Nicholasville. Here I learned that the elder Dr. Young had threatened to cane me on sight; and that he had been heard to say that, if Mr. Davis should die, he intended to have the "old Campbellite" tried for murder. The following day we passed by the house of Dr. Young, but heard nothing from him. I would not have been alarmed at meeting a dozen such men as Dr. Young, for I have long since learned that barking dogs rarely ever bite. On arriving at the place of our meeting, we were happy to learn that Brother Davis had so far recovered as to be able to ride to town, and purchase a Bible, which he was reading with great delight, and that he was among the happiest of living men.

That same year we had happy seasons at Indicott's. Brother Jack Hatlan assisted me in a series of meetings, which resulted in many additions to the church and in infusing new life into the members generally. I was seven years in Carlisle, preaching there one-fourth of my time; at Indicotts one-fourth, and the residue of my time I devoted to evangelizing, either in the employ of the State Board, or of some county coöperation, or some congregation.

I can not now recall the fact whether these years were seven years of scarcity or plenty, in a temporal sense; but I well remember they were years which yielded a copious harvest of souls throughout Kentucky. Those were the palmy days of Johnson, Gano, John Smith, Ricketts, Rice, Hall, Raines, Tompkins, Morton, John Rogers, and others, who spent much of their time in evangelical work.

The South Elkhorn congregation, always foremost in Christian liberality, and most active in every good work, having heard the Macedonian cry coming from the mountain districts of Kentucky, and wishing to respond at once, called me to labor in Estill, Owsley and some

other mountain counties. While in the employ of this
congregation, I devoted half my time each month to this
mountain mission.

On my first trip, I visited Irvin, Miller's Creek and
Proctor, at the Three Forks of the Kentucky River,
with forty baptisms as the result of these meetings. I
was much pleased with the mountain people generally.
It is true, they do not pay as much attention to their
bodies as the people do in the plains, but I am inclined
to the opinion that, according to their opportunities,
they are more attentive to the interests of their souls. It
was not unusual for them to come five or ten miles on
foot to hear preaching; and, after traveling this great
distance, they manifested no weariness whatever, but
would listen for any length of time without complaint.

At that time there was not a wagon in Owsley county,
and very few in Estill. Horses were also scarce, and
saddles a rarity. Consequently, the people accustomed
themselves to traveling on foot almost altogether, so that
it was no great hardship. One lady came on foot eight
miles to hear me, and, becoming convinced that she
ought to confess and obey Christ her Saviour, she asked
her husband if he had any objection to her doing so;
but his opposition was so bitter that she returned home
without submitting to the gospel. The next day, however, she was upon the ground, as anxious as ever to
confess, but, through the opposition of friends, she was
again hindered from doing so. But she would not
give it up, and the following day was upon the ground
again, having traveled in three days forty-eight miles.
She was now so importunate that her husband yielded to
her wishes, and permitted her to be baptized. I shall
never forget the joyful expression of her countenance
when she came forward to own the Saviour. After her
baptism she went on her way rejoicing, and we all rejoiced with her, so joyous and buoyant was she. We met
her afterwards, and observed that she appeared as one
that had been condemned to die but had been reprieved.

Up to this time, there had not appeared upon the

streets of Proctor such a thing as a wagon, carriage, or
buggy. There were people around there who had never
seen a four-wheeled carriage of any kind. All goods
were brought to the town on small crafts, which were
cordelled up the river by boatmen, who made a business
of drawing boats up or down the river.

On my first trip to the mountains, I made the acquaintance of Brother William Rogers, a superior mountain
preacher. He had sown the good seed of the gospel
broadcast over a large district of country: He was industrious and frugal, but, having a living family of twenty-two children (all by one wife), he could not maintain
them and give as much of his time to preaching as the
cause demanded. On my return home, I went to Lexington, and laid his case before the State Missionary
Board, recommending him as the most suitable man
they could employ to labor in his district of the mountains. Consequently his services were obtained by them,
and I believe he remained in their employ to the time
of his death. We were often together during my labors
in the mountains, and I can say with truth that a more
agreeable colaborer I never had in my life. We held
a successful meeting at Proctor, in a large warehouse
which had been fitted up and furnished for the occasion,
there being no house of worship in the place at that
time. The people came in vast crowds to hear — men,
women, children, and even little infants were brought.
The last named did not hear much, but, on the contrary,
by the concerts which they carried on, they kept a great
many from hearing, aside from their mothers. Most of
the time I got along bravely; but, at times, it seemed to
me that every babe in the congregation was squalling,
and that every babe in the whole country was in the
house. Some of our nervous preachers, had they been
there, would have suffered sorely, I fear. These poor
mothers were under the necessity either of staying at
home, or of bringing the little ones with them. These
mothers chose the latter course, and I commended them
for it. Under such circumstances, mothers are rather to

9

be pitied than blamed.   Preachers should cultivate patience in all such cases.   The men, with but few exceptions, were rough-looking fellows, though they behaved with becoming propriety in the house of worship.   You might have often seen them coming to meeting with rifles on their shoulders, except on Sundays, especially those who lived at a distance.   Upon entering the house, they were in the habit of stacking their arms carefully in one corner, together with hunting-pouch and horn, then seating themselves with an air of composure which indicated that they were now ready for the service.

Brother William Rogers, having been reared up among these people, knew exactly how to talk to them. . It excited my admiration not a little to observe how apt and ready he was with illustrations, exactly suited to command and rivet attention, and to carry conviction to the mind.   On a certain occasion he proceeded to meet the false accusation so commonly and persistently brought against us, that we, as a people, reject the Old Testament Scriptures; and, as near as I can recall his argument, it was as follows: "My friends, you have heard it reported that we reject the Old Testament Scriptures as altogether useless, and I want to show you exactly the use we have for both the Old and the New.   A greater mistake could not be made than to say that we have not constant use for the whole book.   Indeed, we teach that the Old Testament is the foundation on which the New rests, and that the New Testament would be void had it not been for the Old.   The two, to be effective, must be taken in their proper connection together.   Some of you have brought your rifles with you to-day, which I will use for an illustration in this connection.   You see this gun has two sights attached to it.   The foremost sight, you see, is a bright bead of silver near the muzzle, or mouth of the rifle.   The hindermost sight, you see, is a small piece of steel, with a very small notch in it.   This sight is placed near the breech of the gun, as you see.   Now let me ask you, What are the uses of those things we call sights?   You answer that they are attached to the rifle to enable us to hit the mark or object at which we aim. In taking aim, you look through the hindermost sight in such manner as to bring the foremost sight in exact range with the object which you wish to strike. You all can see at once that, if you were to use the foresight, without regard to the other, your shooting would be at random, so that, ninety-nine times out of a hundred, you would miss your aim; but when the front sight fills the notch of the hindermost one, and ranges exactly with the mark or object aimed at, you can not miss it if your rifle is good. Now, the Old Testament, with its types, shadows and prophecies, is the hindermost sight. The New Testament, with its exact fulfillment of all the types and prophecies, is the front sight. The object is Jesus Christ, the Son of God and the Saviour of sinners. So that, by looking through the Old Testament on to the New, which is the fulfilment of the Old, we can not fail to see Christ, for the eye will be brought to bear exactly upon Him. You see, then, the use we have for the Old Scriptures, and how it is that neither the Old nor the New can be used to advantage alone."

You may think it strange that I listened to this discourse with divided attention. I was intensely interested in the argument all the way through; but there was something else that equally claimed my attention. It was to see how those sturdy huntsmen listened. They leaned forward, with eyes, ears and mouth opened wide, as if to see, hear and drink in every word spoken. Such listeners are enough to inspire any speaker; and I may add that such speaking as that will make good listeners of almost any people. The secret of it was, that he talked to the people about things which they understood, and in language suited to their capacity.

At the time of his marriage, Elder William Rogers did not know a letter in the alphabet. His wife became his teacher, and, under her instruction, he soon became qualified to read that blessed book which was afterwards his life-time companion. I have heard him speak with much feeling of how much he was indebted to his wife for all that he had been as a preacher of the gospel. By close application he became thoroughly familiar with his Bible, and one of the most successful mountain preachers of the State. He had a fine memory, and held the Scriptures on his tongue's end. He was by nature a man of strong mind, and had a keen sense of propriety. He was humble, really so ; contrasting with the entire class of vain men who, unfortunately, often find their way into the pulpit, to the disgust of all sensible people. There is much meaning in the rough saying, that it is a great thing for any one to have sense enough to prevent him from making a fool of himself. My dear old friend and brother had that kind of sense in an eminent degree.

I attribute the success of William Rogers mainly to the fact that he accommodated his discourses to the capacity of all his hearers. The aged, middle-aged and young alike listened with profound attention to every word which fell from his lips. To use a huntsman's expression, he never overshot his game. There was a simplicity and directness in his discourse that commanded the attention of all who heard him. I have had the privilege of hearing great men and learned men speak, but no man ever interested me more than William Rogers.

It must not be understood that, because the mountain people are comparatively poor, they are, therefore, ignorant. I found in my travels quite a number of persons who were as well informed and, upon all practical questions, as intelligent as the people of the more favored Blue Grass Region. I regret to record the fact that in some places I could find neither Bible nor Testament. I have always been in sympathy with those societies that have for their object the circulation of the Bible, and have been in the habit of contributing something annually to their support. I do not think that the religious world is sufficiently alive to the work of sending the Bible to the poor. If we had the secret history of a single Bible, like that one, for instance, that my mother carried with her to the Territory of New Spain in the year 1801 — how many minds it had enlightened, how many hearts it had cheered, how often it had given strength to withstand trial and temptation — I have thought we would have all loved the book more, and be more active in its circulation. And of all the people on earth, I think we, who claim so much for the Bible, ought to be the most active and untiring in securing this much-desired object. We take the Bible, without note or comment, for our creed, and claim that it is enough as to doctrine, correction, reproof, instruction in righteousness, to thoroughly furnish the man of God unto every good work ; and we ought to spare no pains in putting it into the hands of the people.

At the close of my Elkhorn mission, the Kentucky Missionary Board called Brother William Jarrott and me to labor for a few weeks on the waters of the Kanawha and Coal rivers, bordering on the Virginia line. We labored together upon this tour about six weeks, preaching every day, and most of the time twice a day, to good audiences. We found the people anxious to hear the gospel, and many of them ready to obey. The people in that country had heard many ridiculous stories about our people, and were agreeably surprised to find that we really believed Jesus Christ to be a divine person; that we believed in a change of heart in conversion, and that we taught that every converted man must receive and enjoy the Holy Spirit. We had several successful meetings; brought back to the fellowship several wanderers; baptized quite a number, and re-organized two or three scattered congregations. One young man promised to devote himself to the ministry of the Word, who, as I have since learned, has become an able and useful preacher. I believe he was of the name of Miller. In the town of Moscow, all the meeting-houses were closed against us; so we went to work raising money to build a house for our own people, and succeeded beyond our expectation. So much to the account of a little sectarian bigotry and proscription.

Brother Jarrott had been born and reared up to manhood in this country. Here his kindred and many old friends still lived. He left the land of his nativity when quite young, and before giving any promise of strength or usefulness in the cause of his Master; now he returns in the prime and strength of his manhood, and burning with zeal to tell to friends and kindred the glad story of salvation through the name of a crucified Redeemer. His early familiarity with the habits and manners of the people enabled him to accommodate himself to their understanding very readily, making him quite an able co-worker. His early opportunities for acquiring an education had been poor; but having formed in his mind the purpose of becoming a proclaimer of the gospel, he devoted himself to study for a year or two, and then went into the field and began to practice upon what he had learned, prosecuting his studies as he went, making the Bible his chief text-book, until he became a workman of considerable skill. He was a man of extraordinary physical frame, and of great muscular power. There was no apparent end to his energy, perseverance and endurance. He was endowed with a pair of powerful lungs, could sing tolerably well, and loud enough to fill any common house. Though exhortation was his forte, enabling him at times to carry his hearers almost to sublime hights, yet he was by no means trifling or weak in argument. I have heard him in argumentation deal real sledge-hammer strokes with an unrelenting hand, which were sufficient to break in pieces the idols of false worshipers. William Jarrott had no mercy on error, nor on any who had fellowship with error. He was a man of warm heart, of generous and noble impulses. He could weep over the afflictions and misfortunes of men with a flood of tears; but, if you wished to see the tiger aroused from his lair, you had but to pervert the truth, or show a disposition to deal unfairly with his Master. I have learned to love William Jarrott with a brother's love. William, if what I have said should ever come to your sight, you will know what an old soldier thinks of you, and it may stimulate you to struggle in your arduous labors.

CHAPTER XXX.

John T. Johnson. — John G. Tompkins. — Great ingathering at Somerset.—Spencer.—Owingsville.–J. P. Clark.—Cynthiana.—My neighbors.

Immediately following the Kanawha mission, I was called to the assistance of Brother John T. Johnson, in holding a series of protracted meetings. As might have been expected, I responded to this call with more than ordinary delight. We had been soldiers together in the war of 1812; had shared the same sufferings and perils, both in the march and on the battle-field, in the service of our country. Our experience had been the same in pursuing the pleasures of the world. We had tasted its joys but to know how fleeting and unsatisfying they were. After embracing the religion of our Saviour, we had wandered alike in the mazes of sectarianism and superstition, and at times had been almost lost in the smoke of Babylon. By the same light we had been led out of our troubles and doubts, having exchanged visions, dreams and conjectures, for faith in God and trust in His precious promises. We, therefore, congratulated one another upon the privilege of fighting shoulder to shoulder under the flag of the Prince of Peace, against the errors that had enthralled us, and the enemies that had so long held us in captivity.

We held our first series of meetings together in the year 1846. I believe the first meeting was at Mill Creek, in Fleming county, with a young congregation which had been organized recently by William Brown, a man of wonderful power as a revivalist. At the time of our meeting, my son, John I. Rogers, was preaching for the congregation. The weather was intensely cold, but we continued until abundant success crowned our labors. Our next meeting was at Poplar Plains. This was comparatively a new field for our people. Midway between

Flemingsburg and Poplar Plains was an old Christian
church called Brick Union, which had been established
by Barton W. Stone at a very early day. The congregation was now dissolved, a part of its members going
to Flemingsburg, and a part to Poplar Plains. The
meeting which Johnson and I held at the Plains added
much strength to the little congregation, putting our
cause in that region upon a firm footing. After this
we held. a meeting at Lawrence Creek, some four miles
below Maysville. This meeting resulted gloriously. At
these several meetings one hundred souls were added to
the church, many drooping souls revived, and several
unhappy troubles cured.

.As an evangelist, I have thought John T. Johnson
the best model I have ever known. Perhaps, I ought
not to speak of him as a model at all, for no man could
imitate him. His style beggars all attempts at description. I have read descriptions of him as a preacher,
from the pens of those who are masters in the art of
composition; but the best of them were tame in com-
parison with the real John T. Johnson as you saw and
heard him for yourself.

Though satisfied of the fact that what I may say of
him will fall far short of portraying the man in his true
character, yet I must be permitted to drop a few passing
thoughts as an humble tribute to his memory. He stood
like a lord before the people, and yet no one was awed
in his presence, for his dignity was blended with the
sweet simplicity of a child. He did not wear the dignity
of the world, but it was that of conscious rectitude and
goodness. In coming before his audience, he had the
appearance of a bold, fearless and defiant champion,
every nerve being fully strung and his dark eye flashing
fire. A stranger, dropping into the audience in the
midst of his discourse, would have been inclined to inquire the cause of that strange determination expressed
by the look and gesture, as well as by the words, of the
speaker. A few moments in close attention, however,
would have satisfied the most curious as to the cause.

He would have learned that his Lord and Master had
been rudely assailed; that the glorious Gospel of God's
Son had been perverted; and that, as a consequence, sinners were perishing for want of the bread of life. He
was defending Jesus, his Saviour; he was earnestly contending for the faith once delivered to the saints; he was
pleading for the salvation of souls.

Johnson had practiced law during the earlier years of
his life, during which time he had often been called
upon to plead the cause of the falsely accused before the
bar of human judgment; which accounts for the fact
that his style was that of the advocate, rather than that
of the preacher. He was constantly pleading or prosecuting causes. One very striking characteristic of his
preaching was the faculty that he possessed of making
everything that he talked about a present reality. In
speaking of heaven, you would fancy that he saw everything there, and was lifting you up into regions from
which you too might have visions of God. In speaking
of hell, he seemed to be looking down into the abyss
of torment, beholding the miseries and ruin of lost
souls, and to be listening to their fruitless cries. When
dwelling upon the subject of the love of God, his own
soul was melted with the celestial flame. If the Christian hope was the theme, his whole being became ex-
alted in the contemplation of the meeting of friends and
kindred around the throne of God; then, as if looking down from the celestial hights, he would exclaim,
"Who would not endure a thousand times more than
we are called upon to suffer for the joy of a meeting and
a crown like these?" Then, turning to the sinner, he
would ask, beseechingly: "O sinner, why will you perish
in reach and in sight of such joys? Why not assert your
manhood, and come this very hour to the Saviour, and
live?" He was hopeful and buoyant under the most
adverse circumstances. In all my intercourse with him,
I do not remember to have heard him utter a word of
discouragement more than once. That was at the beginning of a meeting in Flat Rock, Bourbon county,

where, upon our arrival, we found about a dozen persons in waiting, looking as cold and lifeless as the grave. As we left the house that day, Brother Johnson remarked, that the beginning was not favorable for a good meeting. Notwithstanding the bad beginning, however, that meeting closed with about seventy-five additions.

After the Flat Rock meeting, I was selected to hold a meeting at Somerset Church, Montgomery county, in conjunction with Brother John G. Tompkins, which began with the most discouraging circumstances, and ended with the addition of scores to the church. Brother John G. Tompkins was a brother-in-law to Elder P. S. Fall, having married his sister, a lady of fine culture and elegant manners. His career was quite brief, and I may say as brilliant as it was brief. Being a finely educated Virginia gentleman, he was good material to form into a preacher. He was a polished speaker; was systematic almost to a fault; logical, persuasive, and, in the conclusion of his discourse, very pathetic. Had his physical constitution been equal to his mental capacity, I doubt not he would have stood to-day in the foremost ranks among the proclaimers of the Old Jerusalem Gospel. As it was, he accomplished very much good.

About this time, I was induced to move to Owingsville, the old home of Brother John Smith. At the beginning of my work the prospects of success were bright and promising, but the coming among us of John P. Clark so completely blasted all our hopes for good that I returned to my old home again in Carlisle.

Immediately upon my return to Carlisle, I had a call from the American Christian Missionary Board to evangelize in Hamilton county, Ohio, but, not being willing to leave Kentucky at this time, I accepted a call from the congregation at Cynthiana to preach for them once a month, and to make my home in their midst. I believe it was in the year 1852 that I removed my family to Cynthiana, and have been perfectly contented with my situation ever since. I bought a little home of William Withers, who, for years afterwards, was my fast friend and faithful adviser, and whom, if yet living, I would as confidently approach for a favor as any man on earth. He gave me my own terms, and I may say my own time, in which to pay for my home. I found in and around Cynthiana the most liberal and generous people I have ever known. The aged, middle-aged and the young were alike kind and obliging: not for a few days, or months, or years, but during almost a quarter of a century their kindness and generosity have been unabated. I have often thanked God that it was my good fortune to fall in with such a people in the evening of life. Thus far it has been a blessed and peaceful evening, leaving out of view the late unholy conflict between the North and the South. And even in the midst of the troubles consequent upon that unnatural conflict, my friends did not forsake me, but were always ready to comfort and succor me in times of deepest distress. Happy is the man who is surrounded with such neighbors and brethren as I can boast. In the olden times I had known the fathers and mothers of many of these people, and in moving into their midst they recognized me as their father, and treated me accordingly. If I were not afraid of leaving out some of them, I should like to put them upon the Roll of Honor. I will make the attempt at any rate: the Witherses, Ashbrooks, Garnets, Smisers, Pattersons, Shawhans, Wards, Nicholses, Smiths, Millers, Williamses, Remingtons, Walls, Northcutts, Fraziers, Wilsons, Talbotts, Vernons, Amermons, and others.

I was employed to preach once in each month at Indicotts, and, as I have stated, I preached once in each month at Cynthiana. For the balance of my time I was employed to preach under the direction of the State Board in the county of Owen. My chief points of operation in the county were Owenton and Liberty, though I distributed my labors over the county generally. I had very marked success at Buck Creek, where I organized a large congregation, which I believe is still flourishing. I reported that year, as the result of my missionary work, about two hundred and fifty additions.

It is curious to observe how one, starting out from his native place in early manhood, drifts on and on through the shifting scenes of life, until, by some unaccountable turn of the tide, he finds himself in his declining age at the very place where he was born, and among the friends and in the midst of the scenes of his early youth. Such has been my fortune. I feel like one who, after long and tedious wanderings up and down the earth, has come home to die. And I thank God that He has cast my lot in such pleasant and familiar places in my declining age. A few hours' travel would carry me to the place where, more than three-quarters of a century ago, my father built his first cabin in the wild forests of Kentucky, while my mother and I were safely housed in Strode's Station. Much nearer is the sacred spot where my dear lamented wife spent her joyous childhood days. And still nearer stood the cabin where we were made husband and wife, and where I was also married to the Lord Jesus Christ. And yet a little nearer, even in the very neighborhood of my present home, I made my first efforts in preaching.

For a number of years I preached once a month at Indian Creek, and once a month at Mount Carmel. A nobler people never lived than they. When too old to labor for them regularly, these churches adopted a resolution that, whenever it suited me to visit them, I should understand that I was invited; and I rejoice to testify that upon every such visit I was well rewarded for my labor. Grassy Spring, in Woodford county, and other churches were alike kind to me in my old age. Among all these people I felt perfectly at home, and they all deported themselves towards me as dear and dutiful children. With such surroundings, it is not strange that I should be content to spend there my remaining days.

CHAPTER XXXI.

Last visit to Missouri.

Being in my eighty-fourth year, I determined to revisit my friends in Missouri. Leaving Cynthiana the last Monday in April, I arrived in St. Joseph Thursday morning, and experienced a joyful meeting with my son, W. C. Rogers, and his family. This was a long journey for one almost blind and deaf, but I have always found friends to help me along, even in the person of strangers. On the second day of May, I preached at Walnut Grove, five miles out, and had one addition. On Monday morning I went out with my son, and spent the day fishing. On Thursday we went to Stewartsville, and spent two happy weeks with my son Samuel and his family.

My next point was Cameron, where I spent a week with my granddaughter, Mrs. Packard. On Lord's day I preached for the congregation there. The last Tuesday in May I returned to St. Joseph, and preached for the brethren the following Lord's day. Here I met Colonel Burton, who informed me that he had traveled forty miles to see me, for the purpose of inducing me to visit him in Effingham, a short distance from Atchison, Kansas. On the following Thursday I met my only living brother, General William Rogers, of Platte county. On Lord's day morning I met a large assembly, which had gathered there to hear the oldest pioneer preacher of the State. To speak for the last time to those with whom I had mingled for so many years, made it indeed a solemn occasion. Here I met my brother Acre, formerly of Bourbon county, Kentucky. He is now quite an acceptable preacher. On the fourth Lord's day in June I preached two discourses at a basket-meeting at Second Creek. Thursday night I preached at Parkville, and on Friday returned to St. Joseph. On Saturday I went to Walnut Grove, and held a meeting for one week, sojourning with

Herman Johnston, whom I had brought into the kingdom. On the first Lord's day in July I preached in St. Joseph, and the following week I preached in Atchison, where I enjoyed the company of many old friends. On Thursday I went to Colonel Burton's, and filled my engagement with him. Our meeting was a delightful one. Brother Pardee Butler met me here, and impressed me favorably. At one time I entertained prejudices against him, which I am satisfied were unfounded. He is certainly a good and strong-minded man, and of unblemished reputation among his neighbors. Bad men may stand well abroad, but are rarely of good repute at home. On Thursday night I preached at Effingham, and took the confession of a promising young man. On Friday I returned to Atchison, and on Lord's day preached two discourses. My son, W. C. Rogers, organized this congregation some time ago on the old Jerusalem platform.

On Tuesday I took the cars for Leavenworth City, where I met many old Kentucky friends. The following evening I started for Columbia, but was detained by accident twenty-four hours in Kansas City, where I met the beloved Mountjoy, who had been baptized when a small boy in Lawrenceburg, Ky., by my son John I. He is now one of Missouri's best preachers. Here I addressed the brethren at their prayer-meeting, and in the morning hurried on to Centralia, and thence to Columbia. Here I was met by my dearly beloved Brother Wilkes. In Lexington, Ky., his house had been my home by a standing invitation. Brother and Sister Wilkes used to conduct me to my room, and, after seating me in the big chair, they would say, " Now, Uncle Sam, this is your room, and you must do as you please." So you may imagine that I felt at home again when seated in the midst of this family.

On Lord's day, after preaching, I dined at Christian College, which for many years had been presided over with marked ability by the beloved J. K. Rogers, who has become famous as an educator. Here I saw a life-size portrait of Elder Thomas M. Allen, one of Missouri's best pioneer preachers. It was not the likeness before me that crushed my heart as I stood gazing thereon, but it was the recollection of my dear lost boy who, years before, had painted this likeness. I thought of the fatal charge at Augusta, and the mangled corpse of my dear child, the youngest born among my sons. Here let the curtain fall and hide from view forever all but the fact that a nobler, truer heart was never pierced by the ball of an adversary than that which beat in the breast of W. S. Rogers.

On Sunday night I delivered an historical discourse, having been requested to give a brief sketch of my life and labors. My motto was II. Tim. iv. 7: "I have fought a good fight," etc. At the close one confessed faith in Christ, and two united with the church. By special invitation, I visited Missouri University, where I was brought face to face with the likenesses of the former Presidents of the institution, painted by my son, W. S. R. Among them I recognized the beloved Shannon, a great and true Reformer. In his early ministry he was a Presbyterian preacher; but, having been appointed by the Synod of Georgia to deliver a discourse upon the subject of infant sprinkling, after searching his Bible through for proof-texts, and, to his surprise, finding none, he at once laid down his commission at the feet of his brethren, and attached himself to the Baptist church. Subsequently he became acquainted with the views of our people, and advocated with great zeal, until the day of his death, the doctrine of the Bible. From Columbia I went to Miller's Landing, where I preached more than two weeks, on the ground where, in years past, I had achieved for my Master many grand victories. To me this was sacred ground. It was in sight of the graves of my mother, two sisters, and many friends of my youth. Though in my eighty-fourth year, yet, as I stood upon the old battle-ground, I became in feeling young again, and spoke with the strength of my early manhood. On Tuesday after the third Lord's day in August, the evening of my departure, I addressed my brethren and old friends from Acts xx., a part of Paul's charge to the elders at Ephesus. Having commended them to God, and to the Word of His grace, we all kneeled down and prayed together. Then the farewells were spoken, and we parted with weeping eyes, but not as those who have no hope.

From Miller's Landing I went to Grey's Summit, where my nephew, J. J. Woods, was in waiting to convey me to his home. On the following day I began a meeting at Pleasant Hill, which was continued for several weeks. On the fourth Lord's day in August I preached in the morning and at night, and witnessed quite a number of confessions. The brethren prevailed on me to remain for a time. We had a happy meeting, and several persons were added to the church. On Monday I started for Kentucky, and, after a brief rest with friends in St. Louis, I arrived in safety at home, having been out three months. This I intended for my last long journey, and certainly it has been the happiest journey of all.

I have now well nigh spoken all my farewells on earth, and shall soon begin shaking hands with the loved ones gone before. And, though I know not where those greetings shall end, yet I do know where they will begin. I shall greet, first of all, my Father, whose hand has led me all the journey through, and my Saviour, whose grace has been sufficient for me in every day of trial and suffering here. And next, I shall look around for her whose love and goodness have imposed on me a debt of gratitude to God I can never repay. When we meet, shall we not gather up the children and grandchildren, and sit down under the shadow of the throne and rest?

www.ingramcontent.com/pod-product-compliance
Lightning Source LLC
Chambersburg PA
CBHW020603030726
47497CB00007B/2055